"So…" A s[mile tugged at the corner] of his mou[th.] "[Wasn't it you] saying about being sensual?"

Sarah scrambled to correct him. Before Dylan got the wrong idea. "I wasn't talking about being sensual. I mean, not me personally. But you said—"

"No. You said. And what you said was *sensual*." His eyes gleamed.

She refused to be sidetracked. "First of all, what I *said* was *sensuous*. But…" Sarah curled her fingers into her palms and held her arms close to her sides. "What I'm saying is I need your help."

It was a serious request and she'd imagined he'd take it seriously. Of course, that didn't explain why Dylan's smile went up a notch. "My help? To be sensual?"

It was a tempting thought. And not at all in her best interests. Sarah put it firmly out of her mind and tried to keep her voice modulated and her demeanor as professional as possible. Not easy, considering that she was about to humiliate herself.

"I want…" She stumbled over the words and tried again. "I want you to teach me about romance."

Dear Reader,

It's summer, and there's no better time for a visit to South Bass Island in Lake Erie and to Cupid's Hideaway, the wacky bed-and-breakfast run by perpetual matchmaker Maisie Templeton.

This tourist season, Maisie's got her work cut out for her. She has a new gardener, Sarah Allcroft, and it doesn't take an old lady with a keen eye and a belief in happily-ever-afters to know that Sarah needs a little romance in her life. Good thing island police chief Dylan O'Connell is single and looking for a woman to warm his heart—and his bed.

What Dylan doesn't know is that Sarah is on the run. From her job hosting a wildly popular TV show. From the legion of reporters trying to interview her. From a fan who's a little too obsessed.

You can be pretty sure that Cupid's Hideaway will work its magic for these two, just as it did for Noah and Laurel in *Stranded at Cupid's Hideaway* (American Romance #932), and for Meg and Gabe in *Christmas at Cupid's Hideaway* (American Romance #996).

Cupid's Hideaway is a creation of my imagination, but South Bass Island and Put-in-Bay, the island town, are very real, indeed. The island is located just three miles from the Ohio mainland, but it's a world apart, a tiny gem in a lake that can be as treacherous as it is beautiful. At last count there were 128 year-round residents on the island and I'd like to thank each and every one of them for the hospitality I've always found there.

Connie Lane

P.S. I love hearing from my readers. You can e-mail me at connielane@earthlink.net.

Sarah's Guide to Life, Love & Gardening

Connie Lane

HARLEQUIN®

TORONTO • NEW YORK • LONDON
AMSTERDAM • PARIS • SYDNEY • HAMBURG
STOCKHOLM • ATHENS • TOKYO • MILAN • MADRID
PRAGUE • WARSAW • BUDAPEST • AUCKLAND

ISBN 0-373-75076-5

SARAH'S GUIDE TO LIFE, LOVE & GARDENING

This edition published by arrangement with Harlequin Books S.A.

® and TM are trademarks of the publisher. Trademarks indicated with ® are registered in the United States Patent and Trademark Office, the Canadian Trade Marks Office and in other countries.

www.eHarlequin.com

Printed in U.S.A.

For Mary McGuinness,
A great brainstormer, a willing reader and a terrific friend.
Thank you for your help with this one!

Chapter One

What is romance?
It's the question that *Affairs of the Heart*
viewers ask most often. Is romance all about a look?
A touch? Is it something as simple as the scent of
lilacs wafting through an open doorway? Ah, if only
it were as easy as all that! But don't despair, dear
reader. You have *Sarah's Guide to Life, Love and
Gardening*. And Sarah has all the answers.
—*Sarah's Guide to Life, Love and Gardening*

"...until then, this is Sarah Allcroft of *Affairs of the Heart*,
wishing you beauty-filled days, elegant nights and a lifetime of romance."

Sarah held the smile. One second. Two seconds. Three.

"Cut!" Gino Felice, the director, gave the thumbs-up,
and Sarah let go of the breath she was holding along with
the smile that cramped her face muscles and left her lips
as dry as dust. Gino hurried over to where she was perched
on a white wicker settee artfully accessorized with a dozen
chintz pillows in a variety of colors and patterns. Flowers and checks, stripes and watercolor splashes, they all
complemented her blush-pink linen suit to perfection.
Sarah wouldn't have had it any other way.

Gino kissed her cheek. "Gorgeous, darling. Your best

show ever. One look at the tea you set this afternoon..."
There was an assortment of adorable little canapés, finger sandwiches and cookies on a silver tray on the table
in front of Sarah. Gino reached around the Limoges teapot and cups they'd borrowed from a local collector for
the taping and grabbed a sandwich cut in the shape of a
star. He popped the blackberry, sage and cream cheese
concoction into his mouth, closed his eyes and smiled
while he chewed.

"As soon as they see this episode, the good folks over at
the Home & Hearth Network will jump up and take notice,"
he said. "They're going to want you in their fall lineup. I'd
bet my silver-haired granny on it. I wouldn't be surprised
if the phone doesn't start ringing with offers. Very soon."

Sarah wouldn't be surprised, either. Then again, little
ever surprised Sarah.

She simply wouldn't allow it.

Her determination settled in the place that always felt
jumpy before, during and after every taping and, as always, Sarah felt calm and filled with confidence.

By the time Becky Landis raced by to answer the phone
ringing in the outer office, Sarah was smiling again.

"Good show, honey!" Becky was the producer, makeup
artist and wardrobe mistress of *Affairs of the Heart*. She
was also Sarah's best friend. She patted Sarah on the back
as she zoomed by. "You got the directions for those knitted
sachet bags, right?" she called over her shoulder. "I know
we're going to get slammed by requests. Like we always
do. You show women how to craft some charming some-
thing-or-other and they beat a path to our proverbial door.
It's going to get crazier once we go national!" The last
Sarah saw of her, Becky wore an ear-to-ear grin.

Sarah knew exactly why. Once *Affairs of the Heart*
was picked up for cable, she wasn't the only one whose

star would be on the rise. Becky would finally get the chance to work on a network show, just as she'd always dreamed. Gino and the rest of the crew would have the opportunity, at last, to use their considerable talents on a project more challenging than a shoestring-budget show with a tiny local audience.

Sarah, however, was the only one who was going to get thrust, pushed, dragged and swept into the limelight.

Her smile wilted and her insides start jumping all over again.

Almost as much as when Becky called across the studio, "Hey, Sarah!" She held her hand over the phone receiver. "It's *Trend* magazine! They say they heard you're the new diva of romance. They want to know when they can schedule an interview."

Interview?

This time, Sarah's insides didn't simply jump. They did a loop-the-loop. Before she even knew what she was doing, she was on her feet. "Tell them..." Becky was dancing around, too excited to keep still, and watching her, Sarah's panic solidified into a block of ice. "Tell them to call back. Tomorrow."

Anxious to get away before they pinned her down further, Sarah decided to hide out in her combination office and dressing room on the far side of the set.

A good escape plan in the great scheme of things. One that would have been quicker, quieter and far more dignified if she hadn't banged her knee into a corner of the table on her way by. She yelped when teacups fell and scattered. The teapot spilled, and the sandwiches and cookies on the tray turned to mush in a puddle of *lapsang souchong*.

Cookies be damned! Sarah knew exactly how much was—or more precisely, wasn't—in the show's budget.

Their ink would turn from its current shade of pink to bloodred if the Limoges got as much as a scratch.

She made a grab for the teapot at the same time she negotiated the small space between the table and the bank of cameras set up in front of it. She saved the teapot but tripped over her own feet. She would have gone down on her nose if Gino hadn't been there to catch her.

"Thanks." Sarah blew a curl of honey-colored hair out of her eyes and untangled herself from Gino's grasp, anxious to get away—before she did any more damage. She handed him the too-expensive teapot and took off as fast as her sensible pumps allowed.

Once she had the door between her office and the studio closed, she put her back against it and exhaled a long sigh. She congratulated herself.

One more taping out of the way.

One more interview request successfully stalled.

One more bullet dodged.

Again.

How long could she keep going before she got hit right between the eyes?

Rather than worry about it, Sarah sat down at her desk. Though Becky handled the day-to-day aspects of the show and Gino was in charge of the on-camera artistic decisions, it was no secret that Sarah was the real driving force behind *Affairs of the Heart*. After all, she was the one who'd done all the planning and, as part of her MBA course work, the demographic studies.

She'd learned that women in the New England market were champing at the bit for a weekly TV show that reflected their longing for the good old days when *elegance, refinement* and *charm* were as much a part of everyday language as *nanosecond, drive-by shooting* and *Amber Alerts* were today. Armed with the germ of an idea that came to her while she was interning in the accounting office of a local TV station and a loan from a bank dedicated to promoting women's business ventures, Sarah cobbled together all that style, sophistication and gentility into what ultimately became *Affairs of the Heart*. She was proud of the concept and she would have been perfectly happy to nudge the show toward success from behind the scenes.

Unfortunately it was not to be.

The day of their first taping, the woman they'd hired to be their on-air hostess got the flu, and against her better judgment and her vehement protests, Sarah was drafted for duty. The rest, as they say, was history.

The show was an instant hit. And Sarah suddenly had a following and a reputation to live up to. She was the hostess with the romantic mostest. The woman other women watched for advice on every topic under the romantic sun, from scenting linens (lavender for relaxation, lemon to restore energy) to color-coordinating their bedrooms (definitely red and green for sensuality, blues were calming, and beige...well, only if all that was planned for the bedroom was a good night's sleep).

It wasn't as easy as it seemed.

At the same time Sarah kicked off her pumps and poked her feet into the brown imitation-suede moccasins she kept under her desk, she undid the cameo brooch at her throat. She set the pin aside so it could be returned to its owner, the little old lady who lived next door to Sarah, and searched for distraction.

The rough draft of her *Sarah's Guide to Love, Life and Gardening* sat in one corner of her desk, all six hundred pages of it. It called her name, but as she had more and more lately, she firmly ignored it. Because there wasn't a publisher in the world who cared about the hostess of a small-town TV show, the book would never be a book unless one of the cable networks picked up *Affairs of the Heart*.

Since that was precisely what she *wasn't* trying to think about, she decided to shuffle through the day's mail instead. As usual, there were flyers from romantic getaway spots around the country, all hoping to garner a little publicity from a mention on the show. There were also catalogs from lingerie companies.

"One, two, three, four..." Sarah counted under her breath. Seven fan letters from as close as Pawtucket and as far away as Boston. And samples—quickly she scanned the assortment of boxes and padded envelopes scattered over her desk.

Today's samples came from a china manufacturer, a champagne distributor and, if her nose wasn't playing tricks on her, a perfume company. She sneezed, and reaching for a tissue with one hand, she grabbed for the final package with the other. It wasn't until she'd dragged it across the desk that she realized her name was written on the box in big block letters. There was no return address.

Sarah's breath caught and she found herself staring down at the box, her hands poised over the brown paper, her heart suddenly beating double time.

"Crazy," she admonished herself. "Silly. Way too paranoid." And because crazy, silly and way too paranoid were words that weren't in her vocabulary, not to mention her job description, she tore into the package.

The box was nondescript, the wrappings unremarkable. Just like the other, similar packages that had come before this one. And like the silk scarf decorated with red roses that had arrived last month, the nightgown embroidered with tiny rosebuds that showed up a few weeks before that, and the dozen long-stemmed red roses that had been delivered only a couple of days ago, this one didn't include a card.

She braced herself and tore open the box.

Inside was a pair of white sneakers painted with bright red roses.

They were 7½ AA. Her size.

As if it were on fire, she shoved the box away. When she did, a single sheet of paper fell out and fluttered to the floor.

Roses are red,
Violets are blue.
Clumsy in heels,
These sneakers are for you.

"Sarah!" When Becky knocked on the door and called her name, Sarah jumped. She didn't know how long she'd been sitting there staring at the sneakers, she only knew it was long enough. She tossed the box and the accompanying note into her trash can.

"Sarah, I know you're in there." Becky raised her voice. "I've got another call for you. Steve McGee from the local newspaper. He says if you have time, they want to do a profile and—"

Sarah groaned. She put her head into her hands and closed her eyes. When she opened them again, she found herself staring at one of the flyers that had come in the mail, and a picture of a romantic getaway that some innkeeper somewhere, no doubt, wanted her to feature on her show.

It was an ornate Victorian house. Painted bright pink.

"'Cupid's Hideaway,'" Sarah read out loud, refusing to listen to Becky who was still outside the door and as insistent as ever. She kept on reading through three flowery paragraphs about captivating atmosphere and romantic possibilities, but it wasn't until she turned the single sheet of paper over and looked at the item printed in bold type on the back that she really took notice.

"'Wanted: one artistic and conscientious gardener to spend the summer in Put-in-Bay on South Bass Island. Three months of sun, water and Victorian elegance. Room and board included.'"

Put-in-Bay? South Bass Island?

Sarah had never heard of the place and had no clue where it was, but there was one certainty: an island meant isolated, and isolated was sounding better and better by the moment.

"Three months, huh?" She picked up the phone and dialed the number printed on the flyer. In three months she'd know if *Affairs of the Heart* would be picked up by one of the cable networks, and if she tried really hard and got really lucky, that would give her enough time to practice being the Sarah Allcroft everyone expected her to be.

With any luck, it would also give her some time to decide what to do about the stalker with marginal taste and a fondness for roses, the one flower that never failed to make her sinuses twitch.

IF FANTASIES CAME in color and if the color was hot pink...

If they included Victorian gables, turrets and so much gingerbread trim that it seemed like a cake decorator had gone mad...

If they came complete with a wraparound porch and a sign on the front door that proclaimed *Romance Spoken Here*...

If it was all rolled into one, shaken with a touch of wacky and topped with a great big dollop of old-fashioned hospitality...

It would equal Cupid's Hideaway.

At the drive that led to the Hideaway's parking area, Dylan O'Connell slowed the gray Tahoe with the Put-in-Bay police emblem on the side. He was a cop, and a cop was nothing if not logical. Logically, when he saw the bed and breakfast inn that was a bit too everything including too much, he should have groaned. Or at least mumbled a word or two about innkeeper Maisie Templeton's lack of taste.

Instead, all he did was shake his head in a gesture filled as much with admiration as it was with amazement. Hard not to, especially when he thought about the sweet old lady who had brought her romantic dreams to life here in this little corner of South Bass Island in Lake Erie off the Ohio mainland. It was impossible not to admire a woman with more energy than three people half her age and a heart big enough to offer Dylan the room above the garage while his place was being repaired after a nasty water pipe break.

It was unthinkable that he wouldn't be concerned if any of what made the Hideaway so special was ever threatened.

The idea settled inside him like a fishing weight and he remembered the phone conversation he'd had with Maisie earlier in the afternoon. She had a new employee, and Maisie, the woman who loved everyone and whom everybody loved back, was worried.

Sarah Allcroft, the gardener she'd hired for the summer, had arrived on the noon ferry, Maisie had told him. She'd added in confidence that the woman was "a suspicious character."

Dylan parked the car. Technically he was off duty, but he picked up his hat and put it on, anyway. If he had a suspicious character to deal with, he might as well play the police chief role to the hilt.

As soon as he was out of the car, the heavy bass line and screaming lyrics of the hip-hop music that pounded from the other side of the inn assaulted his ears. He cringed. No wonder Maisie had her doubts about the new gardener! He hadn't even met her yet and already he knew that the woman had a taste for music that was low on melody and a little too big on four-letter words.

He rounded the corner, fully prepared to remind Sarah that even though the Hideaway was an X-rated getaway spot for consenting couples, it definitely should have a PG soundtrack. He would have done it, too, if he hadn't taken a gander at what was happening near the steps that led up to the back porch. He stopped dead in his tracks.

Maisie's "suspicious character" was as out of place in a free-and-easy vacation spot like South Bass Island as a hothouse flower would have been if it suddenly sprouted in the bare flower beds. She was short and looked to be slim, though in her baggy clothes, it was hard to tell. She had shoulder-length hair that was more golden than it was brown and eyes that were the same clear blue as the Lake Erie waves he could see beyond the broad sweep of lawn and gardens. Her nose was small and turned up slightly at the end. Her complexion was peaches and cream.

It all added up to the kind of beauty that was sure to turn heads—and had been known to stop men's hearts.

He ought to know. Dylan's did exactly that, then started up again with a funny sort of rumba rhythm that didn't match the beat of the music blaring from the radio at Sarah's feet.

As he watched, she balanced a flat of neon pink impatiens in each hand. She had a garden glove clenched in her teeth and she negotiated her way between a basket of peppermint-striped pink-and-white geraniums and a garden hose. A task that would have been easier and a whole lot safer if the sidewalk hadn't been dotted with puddles and slick with mud.

It didn't take a cop with an eagle eye and a sixth sense for trouble to recognize a disaster waiting to happen.

Dylan darted forward, his voice loud enough to be heard over the screaming guitars and pounding drums coming from the radio. "Here, let me—"

It didn't take a cop with an eagle eye and a sixth sense for trouble to recognize a mistake, either.

Surprising Sarah was definitely a mistake.

Startled by Dylan's sudden arrival, she screeched. The glove fell from between her teeth. She caught a glimpse of it and thinking she'd lost hold of the flowers, she panicked, pivoted and slipped. The flat of flowers in her right hand hit the ground first. Sarah went second. The other plastic flat flipped and hovered in the air. Just before it came crashing down in a sprinkle of pink petals and soil— right in her lap.

By the time it was all over, Sarah was on her butt in the middle of a muddy mess.

"Sorry." Dylan hurried forward and offered her a hand up, but unlike most women who would have welcomed the rescue with open arms, Sarah simply resigned herself to the grimy facts.

"Might as well clean up the mess while I'm down here," she said.

It *was* the most practical approach and, surprised, Dylan did the only thing he could think to do. He crouched down and helped with the salvage operation. He righted one of the flats—the one Sarah wasn't sitting on—and picked up the few unbroken impatiens he could find. He scraped soil off the slate sidewalk and plopped it into the flat, then tucked one plant after another back into place. "You must be Sarah."

She plucked a flower and the wet soil still clinging to its roots from her shoulder and glanced at him out of the corner of her eye. "Do we know each other?"

"Dylan O'Connell. I'm—"

"With the local police. Yeah." She gave his crisp blue uniform the once-over. "I got that part. Are you here to see Maisie?"

The song on the radio ended and another one started up. It was even noisier than the last one, and Dylan leaned forward and raised his voice. "It's loud." When Sarah didn't respond, he pointed at the radio. "The music. It's loud." He reached over and snapped off the radio.

"Sorry!" Sarah's quick smile was apologetic. "I guess I forgot it was on. I was..." Catching sight of the mud, the mess and the flowers crushed and scattered all around her, her expression wilted like the mashed impatiens she yanked out from under her right leg. "I was gardening."

"And I should have let you know I was here before I scared the daylights out of you." Dylan brushed his hands together and stood, looking down at Sarah as he did. Her shapeless khaki slacks were as dirty as her sneakers, and they were caked with mud. The only saving grace of the outfit was her used-to-be-white polo shirt with a bright red cupid embroidered over the heart. The shirt was standard issue for all of Maisie's employees, and this one looked big enough to be worn by one of the burly college kids who stopped by a couple times a week to cut the lawn. Sarah's shirt, though, was open at the neck, revealing a tiny strip of skin every bit as flawless as her complexion. When she reached for another squished flower, the shirt moved along with her, and the grinning cupid—lucky dog!—ended up caressing a breast.

One corner of Dylan's mouth rose in a wry grin and

his rumba heartbeat changed to a cha-cha that did a couple quick dance steps through his chest.

It was time to distance himself. He didn't need temptation and there was nothing as tempting as the prettiest woman who'd stepped on this island in a long time, a damp polo shirt and that little cupid just daring him to—

Dylan forced his gaze away from Sarah and toward the pink monstrosity of a house. "So, first day on the job. What do you think of the Hideaway? It's really unique, isn't it?"

"No guests checking in until this weekend so it's hard to judge the service. I can say that every single room is spic and span. The innkeeper is friendly. The decorating scheme is—" She caught herself and winced. "Sorry. I sound like a guide book."

"You sound like a woman who knows what she's talking about. You mentioned the decorating." Dylan motioned toward the house. "So tell me, if you were writing one, what would your guide book say about the interior design here at the Hideaway?"

For a heartbeat, he wondered what he'd said wrong. At the mention of a guide, Sarah's face went pale beneath its streaks of mud. The next second, she recovered and apparently took the question at face value. Exactly the way he'd meant it.

"You must know all about the Hideaway if you live around here. I can't imagine there's a person on the island who doesn't." Sarah scraped a finger along one cheek and bared a long streak of perfect skin. "Trashy chic. At least that's the notion. There are four guest rooms, each with its own theme. There's Almost Paradise, a sort of Garden of Eden room. Love Me Tender—I peeked in there when I arrived. Graceland meets the worst of the seventies.

Then there's Smooth Operator, which apparently has some sort of James Bond theme and—"

"And then there's romance central. Maisie tells me you're staying in Close to the Heart. At least until the season starts and the first guests arrive." Dylan extracted a handkerchief from his pocket and wiped off his hands. When he offered it to Sarah and she refused, he tucked it back in his pocket. "Talk about romance!" He laughed. "There's more red velvet in that room than in a Nevada bordello."

It was supposed to be a joke. Sarah never cracked a smile. She refused the offer of Dylan's help, too, and instead got to her feet. No chance she was going to get rid of the dirt, but she brushed off the seat of her pants and tucked a strand of hair behind her ear.

"Close to the Heart is very comfortable, I'll give it that," she said. "But it is a little..."

"Flamboyant?"

Sarah's nose crinkled. "I was going to say tacky."

"Think so?" Though he wasn't sure why, Dylan was surprised by her clinical assessment. It was the second time in as many minutes that she'd caught him off guard and it made him more determined than ever to find out what made Sarah tick. Not to mention what made her suspicious in Maisie's eyes.

"I hear the folks who stay in Close to the Heart are more than satisfied," he said, adding a little emphasis to the last word. "After all, there's the heart-shaped bathtub, the round bed, the mirrors on the walls and ceilings..."

All right, so it wasn't exactly fair to tease a woman he hardly knew. But it wasn't as though Dylan could help himself. A beautiful woman. A perfect spring evening. The sound of the waves lapping against the shore. It all added up to one of those magical moments meant for a little harmless fun.

A fact that apparently escaped Sarah's attention.

"The heart-shaped bathtub is as big as the swimming pool at my old high school," she told him. "Can you imagine how much hot water it takes to fill it? Or how much that adds to Maisie's utility bill every month? And the smudges that must get on those mirrors!" A shiver skittered over her slim shoulders. "As for all that velvet and lace...well, it makes me glad I'm working in the garden and not in housekeeping. I wonder how they manage to keep the dust under control."

"That's not the point." He grinned because anybody with a sense of humor would. There was no hotel room—anywhere—as over the top as Close to the Heart. Maisie knew it full well, just as the legion of returning guests who requested the room did.

"When folks come to Cupid's Hideaway, they're usually thinking about other things. Things that don't include dusting and polishing."

Things he shouldn't be thinking of.

Things he *wasn't* thinking of, Dylan told himself.

He cleared his throat and did his best to steer the conversation in a direction that was a little less filled with notions about what two consenting adults might do in that heart-shaped bathtub or that round bed. "Maisie always says that what it lacks in elegance, Close to the Heart makes up for in panache. Seems to me, all that room needs to complete the romantic picture are a few candles, a bottle of champagne..." He spread his arms as if measuring the proportions of a giant-sized vase. "A couple dozen red roses and—"

"Romantic picture?" Sarah frowned. "And roses?" She clumped over to retrieve the basket of geraniums, lifted

it and held it in both hands. "Not a rose in sight," she said.
"Not back here, anyway. There are some over on the other
side of the house." She turned toward the parking lot
where Dylan had left his truck. "They'll require the most
care, so I figured I'd finish this part of the garden first. You
know, get the annuals in so they can start growing before
I worry about the trimming and pruning and such on the
roses."

The plan was pragmatic and straightforward, no-non-
sense and completely without imagination. Apparently,
just like Sarah herself.

It was a fact that might have bothered Dylan if he was
in search of a woman to warm his heart and his bed.

Which he wasn't.

He told himself not to forget it and considered what
Maisie had told him earlier in the day. Sarah might be a
kind of a stick in the mud (with the emphasis on mud)
but she was hardly suspicious.

"So—" he rocked back on his heels "—where you
from?"

Sarah put the basket down on the back steps. She lifted
the individual pots of geraniums out of it and set them in
the dirt in neat, straight-as-soldiers lines. "New England,"
she said, her back to him, her voice muffled.

"And you're here because...?" He let the question hang.

She hesitated before she turned to him, a geranium in
each hand. "Because of gardening."

"Alone?"

As soon as he asked it, he knew it sounded too bold.
Even for a cop. He scrambled to explain himself. "I was
thinking of what Maisie said a week or so ago. She said
she'd hired a summer gardener, but she didn't mention
that gardener coming with children. Or a significant
other."

"Just me." Her expression drooped when she examined the carnage all around her. "Me and my gardening expertise." As if to prove it, she turned around and went back to work, tucking the geraniums into the soil next to the steps. When she bent over, her khakis tugged across her bottom and Dylan smiled.

As soon as he realized it, he wiped the smile away and headed toward the rambling pink garage set along the back property line. Suddenly Maisie's phone call was starting to make a whole bunch of sense.

Dylan's blood ran cold.

He had a feeling that in Maisie's eyes, the only suspicious thing around here was that Sarah was suspiciously single. Dylan was, too, and this was the perfect opportunity to bring them together.

But then, Maisie should have realized that Dylan had a right to his own suspicions.

Heck, it was his duty. He had no choice but to be suspicious of one fluffy innkeeper who, now that both her granddaughters were happily married, didn't have anybody's love life to stick her cute little nose into. The one who might be trying to make a certain police chief her next romantic mission.

"Oh, no!" Dylan mumbled the words and picked up his pace, putting a little more distance between himself, Sarah and that damned cupid that was tempting him to forget every promise he'd made to himself since the day eighteen months earlier when the woman he'd thought was the prettiest woman who ever stepped onto the island stepped back on the ferry and sailed out of his life.

Chapter Two

The modern woman is perfect, dear reader, because
she's always in control. She's cool. She's calm.
She's very collected. She's ready for anything and
prepared for everything. What's that? You say
romance should be spontaneous? Gentle reader, you
are wrong! Even romantic moments can be
enhanced by careful planning. Today's woman
turns unexpected occurrences into part of that plan.
If she didn't…heavens, dear reader! If she didn't,
she wouldn't be perfect, would she?
— *Sarah's Guide to Life, Love and Gardening*

"So…" Eyes twinkling in the candlelight, pink angora
sweater the exact shade of the early May sunset outside
the dining-room window, Maisie walked around to the
side of the table where Sarah was seated and poured coffee from a silver pot. "You were about to tell us,
dear…about your life back home."

She wasn't. As a matter of fact, in the week since she'd
been on the island, Sarah had made sure she hadn't said
one little bit about herself to anyone. She wasn't going to
start now.

She didn't need word to get around that she was a TV

hostess. Especially on a tiny island with a small permanent population and a swarm of visiting tourists that was sure to get larger each day it got closer to the start of summer. Residents didn't have a whole bunch to talk about. Visitors went back to the mainland and spread gossip. She didn't want some eager-beaver reporter to find her.

Or some disturbed stalker.

"You said you were a—"

Maisie's voice snapped Sarah back to reality. "Secretary." It wasn't a lie. Not exactly. Back in Providence when she was working on her undergrad degree in marketing, she'd actually done some temp work. "In a law office."

"An attorney's office. How interesting!" Finished with the coffee, Maisie took her seat again at the head of the table. She arranged her linen napkin on her lap, sipped the pricey shiraz in her wineglass and pinned her second guest with a smile that was nothing less than warm and fuzzy— and nothing short of ruthless.

"Isn't that a coincidence, Dylan? You and Sarah are practically in the same business."

As hints went, this one was anything but subtle. And like every other suggestion and double entendre their hostess had delivered this evening, this one made Sarah's heart jump. Her hands naturally followed suit. She dropped her silver teaspoon and it clattered against the antique china saucer. She winced at the sound, as loud as an explosion against the cupid-infested expanse of the Hideaway's dining room.

In light of what she was planning to talk to Dylan about after dinner, she didn't need to even *think* about happily-ever-afters.

At Maisie's comment, Dylan rolled his eyes, and when their hostess busied herself setting heart-shaped cookies on china dessert plates, he smiled and mouthed to Sarah, "Here we go again."

Sarah didn't know whether she should be relieved or insulted that he wasn't even about to consider the cues Maisie had been dropping like bricks since before dinner started. The ones that said in no uncertain terms that if they hadn't bothered to realize it, Maisie would do their thinking for them: Sarah and Dylan just might be/could be/should be a couple in the making.

Dylan was out of uniform tonight, dressed in well-worn jeans and a golf shirt that brought out the flecks of grass-green in his hazel eyes. A shaft of sunlight ricocheted off the lake and touched his sandy hair with gold. He accepted a plate of cookies from Maisie, then reached across the table, passing it on to Sarah. Even after she already had it in her grasp, he held on to it for a second. "Lawyers and cops don't always get along," he said. "Unless you worked for a prosecutor."

"Prosecute? Oh, no." Sarah set the plate down and tapped a cookie against the rim, getting rid of the extra red-colored sugar sprinkled over the top of it, as well as the jumpiness that bubbled up whenever people were watching her. In this case, the *people* in question included Dylan. She wondered how good a cop he was. Could he see through her story? Straight to the fact that the extent of her law office experience was answering the phone and running out for sandwiches when the senior partner got hungry?

"Our office did probate. Wills. Estates. That kind of stuff. Boring dinner conversation and not exactly work that allows you to follow your bliss." At the same time as she felt the burn of heat in her cheeks that always showed up when she found herself the center of attention, she reminded herself of the story she'd concocted when Maisie interviewed her for the job here at the inn. "That's why I decided to do what I always dreamed of doing. I quit my law office job to become a landscape designer and gardener."

Maisie's smile was as soft as the last of the evening light that shimmered out over the lake. "It's always good to follow where your heart leads. I like to think that's what the Hideaway is all about. Isn't it interesting, you two ending up here at the same time?"

It wasn't.

From the moment Maisie asked Sarah to join her for dinner, then scurried back to the garage to see if Dylan was free this evening, too, Sarah had seen the writing on the wall.

It didn't say anything she wanted to read.

It was bad enough that she needed Dylan's help at all. Worse to admit she needed help with what she needed help with. And way beyond worse (not to mention mortifying, embarrassing and just plain humiliating), because Dylan was the yummiest thing she'd seen since the day she taped the *Affairs of the Heart* salute to chocolate. She didn't need to remind herself that chocolate was bad for her.

Just like falling in love.

"You're not exactly subtle, Maisie." Dylan leaned forward, his elbows propped on the lace tablecloth, and eyed Maisie with the kind of steely firmness Sarah imagined he used on the folks who ended up on the wrong side of the Put-in-Bay boys in blue. "You can stop, Maisie," he said. "We know what you're up to."

Maisie *tsk-tsk*ed away the very suggestion. "Up to? What I'm up to…" She bit into a cookie and licked sugar off her lips. "I'm up to finding out more about Sarah." Maisie smiled in her direction. "We got as far as you following your bliss. Now that you've followed it here...will you stay?"

It was on the tip of Sarah's tongue to say, "Certainly not." After all, she had a TV show to shepherd onto cable. She had a line of sumptuous bed linens and bath towels to design. She had her *Sarah's Guide* to finish.

But she didn't have a screw loose. She knew there was nothing to be gained from laying it on the line. Not if she expected to keep her job—and her secrets—all summer.

"I like it here," Sarah said, and though she hadn't really considered it before, she knew it was true. "I like the slow pace of island life. I like the quiet."

"Which won't last once the tourists arrive in full force!" Dylan crunched into a cookie.

"Maybe not," she conceded. Outside the window, the light was fading to a color that reminded her of the slate gray she'd once touted as the new neutral, and she realized that now that the subject had shifted from her life to island life, she wasn't nearly as tense. "There's a lot going on, a lot of hustle and bustle. But there's a sort of old-fashioned charm to it all, too."

"Yeah. Like all those old-fashioned bars downtown. And the old-fashioned college kids who show up on weekends to drink themselves into old-fashioned stupors."

"But *you* haven't left."

She didn't mean it as a challenge, only an observation. Still, a muscle jumped in Dylan's jaw. "This is my home," he said. "Always has been. Always will be. It's where my parents grew up. And my grandparents. I figure the least I can do is stick around and keep the family name going. Part of the reason I stay is to make sure that those bars and those college kids and all the tourists who will be streaming off the ferries in a week or two don't change the place. Sure, most of the people who are born and raised here leave for life on the mainland. Just like both my sisters and my brother did. I guess I want to make sure that there's always a home for them to come back to."

It was as unrealistic a notion as any Sarah had ever heard. Instead of saying so and risking insulting either Dylan or Maisie, she remarked, "I guess it's the homey part that appeals to me. That's why I think I'd like to settle down here."

It was an offhand comment designed to do nothing more than distract them from asking any more questions about her past. That didn't explain why Dylan narrowed his eyes and studied her with new interest. Or why Maisie sat up, eyes glistening with interest.

"Isn't that wonderful, Dylan?" Maisie declared. "Sarah is going to stay. I knew you'd fit right in with our island family, Sarah dear. As soon as we talked on the phone that first day you called. I knew I made the right decision inviting you to join our staff. This is exactly where you're supposed to be. And it's so convenient that Dylan is staying with us until they finish the renovations on his house, because you two have so much in common. I *know* you're meant to be friends. Or more. It's perfect, isn't it?" Maisie sighed. "Even if you didn't have as much gardening experience as some of the others who applied for the job."

As much experience was putting it mildly. In the days since Sarah had arrived, she'd discovered that there was a lot more to real-life gardening than there was to the kind of gardening she did on her show or wrote about in her book. The physical labor she'd been doing from early morning until late into the evening was a whole lot harder than glancing through Becky's horticultural research and using it as a backdrop to write about what kinds of flowers liked sun and what kinds liked shade. It was far more arduous than putting on a wide-brimmed straw hat and a gauzy dress that drifted around her ankles and strolling through some color-coordinated Eden, taking all the credit for the work someone else had done off camera.

"Speaking of your garden…" Dylan knew Maisie well enough to know that if he let her have her head, she'd be talking about happily-ever-afters again, practically picking out a cottage with a picket fence for them and naming the kids. "I hear there's a chance of frost later in the week."

His comment was enough to make Sarah nearly choke on her cookie. She washed away the lump with a sip of coffee. "It's May."

"It's northern Ohio," Dylan said. "Most folks around here don't even dare plant before the end of the month. And I noticed you've already got most of the annuals in. Maybe that's the way you do it in…"

It wasn't a question, but there was no doubt he expected Sarah to answer it.

Before she could, Maisie chimed in. "Of course she has the annuals planted. I asked her to. The Nelson family is coming this weekend and I wanted the Hideaway to be slicked up and gorgeous. You remember the Nelsons, Dylan. I think you had the pleasure of making Grandpa Nelson's acquaintance a year or two ago."

"The old guy with the bad toupee and the white patent-leather shoes? The one who had the crazy idea that women liked it when he pinched their bottoms?" Dylan groaned. "Guess I'd better get the cell ready for him."

Maisie sniffed. "Not necessary. Grandpa Nelson has departed."

"I'm not surprised," Dylan said. "Probably got his block knocked off by one of the women he pinched."

"Not that kind of departed." Maisie's smile was sly. "He's departed for Arizona. With his new wife. I hear she's thirty-five and quite stunning in a cheap, hot-to-trot sort of way. It wasn't until Grandpa's last trip here to the Hideaway that he was feeling frisky and inspired enough to pop the question. But isn't that what we were saying? If your heart leads you—"

"It wasn't Grandpa Nelson's heart that was calling the shots."

Maisie's cheeks flushed at Dylan's comment. "If your heart leads you," she said, "you'd be foolish not to follow." She glanced from Sarah to Dylan and back again. "Or at least not to peek around the corner and see where it wants you to go."

"Where it wants me to go…" Dylan yawned and stretched. "Sorry. Dinner was fabulous, but my heart and every one of my aching muscles is telling me it's been a long day. Bill is out with the flu. Jake's wife is over on the mainland having her baby and I had to let him be with her. Marsha, who answers the phones at the station, had a root canal yesterday. I can't let the other officers pick up all the slack. I worked a double today and have another one coming up tomorrow."

"Exactly why you shouldn't head over to the garage and hit the hay." Maisie nodded sagely, exactly the right note of authority in her voice. "You're overtired. You'll never fall asleep. Not for hours. Why don't you and Sarah go into the parlor? You can light a fire and a few of those pink candles I left near the stereo. Turn on some Tony Bennett, kick back, relax. Get to know each other better."

"No offense, but—"

Sarah made a choking noise and Dylan bit off his apology. He probably thought she was offended. Little did he know that it was a gulp of panic. She couldn't risk him calling it a night. Not after she'd worked up the nerve—finally—to ask for his help.

She gave him a tight smile and told herself she should at least try to talk him out of leaving. But not so deep down inside, she hoped he'd leave, anyway. Then she could procrastinate a little more.

"Don't feel obligated to hang around on my account," she told him. "I've got plenty to keep me busy. Besides, I can understand how tired you must be and—"

"There is a lot I have to do at the station tomorrow and—"

"I really should be up at the crack of dawn, too, and—"

"Listen to you two!" Maisie's laugh was airy but it contained enough metal to cut off both Sarah and Dylan's half-baked excuses at the knees. "You don't mean it and you know it. Besides, it can't be any later than seven o'clock. You young folks need to learn to enjoy life while you can. Isn't that what romance is all about?"

Romance.

The word skipped through Sarah's head and caused a prickle up her spine. Her hand jumped and smacked into the wineglass near her plate. Fortunately, it was empty and the glass didn't break, but her reaction was all the signal Sarah needed; if just the mention of romance made her lose her focus and her nerve, maybe it was time to rethink her plan.

A retreat was in order. With the door of Close to the Heart locked behind her and her word-processing program open to a chapter of *Sarah's Guide* that was sure to keep her busy long into the night, she could stall a little longer. And wait for another day to face the irrational fantasies—so unlike her—she'd been having about Dylan.

She didn't need to waste brain cells thinking about how handsome he was in that snappy blue uniform of his. Or how scrumptious he might look out of it.

She didn't need to think about the way her insides warmed when she watched him come home to the Hideaway in the evening, either. Or how her heart missed a beat when he waved hello to her before he headed to his room over the garage.

She didn't need to confuse hormones with emotions because she'd done that once before, and all it had gotten her was a whole bunch of heartache. She didn't need to bring sentiment into the mix, because she had three brothers and they had taught her early on that what most people called romance was actually smoke and mirrors. She didn't need to confuse any of it with logic. Because her logic was all she could depend on.

Of course, that didn't mean that she didn't like the little shot of heat that erupted when Dylan grinned at her over the bouquet of carnations arranged artfully in the center of the table.

Rather than think about how much, Sarah pushed back from the table. "I'll get the dishes cleared."

"Oh, no!" Maisie popped out of her chair and started collecting china. "I'm taking care of all this tonight. Meg and Gabe will be back in town in a couple weeks and you know how she is, Dylan. If the kitchen isn't shipshape, she'll get offended and head right back to Los Angeles. Meg's—" she filled in the blanks of the story for Sarah's sake "—my youngest granddaughter. And Gabe was a guest here at the Hideaway last summer. He was on the island following his bliss, too. It led him straight to Meg. They were married last Christmas."

"Charming story." Dylan rose, too, pointedly ignoring the reference to marriage. He grabbed the serving dishes, stacked them and carried them toward the kitchen. Sarah scooped up the wineglasses. Maisie followed with the plates.

"Speaking of Gabe and Meg…" Maisie paused inside the kitchen and waited for the door to swing closed behind her. "There's a lightbulb out up in Love Me Tender. I've tried to change it myself." She rubbed the knuckles of her right hand. "But my arthritis is acting up again and—" She shrugged off what had almost sounded like an uncharacteristic complaint. "Would you go up there and do it for me, Dylan?"

"Sure." He was familiar enough with the Hideaway to know where the supplies were kept. He went to a closet on the far side of the kitchen and came back with a lightbulb. "Bathroom? Or one of the lights over the soda fountain?"

"Actually, it's the one next to the bed." A hand on both their shoulders, Maisie herded Dylan and Sarah toward the door. "Take Sarah up there with you, why don't you, and you two can—"

"That's it!" Even Dylan's good-natured laughter couldn't hide the enough-is-enough fire that sparked in his eyes. Before Sarah knew what he was doing and long before she could react, he grabbed her hand. "We're outta here."

"But, dear—"

"No more." Dylan turned his back on Maisie and tugged Sarah toward the door. "We've had it with the innuendoes."

"But, dear—"

"And with the hints."

"But you could—"

"We're going for a walk."

"I could pack snacks in case you get hungry later." Maisie kept at it, even when they hurried out the back door and dashed down the steps. "And there's a concert in the park tonight, don't forget. You know what they say, a loaf of bread, a jug of wine… I think we could include a bottle of wine in the basket, don't you? After all, we have connections with the local police and…"

She was still talking when they rounded the corner to the front of the inn.

And Dylan was still holding Sarah's hand.

She stopped at the place where the front porch curled around the side of the house and untangled her fingers from Dylan's. "I think we're safe now."

Safe?

That wasn't the way Dylan was feeling. Not when Sarah's hand was touching his. Not safe in the keeping-his-wits-about-him department, anyway.

Grateful that one of them had an ounce of sense, he pulled his hand away from hers and scraped it through his hair. "She's a real character. That old lady has more nerve—"

"More nerve than Dick Tracy. That's what my grandfather used to say."

"Really? My grandfather used to say that, too." He reminded himself that he was the last person likely to fall for Maisie's heavy-handed matchmaking. And found himself smiling, anyway. "Maybe Maisie's right, after all. Maybe we do have something in common."

"Yeah, grandfathers who say corny things."

"And the need to get away from little old ladies who stick their little old noses where they don't belong."

"Like into our lives. All this nonsense about romance!" Her laugh was tight. "At least we can both take a joke."

Was it a joke? Dylan wasn't into the whole macho-man mind-set, but he couldn't help but feel that in her own not-very-diplomatic way, Sarah had just cut him off at the knees.

His pride prickled and in self-defense, he was tempted

to say that he was sure the possibility of romance was a lot of baloney, too. But he'd never been comfortable with lying. Even when it was the easiest course of action.

Yeah, up until a little bit ago, he thought Maisie's attempts at getting him and Sarah together were a little too blatant and a big waste of time. Until that moment when Sarah announced that she was thinking of settling on South Bass. Until his hand closed over hers and the heat that shot through him when they were skin to skin was more than he expected.

He tried not to get ahead of himself. At least not yet. With a woman like Sarah, slow and easy was the way to go. Even though he would have preferred fast and furious.

"Maisie wasn't joking about the concert tonight. You want to go?"

Sarah's eyes widened with surprise, but whether it was good surprise or bad surprise, Dylan couldn't say.

Rather than worry about it, he figured he'd better explain. "I figured with your love of music…"

She gave him a blank stare.

"You know. The radio. Every day when I get back here from the station, I see you working in the yard. And you've always got the radio on."

Her golden brows were silvery in the moonlight. They dropped low over her eyes. "I have the radio on while I work, but I don't really listen. You know what I mean?"

He didn't.

"One kind of music is just like another to me," she explained, and apparently that made perfect sense to her. "It's background noise. You know?"

"I'm afraid I don't. I like music. Rock, classical, a little Sinatra and a lot of Nirvana. That's what they'll be playing at the concert tonight." He caught himself and grinned. "Sinatra. Not Nirvana."

The least Sarah could have done was pretend to consider his offer. "Can't," she said without a moment's hesitation. "I've got a lot to do tomorrow and enough to keep me busy tonight and—"

"Too busy to enjoy the high school band?" Because he was afraid she'd say she was, he didn't give her a chance to answer. "There's bingo at city hall after. Or we might be able to arrange a spin on the carousel over at the park. They're not officially open for the season but... Well, I do have connections."

"And I've got far too much to do." Sarah turned away. "I mean, it's not that I'm not grateful for the offer, but—"

"It's only a concert."

She turned back to him with a sigh. "And we're only walking into the trap Maisie was all set to spring."

"Nah." He refused to think of himself as being manipulated, even by Maisie. Especially by Maisie. He also refused to let Sarah see how disappointed he was by her offhand dismissal. Rather than stand there looking like a loser, he gave in with a shrug, wished her a good night and headed down the road that bordered the lake.

FOR A COUPLE OF MINUTES, all Sarah did was watch him.

That, and give herself a good swift mental kick for letting the opportunity to talk to him pass her by.

"Chicken." She didn't even try to dispute the charge. What was the use, anyway? It was absolutely true. She'd worked up the nerve. She'd had motive and opportunity. And she blew it. Simply because she was being cowardly. And cowardly was something she never was. Was she?

Maybe it was the shame of that ugly truth that finally helped make up her mind.

Maybe Maisie was right and there was some sort of crazy, mumbo-jumbo magic going on at the Hideaway.

Whatever the reason, Sarah ignored the small, panicky voice inside her head that warned that she was getting into something she might not know how to get out of.

She headed to the street and followed Dylan to town.

Chapter Three

Though she is ever polite and always considerate of others' feelings, the modern woman speaks her mind. That doesn't mean she's pushy. Perish the thought! But neither is she wishy-washy. This is sound advice, dear reader, and you must always keep it in mind in life and, most especially, in love.
—Sarah's Guide to Life, Love and Gardening

"So, you do like music, after all."

Sarah tried not to notice (at least not too much) the scent of Dylan's aftershave when he leaned over her shoulder. She was only a few steps behind him when he arrived at the park, and when he stopped to talk to a man carrying a poodle, she stationed herself near the makeshift bandstand. While Dylan chatted, she braced herself against a full-fledged case of the screaming meemies.

The way she felt every time she had to pretend she was the ever-so-together Sarah Allcroft, who existed only in viewers' imaginations.

The way she was feeling right now.

Dylan spotted her as soon as he was done talking to the man with the dog and had come up close behind her. If she leaned back—just a little—she could nestle her head against his chest.

Bad idea!

At least if she was going to keep her head and stick to her plan.

The final pieces of her plan had fallen into place only a couple of days ago. This self-imposed exile in Ohio was a perfect opportunity! She could use the summer to practice the kind of poise and polish her fans expected to see from her—on-screen and off. She could perfect the image of elegance that the media expected and, with any luck at all, she could also bone up on all things romantic.

If only Dylan would agree to help her.

She swallowed down her nervousness along with the panic that sat in her throat like lumpy oatmeal.

"How did you figure it out?" she asked Dylan, her voice breathier than she liked. "I mean, about my love of music. Was it detective work? Or do you have a sixth sense?"

"More like common sense!" His laughter ruffled a strand of hair across her cheek, and rather than think about how nice it felt, she tucked it back into place. "I mean, there's the band." He pointed toward the twelve kids who were setting up and tuning their instruments. "And here you are. That must mean you've decided that you're a music lover."

Because there was no way on earth she could admit that she didn't like music as much as she liked the idea of *Affairs of the Heart* turning a profit and becoming a big, fat success for Becky, Gino and the rest of the crew, she used the excuse she'd been practicing since she left the Hideaway. "Actually, what I decided was that Maisie was right. It's too early to turn in. Figured I might as well kick back and relax. Just like she said."

"Maisie's a smart woman." He gestured toward the

nearest park bench, but it wasn't until he stepped back to allow her to sit down that Sarah realized how chilly it had become.

DeRivera Park was situated in the heart of downtown Put-in-Bay, a street of shops, restaurants and the bars Dylan had mentioned at dinner. The carousel he'd talked about was to their left. The lake was at their backs and, though it was May, a crisp breeze blew in from the north. Hugging her arms around herself and the navy-and-gray plaid flannel she'd put on over her clean Cupid's Hide-away polo shirt, Sarah sat down, took a deep breath and told herself to get a grip.

Now that the moment had come, she wondered exactly how to broach the subject.

So, how much do you really know about romance?

That seemed a little forward. Especially when she and Dylan barely knew each other.

How romantic of a guy are you?

That was a bit too close to the mark when it came to the fantasies that had been plaguing her since the first day they met.

She decided on an approach that was more politically correct.

Even if it was a whole lot less than to-the-point.

"Not exactly a big crowd."

Dylan surveyed the thirty or so people who bustled around, arranging blankets and setting up folding chairs on the grass. He nodded to the police officer who watched the action from the doorway of a pizza parlor across the street.

"About what can be expected this time of year. But, hey, give it a few weeks. This place will be wall to wall with summer visitors. That's one of the reasons the Chamber of Commerce planned this concert for tonight. It's a chance for all of us to take a deep breath before the season starts."

"You must be very busy then."

"Oh, yeah." He didn't seem to mind. "Big crowds. Lots of noise. Everybody zipping around in those golf carts they rent over near the ferry docks. Lost kids, lost dogs, lost golf cart keys. Summer is our busy time."

Grateful for the change of subject and a little more time to stall, Sarah made herself comfortable on the wooden park bench. "And after summer's over?" she asked.

Dylan stretched his legs out in front of him and threw one arm over the back of the bench. "After is when we get to breathe again. The whole place settles down and we have the island all to ourselves. I'm not complaining," he added before she could suggest that he might be. "I mean, summer is how we stay alive. It's when the merchants make the money that sustains them for the rest of the year. But in the fall and winter when everybody is gone…"

"Everybody?" Sarah wondered what the park would be like with icicles hanging from the war memorial cannons and snow piled up against the swings where a couple of little kids were playing. She wondered how lonely it was when the neat little cottages were boarded up against the winter weather and all the sailboats were gone from the marina. "You mean everyone leaves? That the island is deserted?"

"Rethinking what you said about staying?" Dylan's question was a little too pointed. Before Sarah could figure out why, he shrugged and waved to an elderly couple who sat down on the bench next to theirs. "At last count, we had 400 to 450 residents. Some are here only for the summer. Others stay all year. So, no, it's not exactly deserted. And if you're looking for peace and quiet, this is definitely the place. *If* you're looking for peace and quiet."

"I am." It was truer than he could know. Even if she *didn't* hope to make it permanent. "But that's not all I'm looking for. What I really need…" She hesitated.

"Assurance. I can understand that." He waved away what he thought she was anxious about. "It's beautiful here. Even in winter. It's so cold, the snow crunches under your shoes. And so quiet, you can hear your heartbeat." Dylan made a face. "Sorry. I don't mean to sound like a TV commercial. Anyway," he added, as if it would make all the difference, "we do see outsiders, even in winter. Lots of ice fishermen."

"And lots of ice, I bet. I've never been a big outdoors type," she said, then caught herself. "Except for the gardening, of course."

"Exactly what I've been meaning to talk to you about."

"You need advice about tomato plants—I'm your woman!" Sarah poked a thumb at her chest and hoped he didn't need advice about tomato plants. When it came to tomatoes, all she knew was that they tasted good with basil.

"Or maybe you want some ideas about what plants to pair together when you set out your annuals." Chapter Three of *Sarah's Guide*: Color in the Garden…and in the Bedroom. Color was definitely something she knew more than just a little about, and besides, a nice, long talk about the benefits of cooling off the garden with shades of blue and touches of white was as good a distraction as a discussion of island life in the off-season. "Are you going for a garden that's bright and cheery? Or something more somber and police-chief–like?"

"That's not what I was going to ask."

"Then what? If the topic is gardening—"

"Then the question has to be how you talked Maisie into giving you your job."

Nothing like a new wave of panic to keep the old wave at bay. Fortunately, Sarah was saved from answering, at least right away, when the band director stepped up in front of her musicians. The crowd quieted and Sarah took the opportunity to gather her composure and plan her defense.

After the first few notes of the piece, she leaned closer to Dylan and lowered her voice so she didn't disturb anyone. "You heard Maisie," she whispered. "She said it at dinner. Some of the other applicants had more experience than I have but—"

"Some?"

The trombone player hit a sour note, and Sarah pretended she heard that, not the question. "Maisie says she knew I'd fit in best here."

He nodded in time to the music and Sarah breathed a sigh of relief. That was that.

Until the song ended and the crowd applauded.

Dylan joined in, giving the kids in the band the thumbs-up and never once looking her way. "Who am I to contradict Maisie? I'd be more than willing to say she was right if it wasn't for the geraniums."

When it came to topics like profit and loss, market share and residuals, Sarah had an encyclopedic knowledge. When the subject was horticulture, things got a bit fuzzy. As a matter of fact, when it came to most varieties of flower, she knew exactly two things: little and nothing. But lucky her, she'd recently done an *Affairs of the Heart* segment on Mother's Day flowers, and as always, Becky's research was golden.

When the band started the main theme from some movie Sarah couldn't remember and had probably never seen, anyway, she sat up straighter and slanted Dylan a smile.

"Geraniums like sun," she said. "Lots of it. Back at the Hideaway, they're getting oodles of sun where I planted them."

"Uh-huh." Dylan tapped his right hand against the arm of the bench in perfect time to the music.

"They like water. Every day," Sarah added, feeling righteous because this—at least—was one thing she could show Dylan she knew something about. "And they like liquid fertilizer. Once a week."

The least he could have done was acknowledge how right she was. Dylan listened until the song ended. And when it did, he propped his elbows on his knees and twined his fingers together. "It's not where you're planting them," he said. "And it's not how you're treating them. As far as I can see, you're being very good about the watering regimen. It's *how* you're planting them that's got me puzzled."

She demonstrated in the air in front of her. "Dig hole. Stick in plant. Not exactly brain surgery."

"But your rows. They're all—"

The next song was "New York, New York" and it was so brassy and lively, Dylan didn't even try to compete with it. He waited until the kids were done.

"Your rows," he said when the crowd finally stopped its enthusiastic applause. "They're picture-perfect."

"Yes, they are. Thank you."

If she needed any more reminder of why she needed Dylan's help, it was all there in his blank stare. It only took a nanosecond for her to recognize that this was it—the perfect opening she'd been waiting for.

She laughed away the skitter of uneasiness that added an additional chill to the air.

And chickened out.

Instinct took over and made her defend herself. "I like my flowers in straight rows," she said. "It gives them symmetry and makes the viewer feel a sense of order. It's neoclassical."

"It's a waste of perfectly good garden space. Besides, gardens aren't all about light requirements and watering needs. Gardens should be…" Apparently, he couldn't explain. He demonstrated instead, waving his hands. "You know, flowing. Smooth and natural. A little of this here. A lot of that there."

"You mean messy."

"That's not what I said."

"But it's what you're advocating. A little of this here, a lot of that there." The very thought offended her concept of order and Sarah shivered. "Before you know it, you're not seeing individual flowers at all, just getting a sort of overall sensory impression."

"Exactly."

"Exactly?" It wasn't as if she'd never considered the concept, just that she hadn't expected to hear it from a man whose job demanded that above all else, he be rational.

Then again, weren't his *irrational* notions the very reason she'd followed him to the park tonight?

She pulled in a breath for courage. "What you're saying is, you think gardens should be sensuous. Speaking of that—"

"Shhh!" It wasn't until the elderly lady on the next bench hissed and held a finger to her lips that Sarah realized the band had begun another number. Dylan nodded his apology and they both fell silent. Before the kids could finish another bar of the theme from *Rocky*, they got up and left the park.

Sarah recognized a sign from above when she saw one. By the time they were standing in front of the carousel, she'd convinced herself she'd have to have her planned heart-to-heart with Dylan another day.

Too bad nobody told Dylan.

"So…" A smile touched the corners of his mouth. "What's that you were saying about being sensual?"

Sarah's stomach bubbled. She scrambled to correct him. Before he got the wrong idea. "I wasn't talking about being sensual. I mean, not me, personally. But you said—"

"No. You said. And what you said was sensuous." His eyes gleamed.

She refused to be sidetracked. Not by the gleam or by the memory of how nice it had felt when he threw his arm over the back of the park bench and her insides heated along with her outsides.

"First of all, what I *said* was 'sensuous.' But maybe I *meant* 'sensual.' Or maybe…what I'm saying…" She curled her fingers into her palms and held her arms close to her sides. "I need your help."

It was a serious request and she'd imagined he'd take it seriously.

Of course, that didn't explain why Dylan's smile inched up a notch. "My help? To be sensual?"

It was a tempting thought.

And not at all in her best interests. Sarah put it firmly out of her mind and did her best to keep her voice modulated and her demeanor as professional as possible. Not easy considering that she was about to humiliate herself.

"I want…" She stumbled over her words then bravely forged ahead. "I want you to teach me about romance."

One heartbeat. Two heartbeats. Three.

Dylan didn't move. He didn't say a word.

Certain he wasn't listening, Sarah leaned closer and

raised her voice. "I said I need your help. I want you to teach me about—"

"This is some kind of joke, right?" As if he expected some reality TV camera crew to jump out of the nearby bushes, Dylan glanced around. "You're setting me up. Who put you up to this? The guys over at the station? Or Meg. I'll bet it was Maisie's granddaughter, Meg. She always did have a warped sense of humor."

"It's not a joke. You said it yourself. My garden isn't romantic."

"And you want me to—"

"To show me what *is* romantic. I know you can." She rushed to get this over with before her good sense got the better of her. Or before her cheeks got any hotter. "That first day we met, you said Cupid's Hideaway was romantic and you said Close to the Heart was, too. And I think *aesthetically challenged* better describes both the inn and the room. And you said gardens that are all mixed up and messy are romantic, and I…well, the very idea of that kind of chaos makes me break out in a cold sweat. I admit, you're not exactly a guy I would expect to understand this sort of thing, but apparently, you *do* understand, and me…well, I don't. There. That's the truth. I understand what people *think* is romantic, you know, scented candles and soft lighting and perfume wafting on the air. But I don't get it. That's why I figured if anyone was going to be able to help me, you would be the one to do it, so you will, won't you?"

Sarah ran out of air. And nerve. She waited for his response.

Dylan didn't say a word. She swore he didn't blink. Or even breathe.

Finally, after what felt like forever, he turned his head enough to see the monument that dominated the central part of the island. It was more than three hundred feet high, an impressive column of granite erected to commemorate a lake victory in the War of 1812. It was illuminated at night and it glowed like a giant candle in the center of neatly manicured lawn.

"Romance is sort of like the Perry Monument," he said, craning his neck to see all the way up to the bronze urn that topped the column. "It's there. Always. Overshadowing everything. It's as simple as that."

"Simple. Yeah. So I've been told. But—"

"But maybe where you're from, people don't think of romance the same way."

That was, no doubt, supposed to be a clever effort to get her to reveal more about herself. Lucky for her, though, she might be mortified, embarrassed and humiliated, but she wasn't easily fooled. "Maybe where I'm from," she told Dylan, "people aren't so nosy."

He had the audacity to grin. "Just doing my job, ma'am."

"And your job doesn't involve romance."

"My job doesn't, no. As a matter of fact, it's probably the least romantic job I can think of."

"And that means you're telling me no." She should have been relieved. No romance lessons from Dylan meant she didn't have to worry about how she'd respond when he was close. Or how much she'd think about him when he wasn't.

Which didn't explain the thread of disappointment that snaked through her.

"It's okay, really," she told him—and herself—and when she shrugged like it was no big deal, she was afraid it looked more pathetic than casual; so she turned and started walking in the direction of the Hideaway. "I understand. I mean, it's a crazy request and you barely know me and—"

She stopped cold when a cluster of something small and dark suddenly appeared in front of her nose. Startled, she looked around to find Dylan standing at her shoulder.

"Flowers?" Sarah stepped back for a better look. They were violets, their color as inky as the clear night sky. Though she hadn't seen him bend to pick them, they must have been growing somewhere near where they were standing. "You're giving me flowers?"

He didn't say a word. When she didn't respond to whatever it was in that strong-and-silent look he gave her, he clicked his tongue. "Don't you get it? Lesson number one is that flowers are romantic."

"No, lesson number one is that women know better. They aren't bamboozled easily."

He stepped back as if he'd been slapped. "Bamboozle? Who's talking about bamboozling anybody? We were talking romance. And I'm telling you, flowers are romantic."

"Oh, please!" Sarah rolled her eyes and gave herself a mental slap. "I'm sorry I bothered you with my crazy request. I should have known better than to ask a guy for help. Guys don't understand romance. Not any more than I do."

Dylan pulled back his shoulders. Someone had to defend the honor of guys everywhere.

Every crusade needed a champion and like it or not, he'd stepped up to the plate and accepted the job.

"And I'm telling you…" He scraped a hand through his hair. He was still holding the flowers and by the time he was done, they were bent every which way. "Romance is *exactly* what I'm talking about. Giving flowers to a woman—it's romantic."

She eyed the scrawny bouquet. "Then romance is a lot of baloney."

"You don't believe that." One look at the set of her chin and the fire in her eyes and he knew he was wrong. "You do!"

"You bet I do. And I'll tell you why—I've got three brothers."

It was enough of an explanation. At least for her. When Sarah turned and resumed walking, Dylan watched her for a moment. Her khakis were a bright spot in the night. So was her hair. Before she could get too far, he hurried to catch up so he could try to make some sense of a perfectly good evening gone perfectly bad.

"I've got a brother, too," he told her. "And I don't have a clue what you—"

"My brothers, they're all older than me. And all the time I was growing up, I heard about their dating adventures. Listening to them taught me a lot."

"Like…"

"For starters, it taught me that when a guy makes what you call a romantic gesture, he wants something in return."

"Something? Like—"

"Sex, of course."

It was the most sweeping condemnation of men he'd ever heard. And the most ridiculous. "So your brothers are jerks. That means you think I picked those flowers for you so that I could get you into bed?"

"Didn't you?"

"No!" It was true. Sort of.

Dylan winced. He wasn't stupid enough lie to himself. In the week since he'd met Sarah, he had dreamed about getting her in bed, all right. How could he not? He'd watched her work out in the garden and seen how smoothly she moved and how her hair was golden when it was kissed with sunshine. He'd seen her smeared with mud and damp from the spray of the garden hose and couldn't help but notice the delicious curves her wet clothes revealed.

At times like those, he might have been thinking with a portion of his anatomy that wasn't his brain, but he knew it couldn't be kept out of the picture completely or permanently. Any successful relationship had to be based on more than simply the physical. Even if it wasn't going to last longer than just the summer. Especially if it *was* going to last longer than just the summer.

All he'd hoped for tonight was to give her exactly what she wanted, a demonstration of sorts about just what constituted romance. That, and maybe a kiss when he left her at the door of the Hideaway. The way she described it, that alone made him sound like some kind of deviant.

He wasn't sure he wanted to know the answer to his next question. "Are you telling me that sex is completely out of the question?"

"I'm telling you that if that's what a man wants, he should say so. So should a woman, if that's what she's after. After all, it's the completely rational way to handle the situation. The completely sensible approach to modern relationships. It's the adult way to act and it gets rid of all the hearts-and-flowers nonsense. If a guy thinks a woman is so easily impressed that a bunch of flowers or a box of candy can make her rip off her clothes…"

For a second, Dylan had a little trouble focusing. Candy or no candy, flowers or not, he pictured Sarah ripping off her clothes, and it wasn't until she grumbled a sentence about insulting her intelligence that he forced his mind away from the fantasy that pretty much proved exactly what she was accusing him of.

"Now *that's* baloney," Dylan said, reminding himself

that they were talking about the fact that she didn't believe in romance, not the picture that flitted through his mind of Sarah out of those khakis and in some lacy nothing of a garment that hinted at the silky skin underneath. That was definitely *not* baloney. "You're painting every guy with the same brush, and it's not fair. It's perfectly natural for a guy to make a romantic gesture and—"

"And expect nothing in return but a sweet smile and an honest-to-gosh thank-you?"

"Yeah." He stepped back, his weight on one foot, his arms crossed over his chest, and it wasn't until he adopted the defensive posture that he realized Sarah had, too. They faced off like Smackdown opponents, toe to toe and eye to eye.

"You're one hundred percent wrong," he told her, "and I'll prove it. I'll take you up on your request. I'll spend the summer showing you exactly what it means to be romantic."

"And you won't expect anything in return? Nothing more than my sweet smile and a big ol' thank-you?"

"That's right." Dylan stuck out his hand, and Sarah shook it.

Before he could say another word, she plucked the violets out of his hand and even in the dark, he saw her face light up with the sweetest smile he'd ever seen. "Thank you," she said, and still smiling, she turned and headed toward the Hideaway.

Dylan watched her go, too stunned to offer a protest.

And why would he? He'd just agreed to spend his summer teaching the prettiest woman on the island what it meant to be romantic.

And if it also meant that he had to quash the fantasies that had been flitting through his mind about her and accept the fact that, at least for now, anything physical was strictly off-limits?

All the righteous indignation he'd been feeling evaporated in the light of the cold, hard facts.

Apparently, besides being the standard-bearer for romantic men everywhere, he was also the biggest chump in Put-in-Bay, Ohio.

Chapter Four

The modern woman does not indulge in playing
games. There is nothing romantic about it and it
serves no useful purpose. Speak your mind with
your lover! Share your secrets and, most importantly, your fantasies. There's no surer way to ignite
the flamesof romance than with a little honesty—
and a lot of imagination!

—*Sarah's Guide to Life, Love and Gardening*

The last person Sarah expected to see at ten o'clock on a
Wednesday night was Dylan.

Which pretty much explained why she took the chance
of answering the knock at the door of Close to the Heart
dressed in her black and brown plaid flannel pajamas.

"Oh!" Her hand flew to the Avocado Wonder Clarify-
ing Facial Mask that coated her face. "You're not Maisie."

"Nope. Not last I checked, anyway. Only me." He
barely controlled a grin, and when he couldn't hold it
back any longer, he looked over her shoulder and into the
room. "You going to ask me in?" he managed to say.

"Sure. Of course." She stepped back to allow him inside and darted into the bathroom long enough to grab a
wet washcloth and rub it over her cheeks. "I was reading."

"I can see that." Dylan's gaze wandered over the research she had stacked on the bed for Chapter Five of *Sarah's Guide*: Setting the Mood with Scent. Every subtopic had its own folder, color-coded and numbered so it was easy to access.

"Reading isn't romantic," Dylan announced. "Even if you're reading about gardening." He tilted his face toward the mirrored ceiling, the better to try to read the *History of Perfume* label on the top file folder.

Sarah grabbed one of the lacy pillows stacked at the foot of the bed and tossed it over the folders. Not exactly subtle but plenty effective.

"As you may have noticed—" she took another swipe at her cheeks and plucked at one leg of her flannel pajamas "—romance isn't exactly on tonight's agenda. It's late. I worked on the side flower beds all day and broke three fingernails in the process." She held up her hands to prove it. "I'm tired and in the middle of a delicate exfoliation. So what are you doing here?"

"I'm taking you out."

It was as simple as that. At least to Dylan.

Sarah wasn't fooled. One more swipe at her face and she tossed the washcloth into the antique bowl that stood on a nearby table. She eyed Dylan warily. "Does this have something to do with you teaching me about romance?"

"Absolutely."

Okay, she had to give him points for honesty. That didn't mean she had to fall right in with his plan.

"So you think you can waltz in here—"

"Waltzing, now that's romantic!" He grabbed her and whirled her around the room, a maneuver that would have been easier to accomplish if Sarah hadn't kept tripping over her own moccasins.

"No waltzing." She untangled her hands from his and stepped back and out of reach. Better for him, because she had no delusions about how graceful she was. Better for her, because standing that close to Dylan in the red-velvet and gilded monstrosity of a room that practically screamed *Take me to bed* wasn't the safest plan. Not when it came to her hormones or her heart.

"And no going out, either." Sarah was proud of herself. She could sound as bullheaded as he did. "It's late."

"It's only ten o'clock."

"Ten o'clock is late. At least for most working people. Did you know that without at least seven hours of sleep each night, most adults can't—"

His laughter snipped her lecture off.

"I'm being serious," she told him.

"Me, too. I've got special plans and I may not be able to arrange this again for a long time. It's romantic." He dangled the words like bait.

When Sarah didn't bite, he grabbed her hand and tugged her toward the door. "Come on. We're going."

"I can't! I still have avocado mask on my nose. I can feel it. And I'm wearing my pajamas."

Dylan stopped midstride. "Those are pajamas?" He wasn't convinced. "I thought women slept in gauzy stuff. You know, little satin nightgowns, tiny silk outfits, those see-through numbers that are—"

"I suppose you think that's romantic, too?"

Her question seemed to snap him out of whatever fantasy he was having. She wondered if he would have laughed like he did at her facial mask—or if he would have even noticed it—if she'd answered the door in an outfit cut up to here and down to there, instead of in her flannels.

"Crazy," she reminded herself.

Dylan made the mistake of thinking that she was talking to him. "You're right. It is crazy. Lesson number two: crazy can be romantic. And you have exactly—" he checked his watch "—two minutes to get changed and meet me out in the hallway."

She would have argued if he'd been a little slower about stepping outside and closing the door behind him.

But once she found herself alone, her head still spinning from the quick waltz they'd done around the room, Sarah knew she didn't have a choice. He'd only come back and bug her if she didn't get dressed and go wherever it was he wanted her to go with him.

And strangely, as she hurried through washing her face, then tugged on a pair of jeans, a blue sweatshirt and her sneakers, she couldn't help humming.

"THE ROBINSONS WON'T BE HERE at all this year. They're both teachers and I hear they're doing some sort of recertification classes this summer. Then there's the Metzgers." Dylan's gaze swiveled from one side of the street to the other, to a tiny white cottage fronted by what used to be a neat lawn. The lawn was overgrown and filled with weeds, and the house was dark. "They haven't been back for two seasons. Not since Don got sick. He doesn't have the energy to drive down from Detroit anymore."

"That's too bad." Sarah didn't know the Metzgers, but she meant it. "I never stopped to think about it before, but it must take a lot of work to keep a summer home ready and in repair."

"Most of the folks who own property here don't think of it as work. They love the island. Otherwise, they wouldn't keep coming back."

"Except that you haven't talked about the ones who keep coming back!" Sarah couldn't help but call him on it. "All you've pointed out since we left the Hideaway are houses that are empty. You've only told me about people who are trying to sell or rent their property."

The *why* of that hit her like a ton of bricks.

She froze at the spot where the street led in one direction toward the war monument and, in the other, to the downtown shops and restaurants.

"You're telling me all this…?"

"So you can find a place to live, sure." Dylan wasn't the least bit embarrassed at his high-handed tactics. "You can't stay in Close to the Heart forever. One of these days, Maisie's bound to have guests who want to use the room. You'll need to rent a place and, lucky for you, I know all the possibilities. Then again, since you're planning on staying, buying is probably a smarter option."

Sarah didn't need to see the latest statistics on mortgage rates to know he was right.

She didn't need to see her own face to know her cheeks were flaming, either. It was a natural reaction to being trapped like a dirty rat in the sticky web of her own lie.

It wasn't as if she had a choice, Sarah reminded herself. The story about how she was going to set up permanent housekeeping on the island was for Maisie's benefit, designed, executed and kept alive for the sole purpose of making Maisie more amenable to giving Sarah her summer job. And for letting her keep it.

"Maisie says that even if I get displaced from Close to the Heart, there's another room I can use. One that's downstairs and across from her suite."

"Sure." Dylan was familiar enough with the inn and its workings to know. "That's the room she keeps for her own personal guests. But you can't live at the Hideaway forever." He was as certain of his reasoning as he was of his footing in the dark. When they came to a place where the sidewalk was cracked and uneven, he put a hand on Sarah's elbow to guide her.

She stepped as carefully over the crack as she did around the truth. "It wouldn't hurt to start thinking about it." True, even if it wasn't exactly honest. "It wouldn't hurt to start getting some idea of what's available and what it costs."

"Exactly my point. But remember, don't be put off by anybody's first price. There's always room to negotiate."

She wondered if he'd still believe that if he knew how she'd negotiated her way around the truth since even before she'd set foot on the island. Rather than come to the conclusion that he'd think less of her if he knew about her lies, Sarah concentrated on a neon orange sign that glowed from a bar a few hundred feet up the deserted street. Downtown Put-in-Bay was as quiet as a tomb.

"I hope you don't take this the wrong way, but what on earth were you talking about when you said you had a romantic evening planned?"

Dylan held up one hand. "That's another lesson: there's romance in anticipation."

"And in impatience?"

His laughter was his only answer and still grinning, he headed over to the antique carousel. There was a fence around the merry-go-round, and a gate. It was locked but Dylan didn't let that stop him. He reached around to the padlock, gave it a jab at exactly the right spot, and the lock popped open.

When Sarah's mouth dropped open, too, he gave her an aw-shucks grin of innocence. "What? Don't worry. It's not breaking and entering. All the locals know how to open this lock. Besides…" There wasn't much light but he reached into his pocket, took out a small object and held it up for her to see. It glinted. Like metal.

"I have official permission," Dylan said. "From the owner. He even gave me the key to the carousel."

Sarah knew it was best not to get suckered in by what appeared to be the kind of bamboozle job she claimed she never got suckered in by. She still, however, stepped inside the gate and closer to the carousel.

"Ma'am." Dylan bowed to welcome her, and when he offered her a hand, she took it and stepped onto the wooden carousel platform. It moved just a little, and she remembered a visit she'd once made to an aunt in California and how she'd gotten there in time for an earthquake.

"Steady!" He waited while she braced herself against a wooden unicorn, and once she was steady on her feet and set to go, he gave her a tug. He led her on a rambling walk through the painted animals. There were more unicorns and lots of horses, all decorated with carved flowers and ribbons. There was even a pig.

"The seat of honor." Dylan swept his arm toward a huge wooden…

"…fish?" Sarah wondered aloud.

"Not just any fish. This is Pete the Perch. He's famous."

She backstepped away from the animal with its flamboyant tail and gaping mouth. "He's a fish. People don't ride on fish."

"He's the most hotly contested seat on this merry-go-round. People wait in a special line to get on first. So they can ride on Pete." He patted the fish's back.

Sarah didn't move. "I think I'll stand here," she said. "It's a good spot and I can see a whole lot from here." As if to prove it, she looked all around, though what she was hoping to see in the dark was a mystery even to her. "This is a perfect spot."

"But it isn't romantic."

"And Pete is?"

Dylan leaned in close, and because Sarah was wedged between Pete and a white horse with a streaming mane and flashing eyes, she couldn't move. Not when his arm brushed hers. Or when his voice warmed the air. Not when her insides responded in a way that made her want to believe him.

"Pete is very romantic," he said, the words practically brushing her lips. "Besides, local legend says that riding on Pete is good luck."

She gave the fish the quick once-over. "You think?"

"I'm pretty sure."

"And it's not like I don't believe you, but—"

He was tired of excuses. Before she could protest further, Dylan fitted his hands around her waist and lifted her onto the fish.

It was a cool night and Pete's wooden saddle was slick with dew. Sarah threw one leg over Pete's back and clutched the pole that went from the platform to a bar overhead—and right through Pete's head. She settled herself. By that time, she realized that Dylan had disappeared.

She squinted through the dark to see what he was up to, and when she couldn't, she gave Pete a pat. "Romantic, huh?" she asked the fish. "If this is his idea of romantic—"

Just as she said it, all the lights on the carousel flickered on. After the darkness, the lights were blinding and she closed her eyes. When she opened them again, she realized the entire carousel had sprung to life with color. The horse she thought was white was really pale blue. The unicorn in front of her was a shade of green that reminded her of spring grass. Pete wasn't gray like she expected him to be. He was gleaming and silvery, as if he'd just leapt from the lake and the water still sparkled on his back.

She sucked in a breath of wonder. The calliope started playing "Let Me Call You Sweetheart." Dylan stepped out of the cubicle at the center of the carousel. A second after he hopped back on the platform, the carousel lurched forward.

Sarah clutched the pole in front of her with both hands. Even that wasn't enough to steady her. Besides moving up and down, Pete also moved back and forth. The scenery around her swirled.

Dylan moved back toward her, walking from unicorn to horse and from horse to fish. He didn't climb up on one of the animals. He stood at Sarah's side, one hand on the glittering scales painted on the fish's head, the other on the portion of Pete that Sarah had always thought of as the fillet.

"So, what do you think?" When Pete moved backward, Dylan's hand grazed Sarah's thigh. "Romantic enough for you?"

"It's nice." Sarah cringed at her description. A private ride on a closed carousel deserved a little more than *nice*. "It's a beautiful merry-go-round."

"It was built in 1917." The carousel picked up speed and Dylan stepped a little closer. "It's one of the few wooden carousels in the country that's still operational."

Pete moved back. Dylan's hand slid forward. Sarah's thigh tingled.

She swallowed hard, and hoping to distract herself, she watched the fence that surrounded the carousel as it slipped by. At this speed, it seemed solid, like a ring all around them. Beyond it, she could see the street and across from that, the park. The trees and sidewalk spun by. Her head spun right along with them, and the up-and-down motion made her stomach bunch.

Sarah forced her gaze away from the perimeter and back to the carousel itself. Maybe if she concentrated on the lights…

They twinkled all around, and because there weren't any other lights anywhere nearby, they threw funny shadows against the wooden animals. Shadows that moved. Up and down. Around and around.

Kind of like her stomach was doing.

She told herself the lights were a bad idea and forced her gaze to Dylan. Along with Pete, she slid close to him, then farther away. They were nose to nose, then all she could see was the top of Dylan's head.

Pete slid down again and Sarah caught Dylan's smile and saw the lights reflected in his eyes.

"Romantic, yes?" he said.

"It's…" She wondered how to word it, then decided if she tried to find a delicate way to deliver the news, she might not have the chance to speak at all. "I should've told you…"

The music drowned her words. The lights blinded her. Pete the Perch moved up and down. Sarah's stomach did, too.

She timed her movement perfectly and the next time Pete was as close to the base of the carousel as he was likely to get, Sarah scrambled off his back. She pushed past Dylan and staggered to the side of the carousel.

Luckily, they weren't moving very fast; she managed to jump onto solid ground and keep her feet and she kept on going until she got to the fence. She held on tight to it, her eyes squeezed shut, and she didn't dare open them again until she felt her stomach settle.

So it wasn't the most gracious of exits.

Even a nonromantic like Sarah knew that it beat getting sick all over Pete the Perch.

"HOW ARE YOU FEELING?"

Three days after the Pete the Perch fiasco, Dylan figured he knew. He also knew it would be impolite if he didn't ask Sarah, anyway. "Stomach settled down?"

"Yes. Thank you." She was seated at one of the picnic tables that had been brought onto the Hideaway's front lawn in honor of Maisie's annual charity auction. At the mention of the Pete affair, her cheeks darkened, but that was okay by Dylan. The color reminded him of strawberries. Besides, it was better than the pallor she'd had when he walked her home from their carousel ride.

"I'm surprised to see you here." He swung one leg over the picnic table bench and sat down beside her. "Didn't think this was your kind of thing."

"Children's charities? Why not? I think it's great that Maisie does this every year, and I hear it's always a smash. She raises hundreds of dollars for the local softball teams."

"And throws in some of her own so that she can send a donation to the children's burn unit at the hospital on the mainland." When one of the young Hideaway housekeeping staff came by with a tray of tiny cranberry muffins, Dylan grabbed a couple and handed one to Sarah. "I never said it wasn't a good cause. I just figured it wasn't up your alley."

"Why? Because I'm not romantic?" The words were more challenge than question. "In case you've forgotten the details, my last foray into the wonderful world of romance wasn't exactly successful."

Dylan's chuckle was interrupted by Maisie.

"Welcome! Welcome!" Maisie stepped onto the front porch of the Hideaway, and the forty or so people gathered around—mostly women—gave her a round of applause. "It's always good to see so many people here for our little auction. Please, get comfortable. There's iced tea and coffee." She motioned to her right and the refreshment station that was set up there. "And Tanya's coming around with some wonderful snacks. If you spend enough money—" Maisie winked "—I'll even throw in a glass of champagne."

It was the kind of icebreaker the crowd needed. When everyone applauded, Maisie raised her voice. "Ready to go?" she asked.

The answer was even louder applause.

And Dylan sat back to watch the show.

"Here's our first offering." There was an elaborate Oriental screen set up on the front porch, and Maisie reached behind it and revealed the first auction item. Dylan had been to these events before, and though he may not have known exactly what she had back there, he could venture a guess. He turned to see what Sarah's reaction would be.

She had just taken a bite of muffin when Maisie dangled a pair of black satin tap pants and two pasties, complete with tassels.

Sarah coughed and pounded her chest. "The program—" she reached for the printed program on the table in front of her "—it doesn't mention lingerie."

"And Maisie didn't, either." Dylan nodded. He knew why. Maisie knew exactly what he knew. If she made a big deal about exactly what she was selling, Sarah would have dismissed the whole event as frivolous and never would have shown up for the auction. "I'll bet she forgot to mention that what she auctions off are items from the Love Shack. That wacky gift store of hers. She clears out last year's merchandise to get ready for all the new stuff she ordered for this season."

"And all these people come to buy it?"

"They love Maisie. And you have to admit, the Love Shack has a selection like no other store." In the hopes of getting a rise out of her, he wiggled his eyebrows. "It's romantic, you know."

She brushed aside the very thought. "It's impractical. What good is loungewear if you can't lounge in it?"

Dylan watched the way the afternoon sun glinted off the satin tap pants. He whistled low under his breath. "You wear that, I guarantee there won't be much lounging going on."

"Really?" She turned enough on the bench to face him. "And that's romantic?"

"It's as sensual as hell."

"And you think that's romantic?"

"I think—"

"Is that a bid I see from Dylan O'Connell, our police chief?" Maisie's question interrupted him. And Dylan knew there was no fighting it. He nodded and when Maisie declared the outfit *sold,* the crowd cheered.

When one of Maisie's friends, another island senior citizen, brought the tap pants over to their table, Sarah made a face. "They'll never fit you."

Dylan rolled his eyes.

"And now this item…" Maisie switched to items that were a little more discreet. She sold a variety of body lotions, a few boxes of candles and a replica of the cupid sign that hung from the front door. Sarah bought a set of postcards that showed the island back at the turn of the twentieth century and linen tea towels embroidered with tiny violets.

When the tea towels were brought to her by Doc Ross, Maisie's gentleman friend, Dylan leaned close to Sarah. "What, no sexy lingerie?"

"I guess you've got that covered."

"No lotion?"

"Only if it's unscented, hypoallergenic and hasn't been tested on animals."

"Bubble bath?"

"As a matter of fact, I'm a big fan of showers."

Showers could be romantic.

Not exactly what he should be thinking about a woman he hardly knew, Dylan thought, warning himself to steer clear. Especially if the whole point of helping her was to prove that he could be romantic without trying to get her into his bed.

Now all he had to do was remember it.

"Hey!" He perked up when Maisie held the next auction items aloft. "Lace is romantic."

Sarah eyed the two frilly pillows. "You say romance, I say who's going to feel comfortable using accessories like that? I can tell from here that they're made of a cotton and polyester blend and no way can they go in the washer. They're supposed to be throw pillows, but if you have to think about dry cleaning all the time, you'd never feel comfortable throwing them around, and if you're not comfortable with your home furnishings—"

"Then what about that?" Thankfully, the pillows went quickly, and the next item was waiting on the floor of the front porch, right next to Maisie. Dylan pointed at it.

Sarah eyed the item warily before she turned the same wary expression on him. "How can you tell what it is? It's in a big brown grocery bag."

"Uh-huh." He waited for the truth to dawn.

It did, along with a flush that raced up Sarah's neck and stained her cheeks. "You mean there's an item in that bag that Maisie can't show in public…because there are kids around."

"I'd bet my badge on it."

She chewed on her lower lip, considering. Right before a spark of mischief flared in her eyes. Her hand shot up in the air.

"I see a bid from our new gardener, Sarah." Maisie didn't even wait for anyone else to make an offer. "Going once, going twice—sold!"

By the time Sarah handed over thirty-five dollars and the brown grocery bag was delivered and plunked down in the center of the table, Dylan was still amazed. "I can't believe you—"

"What?" Sarah eyes sparked. "You think because I'm not romantic, it means I'm a prude?"

"No, but I know what Maisie puts in those bags and—"

"You mean it's probably one of those items like the glow-in-the-dark condoms she sells in the Love Shack. Or the edible underwear. Or the sex toys."

Her gaze was so level, so matter-of-fact, Dylan couldn't respond. He was grateful when Tanya came around with more muffins. He grabbed one and started munching so that he didn't have to talk at all.

He did his best to pay attention to the rest of the auction, but when Maisie auctioned off a pair of embroidered slippers, his gaze strayed to the brown bag.

When she got two hundred dollars for a framed watercolor of the Hideaway painted by a local artist, he couldn't have said who bought it. And when the auction finished with a one-of-a-kind silk kimono ordered especially for the occasion and it was purchased by Doc Ross, who presented it to Maisie with a flourish, he didn't cheer and clap like the rest of the crowd. He was still wondering what was inside the bag. And speculating about what Sarah intended to do with it.

"So…" The crowd started to break up and Dylan watched Sarah slide off the bench. She stood and lifted the bag, cradling it in her arms. "Aren't you going to peek inside?"

"Nope." She added her tea towels and postcards to the stack.

"I can't believe you don't want to see what you spent your money on."

She shrugged. "Doesn't matter. It's all for a good cause."

"But aren't you curious?"

"Are you?"

"Well, yeah." Dylan got up, too. "I mean, if I spent thirty-five dollars on a mystery item, I would—"

"Cut it out." Sarah gave him a playful poke on the arm. "Thirty-five dollars has nothing to do with this. Neither does romance. You're thinking sex. Pure and simple. Just like I predicted you would."

"I'm not." Dylan had already crossed his arms over his chest right before he realized the pose was the equivalent of having the word *liar* flash over his head in neon letters. "Like I told you before, I think a man can be romantic without—"

"Yeah. Right." Sarah shifted the tea towels, draping them over one arm. She tucked the postcards into the back pocket of her khakis. She dangled the brown grocery bag. "Still thinking romance?"

He forced his arms down and held them tight to his sides. "Of course."

The bag was folded over at the top and there was a hole punched through the brown paper. A hot-pink ribbon was tied through the hole. Sarah tugged one end loose. "How about now?" she asked.

He refused to dignify the question with an answer.

She slipped the ribbon out of the hole and poked it into

her pocket. She unfolded the bag. Before she opened it, she stepped far enough away so that Dylan couldn't see inside.

Sarah peered into the bag. "Wow! I really got my thirty-five dollars' worth."

"Really?" He shifted from foot to foot and craned his neck, more anxious to see inside the bag than he was willing to admit. Especially to Sarah.

She kept the bag well out of reach and way too far for him to see into it. She opened it again. "Yup. Definitely got my money's worth." She grinned over the top of the bag at him. "I wonder if you'd think what's in here is romantic," she asked, then answered her own question. "Nah. My guess is even you wouldn't have the audacity to start talking romance. Not with an item this blatantly sexy." She rolled the top of the bag shut.

"You mean you aren't going to…" Dylan realized his mistake the moment the words were out of his mouth.

At least she had the good grace not to point it out. Instead, she stuck out her hand, and when he was too stunned to do anything, she grabbed his. "This is the part where I give you that big, sweet smile." And that was what she did. "You know, it's all you're expecting in return for showing me a wonderful, romantic time. That and an honest-to-gosh thank you. So—" she pumped his hand "—thank you. See you around!"

Still too floored by what had just happened, Dylan watched her walk away.

He wondered if she had any idea how much her teasing—and that damned brown bag—had turned him on. And decidedly instantly that of course she did.

It was exactly why she'd bought the bag. Exactly why she'd led him on with the mystery of what was inside.

"Congratulations, Sarah." Half in frustration and half in awe for the way she'd managed to work the situation to her advantage, he whispered the words as he watched her disappear around to the back of the Hideaway. "You wanted to leave me tingling from head to toe. You wanted to walk away when I want you so badly that I..." He didn't have to finish the sentence. He could just about taste it.

"Well, you won this round," he muttered.

Chapter Five

Romance is like a delicate flower. It must be
nurtured and tended with the greatest care.
— *Sarah's Guide to Life, Love and Gardening*

No matter how many times she went over it or from how
many angles, Sarah couldn't get beyond the question that
had been nagging her for days.

What on earth had possessed her?

She negotiated her way between a golf cart parked
near the local candy shop and a stroller where a crying
baby was being comforted—sort of—by its frantic
mother. It was late and almost dark. The evening chill penetrated even the green Put-in-Bay sweatshirt she was
wearing with her jeans. She'd just gotten her hair done at
the one and only beauty shop on the island and she wasn't
especially happy that what was supposed to be a trim had
turned into a full-blown restyling.

And still, she couldn't keep her brain from rehashing
every little incident that had happened with Dylan in the
past few days.

What had possessed her to ask for help? From him of
all people? About romance of all things?

It was Thursday night and the unofficial start of the island weekend. Despite the people out strolling, when she turned down the street that led to the Hideaway, she grumbled to herself, "He's licensed to romance now, isn't he? Or at least licensed to show you his idea of romance. Like Pete the Perch. And when he keeps it up, and you find yourself enjoying it, then what are you going to do?"

She was no closer to finding an answer to the emotional quagmire when she reached the Hideaway.

Guests had checked into Almost Paradise that afternoon, and when Sarah started up the walk that led up to the front door, she saw them through the window, crossing the lobby and heading for the Love Shack. She didn't need to bump into some lovebird duo billing and cooing their way through frilly nightgowns and candles with names like Burning Love and Hot for You, their minds clearly on romance. Or at least on what they *called* romance.

"Romance? Romance as in *How stupid could you be to give Dylan the perfect opportunity to try out that romance nonsense on you?*" Sarah mumbled while she headed around to the back of the inn.

"I don't need it, thank you very much," she told herself. "No hearts and flowers for this girl. She knows better than to be fooled by that sort of nonsense. No perfume. No expensive chocolates. No—"

Sarah skidded to a stop at the back of the house.

"Newspapers?"

At the sound of her voice, Dylan looked up from what he was doing. And what he was doing was laying newspaper out, one sheet after another, over her newly planted flowers.

Just to make sure her eyes weren't playing tricks on her, she squinted through the dark and the mishmash of shadows thrown by the light outside the back door. "You're covering up my flowers. With newspaper."

"Yeah. And if you're not too busy…" His eyebrows raised, he motioned toward the newspapers sitting in a neat pile on the back steps. A box of black garbage bags sat there, too, along with a dozen or so bricks that came from the stack Maisie was keeping for the patio—complete with hot tub and tall privacy fence—she planned to add at the back of the house. "I haven't even started the front yet and you've planted a lot out there. We need to hurry."

Far be it from Sarah to argue. Especially with a guy who must have considered whatever he was doing as fairly important. Otherwise, he wouldn't still be wearing his uniform while he did it.

She gathered up the rest of the newspapers, searching her mind for any bit of information that even resembled gardening knowledge.

Lucky for her, her brain clicked into gear. She liked to think it was because she'd learned a lot from hosting *Affairs of the Heart*. She was more inclined to believe it was because of the sharp blast of wind that hit her between the shoulder blades.

"It's cold." She grabbed the Metro section of the Sunday paper and stripped off a page, unfolded it and handed it to Dylan. "You think there's going to be—"

"Frost? That's what the weather guys say. On the Toledo TV stations and the Cleveland TV stations. Not that I trust those folks. But old Charlie Taylor over at the gas station says his knees are hurting like a son of a gun. And when Charlie's knees hurt…"

"Frost."

"You got it." Dylan reached for another piece of newsprint. "I would have gotten here sooner, but we had a situation over near the monument." He backstepped his way through Sarah's neatly planted geraniums, being careful where he put his feet and laying out piece after piece of paper as he went. "Stolen bicycle," he said, arriving at the sidewalk. He straightened and rubbed a hand to the small of his back. "Besides, I figured a gardener would keep an eye on the weather. When I got home, I expected to find you already hard at work."

She refused to acknowledge the unspoken challenge. Or admit that frost was the furthest subject from her mind. Especially when she spent so much of her time lately thinking about how *unfrosty* she felt every time Dylan was around. "I would have been back earlier," she said, touching a hand to her hair and cringing when she realized it was a full two inches shorter than she'd wanted it. "But I got to the beauty shop late and then my appointment ran over and—"

"It's nice."

It was an innocent enough statement. That didn't prevent an emotion that felt a little too much like panic from streaking through her. Every single one of the misgivings she'd been having since the night of the concert burst through her composure, and she swallowed hard. "Does that qualify?"

His sandy brows rose. "As…?"

"Right. Like you forgot." When Dylan moved on to the next row of flowers, she slipped a piece of paper off the pile and shoved it at him. "You can't fool me. I know that guys like you never forget anything."

He smiled at her over the grocery ads. "Does that mean you've spent a lot of time thinking about guys like me?"

He couldn't possibly have known how close to the mark he was.

She hoped.

Her fingers clenched the piece of newspaper into a hundred not-so-neat accordion pleats.

She held it to her chest like a crumbled shield. "You'll be happy to know what a quick learner I am. What you just said, that's banter, and banter qualifies as romantic. See, I'm finally getting the hang of this whole romance thing."

When he flashed her a smile, she figured she didn't have to say it; he already knew. "Let me get this straight. I told you that your haircut is nice, and rather than you accepting my compliment at face value, you assume that I only said it to teach you about romance?"

"Of course."

"And then when I asked a perfectly innocent question—"

"Which it definitely wasn't."

"—you start tossing the word *banter* around. I don't know about where you come from…" For the umpteenth time since he'd met her, he gave her the opportunity to fill in the blank. For the umpteenth time, she ignored him.

A muscle jumped in his jaw. "Folks around here don't use words like *banter*."

"Maybe not. But that doesn't change any of this. That was banter if I ever saw it. Or heard it," she corrected herself. "And I thought you'd be happy to realize it was finally sinking in. You bantered and I recognized that it was romantic."

He didn't say a word, but simply held out his hand.

It took Sarah a moment to realize he was waiting for more newspaper. She slapped a piece into his palm and he walked carefully across the flowerbed toward the house with it. She followed him, stepping around the geraniums and flinching when she felt one squish beneath her sneakers. Even that wasn't enough to squash her spirits. The conversation was over. And she'd had the last word.

By the time Dylan laid down that piece of paper, she was ready with another.

"Nobody ever said I couldn't be romantic." His voice was muffled when he bent over to tuck a piece of paper between a geranium and the reel where the garden hose was kept. When he was finished, he signaled her for another piece of paper. "After all, if I'm not romantic, how are you going to learn what romantic is?"

She was too proud to back down, too taken by the gleam in his eyes to pretend she hadn't heard the question. "No, nobody said you couldn't be romantic. We said—"

"Oh, no, you don't." There was more skepticism than amusement in his laugh. Neither of which made him any less formidable when he stood, threw back his shoulders, and gave her a glare that must have intimidated bad guys from there to Canada and back again. "You said. You're the one who asked for my help."

"And now you're feeling shortchanged. You're thinking you deserve payment of some kind." She pursed her lips, thinking. "Money is the most practical…."

"And the least romantic."

"Dinner is only logical…."

"Only if it's a candlelight dinner."

"Okay, there's always the useful. A gift card for the gas station. A fill-your-cart shopping spree at the local grocery store. A season's worth of trips on the ferry to the mainland."

It must have been a trick of the light; she could have sworn the last suggestion made him wince. He recovered in a heartbeat, and in a heartbeat that made Sarah's heartbeat quicken to a velocity approaching the speed of sound, he was standing less than a hairbreadth away.

"Or a peek inside that bag you won at the auction," he suggested.

She batted her eyes. "I didn't win it. I bought it. And, anyway, that pretty much proves my point to begin with. You're dangling that in front of me like it's a worm and I'm a fish. You're pretending what I bought is romantic and you expect me to believe it. Even though we both know it isn't romantic at all. It's sexy. Plain and simple. That's all there is to it. Like every single item in the Love Shack is sexy. You probably expect me to believe that the sex toys and the edible underwear and all that other stuff in that crazy gift shop is romantic, too."

He whistled low under his breath. "You bet it is! There's the incense, the aphrodisiac teas, the little chocolates shaped like—"

"And I say it's all a con. An excuse to get a woman into bed."

"Depends on the bed." He wiggled his eyebrows. "Depends on the woman."

"But still proves my point." She backed away. Partly because she needed room to unfold the next piece of newspaper. Mostly because when she was standing too close to Dylan, it was too easy to believe his romantic soft soap. With a little distance between them, she was able to breathe. The oxygen kick started her brain and she remembered that romance was just like those soap bubbles. It floated and flitted—and ended up exploding in your face.

When Dylan moved forward, Sarah moved back. Another geranium met its fate beneath the sole of her sneaker. Without another word, he went back to work. When he finished another row of flowers and stepped out onto the sidewalk, Sarah was ready for him.

"Lucky for us I like my rows of flowers neat, instead of messy, huh?"

Okay, so it was unfair of her to take advantage, especially when he was helping to save her flowers and maybe her summer job. Sarah couldn't help getting in the dig. Especially since it there was a chance—small though it was—that it might force the subject to change.

"If my rows were planted all…" She made the same kind of motion he'd made in the park the night he questioned her gardening skills, swirling her hands through the air in front of her. "If they were all artsy and flowing, it wouldn't be nearly as easy to step through them."

"If they were all…" He waved his hands in the air too. "We wouldn't need as much newspaper. Or garbage bags." He motioned in that direction, and though she was tempted to pretend she didn't know what he was hinting at, Sarah figured she'd better not press her luck. Anxious to steer their conversation away from romance and onto a subject that was safer—even if that subject was gardening—she plucked a garbage bag out of the box, fluffed it open and split it down one side.

Dylan laid the plastic over the newspapers, then weighted down the edges with the bricks.

"I'm sure professional gardeners have more sophisticated methods of keeping the frost off flowers." He paused to give her time to jump in and tell him exactly what those methods were, and when she didn't, his smile was strained. "This should work fine. You'll have to get the plastic off bright and early tomorrow, of course, before the sun hits and bakes your flowers to a crisp."

"I know that." She didn't. She wondered if he'd guessed. If that was why he'd mentioned it in the first place. Rather than have him point it out, she headed over to the north side of the house, the shady spot where she'd planted the hot-pink impatiens and added some yellow and purple zinnias, simply because she liked the juxtaposition of the colors.

By the time Dylan caught up, she was ready. She held a piece of newspaper out to him.

He stopped a little too far away to take it and shoved both his hands into the pockets of his slacks. "You've been thinking about it a lot, huh? About me teaching you romance?"

So much for trying to distract him. She offered him a smile. "I haven't been thinking about it at all."

He plucked the paper out of her hands. "You're a lousy liar."

"And you have an overactive imagination."

"Oh, yeah?" He chuckled and got to work on the zinnias and impatiens, and this time when he reached for another sheet of paper, he paused to give Sarah a careful examination, as well. His gaze skimmed her sneakers, her knees, her hips, her waist. It stopped for a second at the place where fat white letters proclaimed Put-in-Bay across her chest before it skipped up to her mouth. "If you weren't thinking about romance, why did you jump down my throat the second I complimented your haircut?"

"I didn't jump down your throat." She stepped over the low-growing purple salvia that she'd used as a border around the taller flowers. "I was simply protecting my interests. If you're going to act romantic—"

"That wasn't romantic."

"But if it was—"

"It wasn't." The bed was small and he finished with it sooner than Sarah anticipated. When he stood, her nose was practically pressed against his badge. "Now this…this could be romantic."

Sarah didn't see how. Because she knew what she was feeling was all about hormones.

She forced her gaze up from the badge and managed a smile. "Technically, we never said you couldn't try."

His voice dipped along with the look that touched her eyes and grazed her lips. "I haven't even started trying yet."

"Go right ahead. Because remember, we said you could talk romance and you could act romance and you could teach me all about what's romantic and what isn't. But you can't want to get me in bed as a result."

He winced.

Sarah grabbed the stack of newspapers and headed for the next flower bed. "Guess I know what that hair compliment was all about."

"The hair compliment was all about the fact that your hair is cut and that it's very nice."

"And that you want to get me in bed."

Behind her, she heard his exasperated sigh. "Whether I want to get you in bed or not has nothing to do with your hair."

She got as far as the front walk and whirled to face him. She hadn't realized he was following so close; her stack of newspapers poked his chest. "But it does have something to do with you telling me my hair's nice."

Dylan opened his mouth, then snapped it shut again. He scraped a hand through his hair. "Give me those," he said, and before she could, he snatched the newspapers out of her hands.

Here at the front of the inn, both sides of the walk were bordered by a two-foot-wide swathe of pink and purple petunias. Dylan plunked the stack of newspapers on the sidewalk along with the box of garbage bags he'd brought along from the back of the house. He got to work on the right side. Sarah took the left.

Dylan didn't have to watch to know exactly when Sarah stopped working and starting watching him. The chilly air heated a little. So did his gut. Rather than let his urges take over—and prove that she was right all along—he kept on working. He'd been meaning to feel her out, in the strictest sense of the phrase of course, and not the one that popped into his head when he watched her bend over to lay down another piece of paper. Now was as good a time as any.

He was almost all the way to the front walk and the grinning cupid sign that sat in one corner of the front lawn. He waited until Sarah had a garbage bag between her teeth and was tearing it along one side.

"I got a phone call today," he said. "About you."

Her fingers froze. Her shoulders tensed. She stared at him, wordless, for a second or two, but she didn't ask what he was talking about. Which told him he'd been right on the money from day one. Sarah was hiding something. From Maisie. From him.

He reached for another piece of newspaper. "Aren't you going to ask who was looking for you?"

The garbage bag split and she laid it over the newspapers before she scrubbed a finger across her lips. "I can't imagine who would be calling you about me. I don't know anyone here on the island."

"I didn't say the call came from anyone on the island."

She went still again. The way he'd seen a rabbit do in the fields over near the airport when he came on it suddenly and it wasn't sure if it should play statue or turn and run.

"All they wanted was to know where you were."

"You didn't…" She swallowed her words and turned away from him. By that time, Dylan knew he couldn't string her along anymore. Whatever she wasn't telling him, it was big. And frightening.

And he felt rotten for making her worry.

He stepped over the rest of the petunias and came up

behind her, touching a hand to her shoulder. "Sarah, if you're in some kind of trouble…"

Her laugh was a little too high-pitched to fool him. "What are you talking about? What kind of trouble can a gardener get into on an island this size?"

"That's pretty much my question."

She turned to Dylan and his hand stayed on her shoulder. "I appreciate your concern. All you can do to help is tell me what you told him. If he knows I'm on the island—"

"Sarah!" The anxiety in her expression tore into Dylan like a knife. "When you made your hair appointment yesterday, you didn't leave a phone number. Jean and Cheryl over at the beauty shop knew you were working here at the Hideaway, but they didn't know where you were staying and they figured since I pretty much know everybody and everybody's business here on the island, that I would be able to locate you. You were late and they called me."

He'd never been slugged by a blonde before.

Not that the punch on the arm she gave him qualified as a slug. The relief behind it, though, was unmistakable.

Dylan threw his hands in the air and backed away from her. "All right! I admit it, I deserved that. But give me a break, will you? If you need help—"

"Gardening help? Or is your mind running in some other direction?" Her eyes were the color of sapphires. Just as hard, too, and her jaw was rigid. "Let me guess, you were hoping to scare me, then race to my rescue. To play knight in shining armor and garner a few gratitude points. Thinking that would be a quicker way to get me between the sheets?"

"No! Yes! I mean, no, not the between the sheets part. Maybe the knight in shining armor part. But let's face it, that sort of goes along with my job description. Besides, you haven't left me with a lot of options. You haven't exactly been open and approachable. I've tried asking about your past. And when I do, you clam up like a...well, like a clam."

"So you decided to scare me into a bonding moment? Well, isn't that romantic!"

It wasn't. At best, it was miscalculated and badly timed. At worst, it was just plain boneheaded.

He was actually ready to admit it. Except that by the time he realized he needed to, Sarah was gone.

Chapter Six

Have we mentioned secrets? Secrets shared between
lovers are the best kind. But secrets kept from one
another…are you trying to sabotage your romance?
—*Sarah's Guide to Life, Love and Gardening*

"Whatcha up to, Chief?"

Officer Jake Moore's cheery greeting snapped Dylan
to attention, and he found himself with his fingers poised
over the keyboard of the office computer.

What *was* he up to?

Before Jake could walk around to the other side of the
desk and see what he was doing, Dylan hit the close button on the program that was open in front of him. The one
he was about to log on to. Just as he'd almost done a half
dozen times since Sarah landed on the island.

"Up to? Nothing."

Jake gave the computer screen a sidelong look. "You're
doing a background check."

"Nah." Dylan got up and went over to the coffeemaker.
He poured himself a cup in the mug that said *Chief* on it
in fat blue letters and added more sugar than he knew was
good for him. He liked his coffee strong and sweet, and
because even in a small town a police officer never had

time to linger, he'd learned early on in his career to drink it very hot. He leaned back against the table where the coffeemaker shared space with the department fax machine and took a sip. "Nobody around here worth doing a background check on, is there?"

Jake pursed his lips. "Is there?"

Dylan groaned. "Come on, Moore, don't pull that cop routine on me! I taught it to you, remember? Answer a question with a question. Make the person you're interrogating feel guilty."

"Do you?"

"Do I what?"

"Feel guilty?" Jake was a tall, skinny kid with an honest face and big ears. His hair was pale, like his skin usually was. Except at times like now when it flushed with color. "It's gotta make a fella wonder, Chief. What you might have to feel guilty about."

"Nothing."

It was true. Sort of. Time and time again since the day last week when his joke about the phone call fell flat against the terror that sparked in Sarah's eyes, he'd weighed the advantages of doing a thorough background check on her. That was the guilty part.

But just as often, he consoled himself, he'd talked himself out of it. And that meant he could forget the guilt.

Sure, he'd taken the first step. He'd checked into Sarah's driving record and he wasn't surprised that she didn't have so much as an outstanding parking ticket. He never went any further and he couldn't say why. He hadn't checked her credit rating. Or criminal records.

Mostly because it felt like an invasion of privacy.

Partly because he wasn't sure he wanted to find out whatever it was that Sarah was hiding.

All of which were perfectly good excuses, even if they weren't reasons.

Which didn't explain why Dylan felt guilty, anyway.

He pushed away from the table and stalked into his office. "It's not exactly like I'm eavesdropping or spying or sticking my nose where it doesn't belong." He was talking to Jake, but reminding himself at the same time. "I'm doing my job."

Jake followed him. He leaned on the door frame. "Always said that about you, Chief. Always said that you were the best at doing your job of anybody I know."

There was a stack of papers sitting on one corner of his desk. Monthly reports. Dylan slid the papers in front of him and dropped into his chair. "So it's Memorial Day and the official start of our summer season. The island is crawling with tourists and there has to be more for you to do than hang around here and give me the third degree. Maybe you'd better get outside. And maybe you'd better leave me in peace so I can get this paperwork taken care of and I can get outside, too."

"Maybe." Jake had a mug of coffee, too. He'd only been on the force a little less than two years and he'd yet to develop the talent for drinking coffee so hot that it would make a civilian's mouth combust. He blew on the steaming liquid before he took a careful sip. "Only I supposed...you know...I supposed maybe you'd want to talk about it."

When he sat back, Dylan's desk chair squeaked. "It's not that I don't appreciate your concern. But honest, Jake, I don't need a heart-to-heart. Save the big daddy talks for that son of yours."

Even though he wasn't invited, Jake dropped into the chair that faced Dylan's desk. "Believe me, I've been practicing. I've talked to Connor about how drugs are bad for him and how important it is for him to find the right college. Haven't gotten up the nerve for the birds and bees talk yet." Jake's cheeks got redder. "But hey, he's only three weeks old. He's not exactly ready for that one."

"And you think I am." It wasn't a question. If he was smart, Jake wouldn't have responded.

Apparently Jake wasn't as worried about smart as he was about his boss. "Can't have it. We talked about it, you see. Me and Marsha and Bill and the rest of 'em. We don't like the idea of you mopin' around."

The Put-in-Bay Police Department was housed in the basement of the redbrick town hall. In spite of the lack of windows and the walls that were painted utilitarian gray, it had never felt claustrophobic.

Until now.

Dylan finished the rest of his coffee in one long swallow and got up. He sidestepped the chair where Jake was sitting. "I never mope."

The sound Jake made was half grunt, half laugh of disbelief. "You did your share of moping when Lisa left."

Jake recognized his mistake the second the words were out of his mouth. As if he expected a California-style rock 'em sock 'em earthquake, he clutched his coffee mug in both hands and held on tight. He refused to meet Dylan's eyes.

And Dylan refused to let ancient history get in the way of what was supposed to be the rest of his life.

"Kind of hard not to mope," he said, "when the woman who claims to love you more than life itself suddenly decides that life on an quiet little island isn't exactly her idea of happily ever after."

"Sorry." Jake dared a look at his boss, then looked away again. "We wouldn't even care but—"

"You know, it's not exactly comforting for me to think

that I'm the number one topic of gossip in this office." Dylan headed to the outer office, raising his voice so that Marsha, who was working dispatch, and Lillian, who was cleaning both of the town's empty jail cells, were sure to hear. "I'd like to think you'd all have more important matters to talk about."

Jake shrugged. "Not really."

Dylan rinsed out his mug, then slammed it onto the rack near the coffeepot. "Then find something. Look around. There's got to be something you can do to keep busy."

"I could run that background check for you."

For a second, Dylan was tempted to take him up on the offer.

"Nah." He dismissed the idea before it had a chance to fully form because he was afraid that once it did, it would sound even better. "It's not right."

"Heck, Chief, we do background checks on people all the time."

"Yeah. We do background checks on people. People we arrest. People who are disturbing the peace. Or shoplifting. Or acting like total idiots because they've had too much to drink. Not people we know."

"And not people we like." Jake's hat was on the desk that the patrol officers shared. He picked it up and twisted it in his hands. "But you know, that's not exactly true. Before I married Tracy, I checked up on her," he said, and added quickly, "Don't you ever tell her I told you that."

The idea of Jake being that diligent—or that suspicious—struck him as odd, and Dylan laughed. "What did you find out about her?"

"Not much. But remember, she was from Sandusky." He turned to face the general direction of the lake and the Ohio mainland beyond. "Never can tell about those big-city girls."

"Well, I can tell." Dylan paced over to the door that led into the mayor's court. It was a holiday and there was no one in there, so he took a couple of steps inside the room before he swung around and marched back the other way. "I've always been good at reading people. And in my own mind, I knew I had it all down pat. Sure, Maisie said she was suspicious—"

"Suspicious to Maisie means she can't figure out why a woman and a man aren't...you know."

"Exactly." To emphasize his point, Dylan pounded his fist into his palm. "That's what I thought. All along, I figured that Maisie wanted to get us together. And I still think that's true. But then last week when we were working to save her flowers from that last frost..." He remembered that night. "Sarah's got a secret," he told Jake. "And she doesn't want me to know about it."

Jake glanced at the blank computer screen. "Then a background check seems like the most logical solution."

It did.

Dylan stepped toward the computer. The instant gratification would be nice, but he knew that someday he'd regret it if he sat down and did a search through all the usual sources. "I can't," he said. He stopped three feet from the computer and eyed it as if it was a snake, reared up and ready to bite. "I know that's crazy. It's my job to make sure that the island is safe. It's my job to protect people. But hell, I feel like I'm violating her privacy. And her privacy is something she obviously values very highly."

"Yeah, so did Tracy." Jake clapped his hat on his head and walked toward the door and the stairs that led up to street level. He opened the door and stopped, his back propped against it. A rush of warm, late May air streamed inside. "You know, when I first met Tracy and did that background check, I stopped when I got as far as the Department of Motor Vehicles. Figured if a girl from the mainland could live twenty-one years and have only one speeding ticket to her name, that said a lot about her character. I was tempted to dig a little deeper and I might have done it, too. Except by that time, me and Tracy, we were pretty close, and I didn't need to investigate anymore. She told me everything I needed to know about her."

"Great." Dylan mumbled the word while he watched the door swing closed behind Jake. "Just what I need, advice about my love life from a guy who's young enough to be my kid brother. It's not even like he's right." Dylan went back into his office and flipped through the stack of monthly reports, but instead of seeing the facts and figures he'd have to go over with the mayor the next morning, he pictured the way Sarah's eyes glittered in the moonlight. The way her mud-stained khakis were smooth over her hips.

He caught himself on the verge of a sigh and slapped the reports onto his desk. "It's not like I'm waiting for some big bonding moment," he told himself. "It's just that Sarah's worried. And I—"

"Chief?" Marsha called to him from the outside office. "Got a call here from Bill. He's at the marina. Says he needs assistance and needs it fast."

"Great." This time when Dylan said the word, he meant it. A little action would put his mind back where it belonged. And off a certain gardener who was haunting his dreams.

He hurried to the door and raced up the stairs. He hit the sidewalk at a quick jog. The Municipal Marina was right across the street from DeRivera Park and only a stone's throw from the police station. Even before he got there, Dylan saw that there was some sort of commotion on one of the docks that stuck out far into the water. A group of people was gathered around one of the boats and other people were running over to see what the excitement was all about. Somebody was pointing toward the mast of one of the sailboats. A woman nearby was fighting to get onto the boat. She was being held back by the crowd.

In the middle of it all was Bill, his hat off, his face red. He was trying to yell over the noise of the crowd, trying his best to maintain some peace and order.

It wasn't working.

Dylan picked up his pace and didn't stop until his feet were pounding the wooden dock.

That was when it hit him. That the lake was only a couple of feet under the soles of his shoes. He swallowed down the sudden lump of terror in his throat and headed out to help Bill, wondering as he did what the folks in the crowd would say if they knew the ugly truth.

That the police chief of an island town was scared to death of water.

WHAT WAS RIGHT was right.

At least that was what Sarah told herself after the excitement on the dock died down and the crowd cleared out. Once again, she could hear the soft lap of the waves against the shore and the bass beat of the music coming from the bar across the park. That, and the words that kept pounding through her head.

What was right was right.

And if there was one subject Sarah Allcroft knew about, it was the right—and the wrong way—to do things.

It would have been wrong to stand in the middle of the crowd, caught up in the excitement and not admit (at least to herself) that a breath of relief whooshed out of her when Dylan appeared from out of nowhere and took charge of the situation. It would have been silly to pretend she wasn't at least a little bit impressed when he hopped onto the sailboat where a screaming woman who'd taken the whole Margaritaville atmosphere a little too seriously was fighting to climb the mast so that she could rescue a stray kitten that was up there and refused to come down. After all he did—for the woman and for the little cat—it would have been a lie to say that she wasn't proud of Dylan.

Not to mention how yummy he looked with his sleeves rolled up above his elbows, his uniform pants nice and tight across his butt, and his muscles straining when he shimmied up the mast himself and brought the frightened kitten down cradled in the crook of his arm.

It would have been really wrong if she didn't tell him— about the how-proud-she-was part, not the how-yummy-he-was part. Even if the last time they were together she'd nearly been careless enough to reveal that she was hiding out on the island—and afraid of who might find her.

She was ready for Dylan the second he stepped off the dock.

"That was pretty cool."

He was surprised to see her. But he wasn't disappointed. A smile tugged at one corner of his mouth. "All in a day's work, ma'am."

"Maybe, but where's it written that the boss has to do the grunt work?"

As if he was sharing a secret, he leaned in close. They were standing in the shade of the huge old oaks that ringed the park, but his skin was still warm from the sun out on the dock. The heat wrapped around Sarah like a blanket. "Bill's afraid of heights. I couldn't make him climb that mast. Besides, if I let that crazy woman try and get the cat herself, I know she would have fallen in the lake. So I had a choice: climb or swim. I'll take climb any day."

"I've always heard that folks call the fire department for stuck cats."

"Fire department around here is volunteer. And it's a holiday for them, too. Figured as long as I was on duty…" He rolled back on his heels. "Any chance you were impressed?"

She'd already put herself out on a limb; there was no use making it any easier for him. "A little," she admitted. "Didn't know you were a cat lover."

He raised his eyebrows. "Maybe just a lover."

Sarah laughed. "Now you're pressing your luck!"

"Am I?" He was laughing, too, but that didn't prevent him from stepping even closer. "You never know until you try."

Sarah backed away and pretended to be surprised. "Why, Officer, does that mean you're admitting defeat? That you're willing to confess that a guy would rather dispense with all the romance nonsense? That he'd rather get a woman in bed right off the bat without ever trying to hoodwink her with the hearts and flowers?"

"You never give up, do you?" The way he said it, she wasn't sure if it was a good trait or bad. "Can't we have a conversation without you turning everything I say inside out and upside down? Or maybe…" His smile sparked. "That's it! You're the one pushing this agenda." He pointed an accusing finger at her. "You're pretending you don't understand romance because it's your way of begging for romantic gestures."

"Not true." Taking in the scenery was better than having to face the *gotcha!* that sparkled in his eyes. Sarah whirled around and started walking. "I'm simply pointing out—"

"—that you can't stop thinking about what a romantic guy I am. That you can't stop thinking about me."

Even though the only traffic was golf carts and they were moving as slowly as snails, she stopped to check for traffic before she crossed the street. "You're awfully egocentric."

"Is that a compliment?"

"It's an assessment. And in case you didn't know—"

"I know what egocentric means. Maybe I'm not the only one who's way too impressed with himself. Or herself."

They were smack-dab in the middle of a long walk that led up to a pier where a seafood restaurant shared space with a bar and an ice cream parlor. She had to move closer, then back up again to avoid the folks walking in and out. While she was at it, she figured she'd better keep her voice down, too. She'd already seen more than one person point at Dylan and whisper about how heroic he'd been rescuing that cat. No use bursting their superhero bubbles.

"If you're suggesting that I'm the one who's conceited, well, you're wrong," she told him. "On the contrary, when it comes to self-assessment, I'm very much in touch with reality. I know my weaknesses. And I know my strengths."

He nodded and crossed his arms over his chest, stepping back a smidgen to give her a quick once over. "Go ahead," he said. "Tell me."

"Tell you…?"

"Your weaknesses. Your strengths."

She was caught short. And directly in the spotlight she tried her best to avoid. Of course if she let on, he'd never give her any peace. Resigned to her fate, she decided to get it over with as fast as possible.

"Very well." She stood up straight and forced herself to display the kind of composure she showed in front of the camera. Now, just like then, her stomach jumped and her heart beat double time. Now, just like when the camera lens was turned on her, she hoped she didn't trip over her words.

"Okay. My weaknesses, by Sarah Allcroft." She cleared her throat and hoped Dylan assumed the color in her cheeks was from the sun. "Well, for starters, my eyes are too close together."

Dylan chuckled.

"And my nose is a tad too thin."

He didn't comment.

"My hair gets washed out in the summer sun. You know, sort of a brassy color that makes it look like the blond isn't natural. And believe me, it is. Then there are my breasts…well…" She poked her thumb at the blue T-shirt she was wearing with her denim shorts. "I'm sure you've noticed that there isn't much there."

If he hadn't before, he sure noticed now. Before he spoke, he had to wrench his gaze away from the blue T-shirt. By the time he did, his pupils were dark with an emotion so much like desire, it nearly took Sarah's breath away.

He cleared his throat, too. She'd done it to center herself, to steady her voice and her mind so she could concentrate on the matter at hand. But Dylan?

When Dylan did it, Sarah swore he was struggling to catch his breath.

"And your strengths?" he asked.

"Well, if I have to point them out, maybe they're not as strong as I imagined." She didn't give him a chance to tell her she was right. "I'm a better-than-average businesswoman," she told him. "Levelheaded. Logical. Analytical." She knew it was all true and that was enough to give her at least a tiny shot of confidence. Too bad her hands were trembling. "I can hone in on a market trend before anyone else. I can tap into other people's talents and bring out the best in them, mostly because I'm able to objectively analyze my own talents and know where they need augmenting. Case in point: I know I'm a little deficient in the romance department. I suspect that you're not. Hence, I asked for your help. So you see, I'm not the least bit egotistical. I also, in case you haven't noticed, have an extraordinary gift for pairing unusual colors and a sense of style that is, to put it quite bluntly, far above the norm. Oh!" So he didn't get the wrong idea, she made sure she gave him a smile wide enough to charm the birds out of the trees. "And I'm a hell of a gardener."

"You're a hell of a storyteller, too, but I'm not even going to bother to point that out because I'm enjoying listening to you so much I don't want you to stop."

"Well, I am. Stopping, that is." She folded her hands at her waist. "Enough said."

"Right." Dylan latched onto her arm and tugged her toward the far side of the pier. "Let's get dinner."

"Aren't you working?" The feel of his hand against her arm was nice, but she figured she'd better protest, anyway. Before she got too used to it. "Aren't you on duty?"

"Even cops have to eat. And before you bring out the stereotypes, let me point out that I don't even like doughnuts." He yanked his wallet from his back pocket. "Two," he told the guy with the hot-dog cart who was stationed near the pier. "One with extra mustard, lots of ketchup and a big glop of relish and the other..." He paused, waiting for her order.

"Plain."

"That's your problem," Dylan said. The vendor handed him the first hot dog, which he passed to Sarah. "You have a complete lack of imagination."

"I do not!" She drew back her shoulders. "Why, I'll

have you know that I was the first person in Rhode Island to—" She realized her mistake the second the words were out of her mouth. She couldn't call them back and she didn't want to explain, so she bit into the hot dog.

Dylan didn't push. He took his own hot dog, paid the vendor and walked over to a park bench that faced the water. Sarah was right behind him. He sat down, took a bite and didn't say another word until he chewed and swallowed.

"Don't feel so bad," he said. "I knew you were from Rhode Island."

Sarah sank down on the bench next him. "What else do you know?"

"What else should I know?"

"Nothing." She wasn't all that hungry anymore. She picked off a piece of the hot dog bun and tossed it into the water. Instantly, a mother duck and five ducklings swam out from under the dock. They scarfed down the bread and quacked for more. Sarah obliged, giving them one more hunk of bread before she took a bite for herself.

She chewed and swallowed before she spoke. "I lead a pretty boring life."

"And whatever happens in it isn't any of my business."

"I didn't say that!" She turned on the bench to face Dylan and wished she'd been a little slower. Then she wouldn't have seen the flash of disappointment that clouded his expression. At the same time she wondered why it made her feel so rotten, she gave the rest of the bread to the ducks, wrapped up the hot dog in the slick paper it came in and tossed it into a nearby trash can. "What I meant to say is that there isn't anything to know. I'm a gardener. Can't get much more boring than that."

"You don't say much about yourself."

"My point exactly. There's not much to say."

"Family?"

She wouldn't have said a word if she didn't feel guilty. She wouldn't have felt guilty if she didn't realize that by shutting him completely out of her life, she was making him think that he was missing out, though he didn't know on what. And that like it or not, by shutting him out, she knew that she was missing out, too.

"Three older brothers. I told you about them. Always on the make. Always on the go. Real eager beavers. Danny has his own accounting firm. Jeff's been in the army for years and a couple of months ago, he was promoted to major."

"That's two."

"Yeah." She hesitated, then was instantly sorry that she did. She was an adult. She could certainly talk about family dynamics without sounding like a bitter teenager. Maybe.

"Number three is Matthew, and after they made Matthew, they threw away the mold. He's Mother and Dad's pride and joy. The best and the brightest. The smartest and the best-looking. The most likely to succeed, blah, blah, blah. Four-year scholarship to Harvard and they haven't stopped talking about it since the day he packed his bags and moved to Boston. For the record, that was twelve years ago. All the years we grew up together, Matthew was…"

It was kind of hard to explain.

Sarah tried, anyway.

"Matthew has a warped sense of humor. He's the brother who was always playing the practical jokes. The one who always ended up embarrassing me."

"How? How did he embarrass you?"

Heat flared in Sarah's cheeks again. "Well, one summer at the lake Matthew put a frog down the back of my bathing suit. Or there was the time in eleventh grade that I got a Valentine's Day card from a secret admirer and he convinced me it was from Chris Trebecca, the star of the varsity football team."

"It wasn't."

Sarah felt heat all the way to the tips of her ears. "There I was on the other side of the cafeteria, watching Chris open the card I sent him in return. I think it was when I saw him mouth the words, 'Sarah who?' that I figured out that Matt was behind the whole thing."

"That was then. What about now?"

"Now?" Sarah could only shake her head in wonder. For all the humiliation he'd caused, Matthew was also the most adventurous of her brothers. And the most successful. "What's that old saying about a leopard not changing its spots? That's Matthew. He's the slickest salesman you're likely to meet this side of a used-car lot. You know the type—so charming, it hurts. It's no wonder he's doing really well out in California. He's in commercial real estate. Has one of those teams. You know, they run around and do all the work and Matt makes the big bucks and gets all the glory."

"Impressive."

"You think so?"

"Don't you?"

When she was feeling charitable, she did. At other times…

Sarah sighed. "All my brothers are successful guys in their own way. And not one of them is about to let anyone forget it."

"Must be tough growing up with that kind of competition. A family of overachievers. Parents who take a lot of pride in their children's accomplishments. Is that why you became a…" He paused for the briefest of moments. "Gardener?"

"I became a gardener because I like planning a garden and working in the soil and nurturing the plants. And I deal with my brothers the way I've always dealt with my brothers. I may hide it well under my mild-mannered gardener exterior, but you should know, I can give as good as I get."

"I'll bet." He didn't even try to hide the smile that brought out a dimple in his left cheek. "You know, there are some folks who think that cops are more than just keepers of the peace. That we're sort of counselors, psychologists. you know? That we have to have the ability to size up a situation and analyze it lightning-quick. We don't often have the luxury of making mistakes."

"Is that what you're doing? Analyzing me?" Sarah uttered a nervous laugh. Maybe because even a hint of having herself and her motives analyzed sent a wave of pure panic through her. "So what's the diagnosis, doc?"

Dylan cocked his head, considering. "I think…" She didn't realize there was a crumb of bread on her T-shirt right near the waistband of her shorts. At least not until he reached over to flick it aside.

It was an innocent enough gesture, but Sarah felt every inch of her body respond. Her temperature shot up as high as the boat mast Dylan had climbed. She tensed, expecting more at the same time she feared it. And wanted it.

Dylan didn't move back when he was done. His left arm brushed her right and his mouth was only a hair's breadth away. "I think there's more going on than just a little sibling rivalry," he said. "You resent your brothers, don't you? You're mad at them because they were callous jerks who turned you off to romance."

"And if they didn't?"

"Ah, if they didn't!" He leaned a little closer. "If they didn't, you never would have asked for my help. And if you never asked for my help—"

"Sarah!"

At the sound of a man calling her name, Sarah jumped as if she'd been touched with a hot poker. She'd been so lost in the warmth of Dylan's eyes, so wrapped up in the way she felt with his skin against hers and his voice caressing her like sunshine, she'd forgotten they were in public and that being with Dylan didn't mean she was safe.

"Hey!" Dylan's hand closed around her arm. "You're as pale as a ghost!"

She didn't have as much as an inkling of what her stalker looked like, so she knew it wouldn't do any good, but she scanned the park anyway. When she heard the man call out again and saw him hurry over to a woman rocking a baby in a stroller, she felt like a balloon that had been pricked with a pin.

She knew a strategic mistake when she made one and this was a whopper. Rather than admit it and get herself into a conversation she didn't want to have, she decided a little denial was the way to go. She turned around and gave Dylan a quick smile. "You were saying?"

"Me? Nothing much, apparently." The warmth in Dylan's eyes evaporated. His voice was as tight as the muscle she saw jump at the base of his jaw. He stood. "It's getting late and I've got to get back to the station. It's a holiday and that means it's bound to be busy tonight."

"Sure." Sarah stood, too. "Thanks for the hot dog."

He had already started walking in the direction of the police station and he stopped and turned to her. "Not going to use me buying you a hot dog as an excuse to accuse me of coming on to you?"

"Not this time." She managed a smile. "I read somewhere that it's not fair to do that to a superhero."

"Is it fair to lie to a superhero?"

"Lie?" She crossed her heart with one finger at the same time tucked her other hand behind her back. "Why, Officer, I'd never lie to you."

He took her at face value, nodded and walked away.

Sarah let go the breath she was holding. But it wasn't until she saw Dylan cross the street and turn toward the police station that she dared to uncross her fingers.

Chapter Seven

Nothing says romance like flowers!
—*Sarah's Guide to Life, Love and Gardening*

"I told you, Becky. Just like I told you last Tuesday when we talked. And the Tuesday before that. I'm fine." Sarah did her best to sound chipper. Becky Landis, her *Affairs of the Heart* producer, was a first-class worrier. No use giving her any more to worry about. "As right as rain," Sarah chirped. "As perky as—" She was standing in the middle of the sidewalk that led up to the Hideaway's front door and she looked down at the petunias that edged the walk and winced. "As perky as my petunias aren't."

"Unperky petunias? That sounds serious." Becky obviously didn't recognize the gravity of the situation. There was a chuckle beneath her statement. "Maybe your petunias would perk up if you'd do an old pal a favor and show your face here in Providence. Just so I know you haven't jumped ship and decided that you're never coming back."

"I'm not kidding, Becky." Becky wasn't kidding, either, but now was not the time to get into that. Sarah scanned the length of the walk. Her stomach clenched. Right before it did a back flip. "My petunias have gone p-tooey!"

Becky clicked her tongue. "You never listen to your own advice. Not about flowers. Not about romance."

The comment hit a little too close to home, and Sarah held her cell phone away from her ear and eyed it suspiciously, wondering how Becky could have zeroed right in on the Dylan problem when they were supposed to be talking petunias. "Forget romance! I've got major horticultural issues here. My flowers, they're all…" She stooped down for an up-close-and-personal with the disaster. "Some of them are brown and crisp. Some of them are brown and mushy. Some of them…" She poked her finger at one of the flowers and it drooped. "Some of them are brown without the mushy. Petunias aren't supposed to be brown, are they?"

She didn't have to see Becky to know she was sitting behind her desk, shaking her head in wonder. "What color were they when you planted them?"

"The petunias were purple." Sarah scanned the rest of the beds. "The salvia was purple and pink. The impatiens was a sort of flamingo color and now…" She gulped. "They're all brown."

"Too much water," Becky said. "Or not enough. Is it hot there?"

It was. "Around here, they say that if you don't like the weather, you should wait five minutes. They're right. Last week it was so cold we had to cover the flowers so they wouldn't freeze. And today—"

"We?" She heard Becky's desk chair screech, the way it did when a topic caught her interest and she sat up straight. "What's going on there that I don't know about?"

Sarah poked the toe of one sneaker into the flower bed. The nearest flower collapsed. "What's going on is that I'm going to lose my job."

"Good. Then you'll come home."

It was bound to come to this. Like it did every Tuesday afternoon when Sarah called Becky. She knew it the minute she dialed Becky's number. She remembered the speech she'd given Becky before she left Providence, the one that was all about giving herself a break before the media frenzy began. The one that didn't include any mention of the stalker because Sarah had never told Becky about the anonymous gifts or come right out and said that the whole stalker scenario scared her to death. She knew Becky would make a big deal out of the whole thing—a big deal that was sure to include the media.

Anyway, no use two of them losing sleep.

"We've been over this. How many times? It's only for the summer, Becky. Just for a change of pace, a change of scenery, firsthand experience with the charming country inns and beautiful flowers and this whole hokey notion of romance. You know, exactly what I talk to viewers about every week. It will make the show better."

"Well, it's making me nervous." Becky was a short, round woman with a good head on her shoulders and the tenacity of one of those little terriers that goes into a fox den and doesn't come out until it got the varmint in its teeth. "I'm getting calls, Sarah. Lots of calls. You're on the verge of major stardom and nobody can understand why you're not around for interviews. I even heard from some new mag, *Elegant Living*, or some name like that. The reporter's name is Jason and he's a real sweetie. He's talking about using you for the cover of the premier issue. The cover, Sarah! He practically begged me for your phone number."

Her breath caught. "You didn't—"

"How could I give it to him? You changed your cell number before you left town and you haven't even bothered to give it to me. I didn't want to humiliate myself by telling him that I can't get hold of you, that I only talk to you when *you* call *me*. Am I getting through to you, Sarah? Do you understand how really important all this is?"

She did. If only...

Sarah shrugged away the nervous tattoo that started up inside her chest every time she thought about Providence. Bad enough she had the stalker to worry about. Worse that the media was circling like sharks with chum in the water. Way worse if she ever gave an interview and tripped over her own common sense and her insecurities—and admitted that the whole romance shtick was nothing but a means to an end.

In this case, the end was a business empire designed to outdo that of any other lifestyle diva. The means...well, the means was pretty much preying on the fantasies of a whole bunch of women raised to believe that when a man offers a romantic gesture, it's out of the goodness of his own heart. And not because some other portion of his anatomy was in charge.

Before Sarah even realized she was doing it, she found herself stepping over the dearly departed petunias so she could see beyond the Hideaway and back toward the garage. Once she did realize she was doing it—and who she was hoping to catch a glimpse of—she gave herself a shake and reminded herself to keep her mind off a certain police chief. And on the matter at hand.

At the moment, the matter at hand was publicity.

And how desperate Sarah was to avoid it.

"What, they're going to take my picture for the cover of some new glossy magazine as I'm tripping over one of the props on the set? Or maybe I could pose with the petunias I forgot to water. Or the ones I watered to death. That would make a terrific photo spread." She laughed so

Becky wouldn't know how much the publicity really bothered her. "I can't be what they want me to be, Becky. You know that. You talk to this Jason guy. You can give him the skinny better than anyone. You know, get into all the facts and figures, the market trends, the sociological implications."

"I could. But that's not what he's after. That's not what *any* of them are after. They're asking for you, Sarah. It's your own fault. You're the one who embodies elegance. You've got it all down pat, the refinement and the charm and the—"

"Dead petunias."

"Yeah, that, too." Becky sighed and her frustration was evident, even across the miles. "What do you want me to tell him?"

"Exactly what you've told all the others. I'm on sabbatical. I'll be back soon."

"Will you be?"

"Of course!" There had never been a moment's doubt in Sarah's mind. She was only hoping that by the time she did get back, she would be ready to face the Jasons of the world. And her stalker would have grown bored and disappeared beneath the rock he'd crawled out from under. "It's only for a little while longer. We don't go into production again until the fall, so there's not much that I have to take care of. Besides, you're the most conscientious person I know, Becky. You know all about responsibility. You wouldn't want me to leave these nice folks high and dry, would you? Like I left the petunias?"

There was a sudden purr of interest in Becky's voice. "Any particular 'nice folk' you're talking about?"

Again, Sarah made a face at the phone. She knew Becky was a first-class producer; she didn't know she was clairvoyant.

"You know I don't believe in that romance nonsense."

"Uh-huh. But you didn't say no."

"And even if I did…" Like it or not, Sarah couldn't help herself. For the second time in as many minutes, her gaze strayed past the pink Hideaway and toward the pink garage. Determined it wouldn't happen again, she stepped back over the petunias and onto the sidewalk, putting the hulking Victorian between her and the temptation that was temporarily staying only a short distance away.

"Even if I did believe in romance," she told Becky—and herself, "it wouldn't make any difference. This place is like the land that time forgot."

"As in dinosaurs in the woods? Or are you talking about a town full of bumpkins chewing on straw and spitting tobacco?"

Sarah cringed. Not only wasn't it true, but it didn't tally with the picture of Dylan that kept flitting through her mind. Bumpkin? Not a chance. "That's not it at all. It's just that the people who live here…well, they live here. All year long." She remembered what Dylan had once told her about the island in winter, the crunch of a new snowfall, the quiet that enveloped the place. "He loves it here and he's never going to leave. And he wants a woman who loves it as much as he does."

"Aha!"

It wasn't until she heard the satisfaction in Becky's voice that she knew she'd made a tactical error.

"I meant *he* in the generic sense," Sarah said. "As in *all of mankind.*"

"And I just fell off a turnip truck." Becky snickered. "And speaking of turnips—" Sarah heard Becky shuffle papers on her desk "—I've got to get your approval on the sketches for this packaging. You know, that seed company that wants to produce the line with your name on it."

"I'm selling turnip seeds?"

"Not turnips. Flowers. Remember? It was your idea. All the old-fashioned varieties and the packaging is so Victorian, you won't believe it. We've got morning glories and hollyhocks, marigolds and zinnias and—"

"Zinnias." Sarah sighed. "They're dead, too. I can't believe Maisie hasn't noticed this mess yet. And what are her guests going to think? They're coming here to stay in romance central, and instead, they're checking into the Bates Motel."

"And you're not listening to me!" Becky gave a muffled shriek. "The sketches need your approval."

"I'll do it when I get back."

"It can't wait. I have to send them to you, Sarah."

It was silly to hedge. Silly to hesitate. It wasn't like Becky was going to slap her address onto that flashing news ticker on Times Square. She trusted Becky more than that, and so Becky would know it, she gave her the address of the Hideaway.

"Ohio." Becky was skeptical. "I knew you were trying to get away from it all, but really, Sarah, Ohio?"

The tiny thread of possessiveness Sarah felt when she realized Becky was making fun of the island surprised her. Rather than think about it, she simply told Becky, "This is a small island. And the folks over at the post office talk to everybody. And everybody knows everybody. Make sure you send that stuff in a plain envelope. No *Affairs of the Heart* logo. Not even a return address."

"I know. I get it." Becky was satisfied that she'd won at least one round of their weekly fight. "I swear to you I'll burn the piece of paper I wrote your address on. I'll go to the mailbox wearing dark glasses and a false nose. I'll—"

Sarah laughed because she knew that if she asked her

to, Becky would do exactly that. She was still smiling when she promised they'd talk again the next Tuesday afternoon and disconnected the call.

"I hope that smile on your face means that you're thinking about your petunias being in a better place."

At the sound of Dylan's voice, Sarah jumped. So did her heart. She spun around and found him studying the long row of dead flowers. He was dressed in his blue uniform, but his hat was off. He held it respectfully over his heart.

"They're dormant." Even Sarah was surprised at the audacity of the words that fell out of her mouth, but once they did, she had no choice but to back them up with something that at least sounded like enthusiasm. "They'll perk up. You'll see."

"Uh-huh." He switched his gaze from the petunias to Sarah. "Too much water," he said. "Or not enough."

"That's what Becky said." She tucked her phone into the pocket of her khaki shorts. "I don't think so, though. I think they simply need a little TLC and some recovery time and once they have it, they'll reward us with a showy display of—" She realized she was repeating Chapter 4 of *Sarah's Guide* ("Beauty in the Garden") word for word and stopped herself before she could sound even more lame.

"You're the gardener." Dylan put his hat back on his head and checked his watch. "The way I see it, you're also the gardener who should be off work right about—" he waited while the numbers on his watch changed from four fifty-nine to five o'clock "—now. Get cleaned up. We're going out to dinner."

"We are?"

"Absolutely." He took her by the elbow and piloted her toward the Hideaway. "You see, I've decided that I'm playing this all wrong."

"Playing?" When they got to the front steps, she untangled herself from him. "I didn't know we were playing."

"We aren't. *You* are. And I've been watching from the sidelines. But that means I've been playing it all wrong."

She shook her head. "You'll have to excuse me, I've been out in the sun all day. I guess my brain is a little fried. You said you weren't playing, but we were playing, so now you're playing—"

"What I said was that I wasn't playing. And you aren't playing by the rules. That means that I've been playing it all wrong." He puffed out his chest. "Time to take charge. Like any self-respecting police chief should."

"And you're taking charge of…?"

"You!" Dylan nudged her toward the steps. "Get changed. And dress up. We're going to a white tablecloth, candlelight kind of place."

Sarah backed away from him and the encouraging hand he had at the small of her back. "That sounds suspiciously romantic to me."

"Think so?" His expression brightened. "That means we're at least making progress. There was a time you wouldn't have recognized even that little bit of romance, not even if it came up and bit you."

"Ha!" It was the only logical response to a statement that outrageous. Especially since it was true. Sarah pulled back her shoulders and stood sneakers to highly shined shoes with Dylan. "What are you up to?"

"Me?" He had the nerve to look indignant. "Technically, what I'm up to is teaching you about romance."

"And nontechnically?"

He hadn't expected her to pay that much attention to his phraseology. But he wasn't about to back down. "Nontechnically…" He gave her a smile. "I finally figured out that even though you asked for my help, you really don't want it." When her mouth fell open, he held up one hand to stop whatever it was she was going to say. "Or you really do want it and you're going to make me work harder for it than I should have to. Simply because you've got this wacky notion about how guys can't be sincere about romance. At least that's the excuse you use. And that's when it hit me."

"About the playing and the not playing and the not playing it right."

"Exactly!" His smile inched up a notch. "You see, every time I try to do what I promised I'd do, every time I show you what's romantic, you back off."

"I do n—"

"Oh please! Do I need to remind you about Pete the Perch?"

Sarah sniffed her indignation. "Pete the Perch was physical, not psychological."

"Well, you're going to have your chance to prove it. Because from here on in, I'm taking my mission very seriously."

"And your mission is…?"

"To teach you all about romance." Dylan smiled, clearly pleased with himself. "It means I can walk romance and I talk romance. Heck, I'd even go so far as to say that it means that not only do I want to invite you to a romantic, candlelight dinner but that I'm duty bound to do it. Get it?"

She didn't. At least not that she was going to admit.

Before she had a chance to try to reason her way through his argument, he put both hands on her shoulders, turned her around and gave her a little push toward the inn. "The only way I'm going to help you is to start being romantic."

It was hard to argue with a man who was so sure of himself.

It was hard to argue with a man who was so damned delicious in that crisp blue uniform of his with his hat at a cocky angle and a self-satisfied expression on his face.

It was impossible when both men were one and the same.

As she climbed the stairs and headed up to Close to the Heart to shower and change, Sarah knew she'd gotten herself into the exact situation she'd been trying to avoid.

Trouble was, when she saw Dylan with his arms crossed over his chest and his hazel eyes glittering, as if he could barely wait until they were together again, she wasn't sure she even wanted to try.

No sooner had the front door closed behind Sarah than Dylan heard the sounds of footsteps on the slate walk. Maisie scurried around from the side of the house.

"So what do you think?" he asked.

She didn't have to ask what he was talking about. "I think you handled that well, dear." She patted his arm. "Sarah is a headstrong woman. She's accomplished and mature. It's only natural that she expects any man in her life to be the same."

"It doesn't feel mature. All this beating around the bush." Uncomfortable, Dylan rolled his shoulders.

"But you're determined to go through with it? You're going to comply with her wishes and try to teach Sarah about romance?"

It wasn't the first time that Maisie had brought up the objection. Politely. And in her own grandmotherly sort of way. None of which made it any less pointed.

"It's not exactly like I'm being underhanded." Dylan gave her the same explanation he'd given her earlier in the

day when he first broached the subject with her and asked
her advice about china and crystal. "Everything is completely aboveboard. No fine print. And that's what really
gets to me. Why should I have to talk her into it like it's
some sort of trap? Why can't a woman take a guy at face
value?"

"Oh, I think most women do. Unless something's
soured them on romance and men in general."

Dylan stared at the little old lady. "Her brothers." Apparently, Maisie didn't know this part of the story. He
filled her in. "Three of them, each a bigger jerk than the
last. Boasted about how easy it was to use a little romance
and a whole bunch of blarney to get their dates into bed."

"Terrible waste of romance!" Maisie frowned. "Unless
it's done with a great deal of finesse, of course, and with
the idea that both lovers know it's all part of the delicate
game of seduction."

"I don't think there was anything delicate about this
game. These guys were bragging to their sister, for God's
sake. Strikes me that all they were trying to teach her was
that guys could be stupid and that women were even more
stupid for falling for it all."

"That would explain it, of course." Maisie nodded.
"But not completely. There's something else here. Mark
my words. Sarah is too smart not to recognize a knuckle-
head when she sees one. Doesn't take a rocket scientist
to figure out that her brothers are knuckleheads of the first
order, and I've never even met them. No, no. There's
more. Now, Sarah isn't exactly the kind of person who
opens up and shares. No doubt because she thinks if she
does, she's calling attention to herself. But I suspect she's
been burned. Had her heart broken."

"Are you're worried that I'm going to break her heart
again?"

Maisie's silvery brows dipped low over her eyes. "Don't be silly, dear. You're much too honorable a man to do that." The phone rang from inside the lobby and she scrambled up the steps. She already had the door open when she turned to him. "You see, it's not Sarah I'm worried about."

Chapter Eight

There are those who say any place can be romantic. It's
hard to argue with this—at least in theory. It is lovely to
believe that a brickyard could have the ambiance of a
candlelit bower. It is also completely impractical! Please,
ladies, keep this in mind. Presentation is everything, in
food and in romance. Soft colors, gentle fragrances, the
drifting scent of potpourri…it all adds up to the kind of
romance that cannot be achieved in any other way.
                              —*Sarah's Guide to Life, Love and Gardening*

A quick shower, a change of clothes and Dylan was back
at the bottom of the Hideaway's front steps in less than
an hour, wishing he'd set a hard-and-fast time to meet
Sarah. Then he could be back at his room above the garage, pacing. Instead of pacing here.

"Dumb," he told himself, smoothing his tie and shift-
ing the sportcoat he had hooked on his thumb and flung
over his right shoulder to his left. "Silly to be nervous. It's
only a date."

Except that it was—if you didn't count Pete the Perch,
which was more of a disaster than a date—a first date. A
first date with Sarah. And Sarah was the most appealing
woman he'd met since…

Maisie's last words to him crackled through Dylan's

head. Then and now, he refused to listen. Maisie was a worrywart. She was too tenderhearted. She was way too concerned about everybody's love life. Even when the everybody in question didn't have much of a love life.

Then again, maybe that was exactly why she was so worried.

Dylan paced up to the stairs, back toward the street, around and toward the stairs again. He had started on the third go-round when he heard a door close from somewhere inside the inn. He hurried back to the porch and stationed himself at the bottom of the stairs. As if he'd been there all along, calmly waiting. His heart beating double time, he waited for the door to open.

In the fantasy that had been taking shape inside his head ever since he'd planned tonight's dinner, he pictured Sarah in a summery dress cut high above her knees. It would be flowery, he hoped, in keeping with the romantic theme of the evening. It would have a hint of pink in it to bring out the pretty color in her cheeks and a sash tied snug to show off her slender waist. She'd be wearing sandals, he'd decided, her toenails the color of cotton candy and her steps as light as butterfly wings. Heck, she was a gardener (sort of) and even if it wasn't technically summer, it was the first week of June and officially island vacation time; she might even have a flower in her hair.

When the door swung open, he held his breath.

And let it out again with a whoosh when Sarah stepped onto the porch.

"You're dressed like you're going to court!"

She straightened the jacket of the gray pin-striped suit she'd put on along with a white Oxford shirt and practical black pumps. "But this is my best outfit." She looked down at herself in dismay. "I can change. Really." She started back toward the house. "I'm not sure what I have to wear, but I—"

"No. You're fine. Honest." Dylan stopped her before she had a chance to open the door. Partly because he didn't want to inconvenience her. Mostly because he realized that now that she was here, he didn't want her to leave.

"You look fine." He couldn't imagine that Sarah would ever *not* look fine. Even if he did prefer that her skirt didn't cover her knees. He gave her the thumbs-up. "You're perfect." He stepped back and made a sweeping gesture toward the street. "Your carriage awaits."

"My carriage looks a whole lot like Maisie's golf cart." She headed down the steps and walked along at his side. "You're sure you want to be seen in public in that?"

Like everything else about the Hideaway, the golf cart was over the top. Pink. Fringe hanging from the flat-top roof. Rhinestones studding the steering wheel cover and a grinning cupid painted on the side.

"It's this or that." He pointed toward the gray Tahoe with the Put-in-Bay Police emblem on the side. "Besides, when I make a romantic gesture, I go all out, and nothing says romance like Maisie's golf cart!" He shot her a smile and held out his hand to help her into the cart, and he considered it a minor victory of sorts when she actually let him do it.

When she was settled against the pink plush seats, he waited to see what she'd think of his second romantic gesture, the geranium he'd stuck in a water bottle and left in the cup holder that was molded into the front dash.

She noticed it instantly and her mouth dropped open. "Betty and Dorothy Depp's geraniums! I'd recognize that salmon color anywhere." There was horror in her eyes when she looked down the street at the Hideaway's closest neighbor. "You picked one of their geraniums? Are you out of your mind? The Depp sisters already give Maisie enough grief about the traffic the Hideaway attracts. And they're practically obsessive about their geraniums. They'll have your head!"

He didn't doubt it for a minute. He only wished Sarah realized that was what made the purloined petals all the more romantic. That, and the fact—mundane as it was— that he didn't have much of a choice.

"I was going to do an arrangement of zinnias, but...well..." He couldn't bring himself to say anything else about the flower beds on either side of the front walk. It was too painful. "The Depp sisters will never miss one little geranium."

She narrowed her eyes. "And here I pictured you up-holding the law."

"There are exceptions to every law. A perfect spring night and the prettiest woman on the island..." He hurried around to the other side of the cart, shrugged into his sportcoat and slid behind the wheel. "Those sound like two perfectly plausible exceptions to me."

"Exceptions. But not all that plausible."

"What?" Laughing, he leaned closer to her. "You don't believe the perfect spring evening part? Or the part about you being the prettiest woman on the island?"

"You said I'm dressed for court."

"I meant for courting."

"You're schmoozing me."

"I'm complimenting you. Because it happens to be true."

She tried not to smile. It didn't work.

So, Sarah did appreciate a compliment as much as the next woman!

The revelation should have left Dylan feeling pretty

satisfied with himself; he'd discovered a chink in her armor. Instead, it sent a wave of warmth through him. He knew more about Sarah than he knew a few minutes ago. It wasn't much. But it was a beginning.

Like all cops, he wasn't content to stop halfway. Not when he had one small success under his belt and was one step closer to putting together the pieces of the mystery that was Sarah. He started the golf cart and did a wide U-turn to head downtown. "So—" he maneuvered the cart around a group of tourists who had come to ogle the Hideaway "—who's Becky?"

He'd caught her off guard. Exactly as he intended. It took Sarah a couple of seconds to recall that she'd mentioned the name earlier in the evening when he came home and found her talking on the phone. She smoothed a hand over her Wall Street skirt. "Becky's a friend."

"Back in Providence?"

"Yes, back in Providence."

He nodded. A little farther up the street, Bob Hesmett was standing outside his house in red-and-white striped boxers and a sleeveless undershirt. Dylan slowed the cart so he could wave and ask Bob about his recent open heart surgery. When he was done, he skirted a puddle caused by somebody's lawn sprinkler, slowed down to let three cyclists pass and turned on a street that was bordered with neat grape arbors.

"That's it?" Sarah's voice told him how uneasy she was. "That's all you're going to ask?"

He pretended surprise. "You mean about Becky? What else is there to ask?"

"You're not going to try and wheedle more information out of me?"

He pursed his lips. "Should I?"

"No! But I can't believe you'd take the trouble to ask about Becky and then simply leave it at that."

"It wasn't any trouble."

"And you don't care who she is or how I know her."

"Sure I do." They were on the main road that led past the airport and into town. This time of the evening, there were a few other golf carts around, but it was hardly a challenging drive. Dylan slid his right arm across the back of the seat. He beeped at a couple of little kids playing in their front yard who recognized him and waved. "I'd like to know all about Becky. Because I'd like to know all about you. But if you don't want to tell me, that's fine by me."

"You're not going to try to get me to tell you about my past."

"Nope." Dylan stuck out his arm to indicate a left turn and took the next corner at a precipitous fifteen miles an hour. "That wouldn't be romantic, and as I pointed out earlier…"

"Tonight is all about romance."

He grinned. "I'm glad you noticed."

"I did. And it's not that I'm not grateful for dinner and the flower and the drive, but…"

Dylan stopped the golf cart in a parking place in front of city hall. He shut it off and turned in his seat so that he was facing Sarah. "You're suspicious of my motives. Because of your brothers."

"Yes." She bit her lower lip. "And no. It's going to sound stupid."

"I doubt it."

"It's juvenile."

"So it's juvenile." He told himself to take it slow and easy and somehow found he was holding Sarah's hand, anyway. When she didn't pull away, he twined his fingers through hers. "Tell me, Sarah, what gave romance such a bum rap?"

She sighed. "More like *who* gave romance a bum rap. Tony DiMarco."

"Tony Di—"

"DiMarco. Yup. Second year of college. See, by then, I'd pretty much figured out that my brothers were goofballs."

"I'm glad."

"Yeah. So was I at the time. So with my newfound knowledge that my brothers were goofballs and this sort of epiphany that romance was still very much alive and well in the world, I decided to romance Tony DiMarco."

"Was he hot?"

"Hey, I was twenty. I'm not sure I knew from hot at twenty. But I did know cute. And Tony DiMarco was way cute. So I wrote him corny notes and sent him funny pictures. I bought him flowery cards and even wrote some very bad poetry."

"And he dumped you."

"Nope. He asked me to marry him."

"That was good." One look at Sarah's expression and he amended the statement. "It wasn't good."

"It was. At least until I found out what he was really after."

"Sex."

"Oh, please! You think I'm a nun or something?" Sarah rolled her eyes. "If all Tony wanted was sex, believe me, he would have been a happy man and we'd probably be married with a gaggle of kids, a couple of dogs and perfect little lives."

"Then what happened?"

"The world's longest engagement, for one thing. And I never caught on." As amazed now as she had been then,

Sarah shook her head. "Did I mention that my father has one of the most successful computer consulting firms in New England? And guess what Tony majored in. It seemed like synchronicity, like this wonderful twist of fate that had brought me together with this great guy and Tony together with my family. Tony was brilliant. And by then, he was just like one of the family. After graduation, Dad gave him a job and a partnership, along with some hefty stock options."

"But I already know there's no happily ever after to this story."

Her grip tightened on Dylan's hand. Just a little. "It was Valentine's Day and I stopped by the office with a cute card, his favorite chocolates and a special little surprise I picked up at the local lingerie shop. That's when I heard Tony on the phone talking to a friend from out of town. He was, to put it mildly, telling the guy what a sucker I was."

Dylan winced. "Not a pretty picture."

"No, it isn't. Not then. Not now." Sarah untangled her fingers from his. She sat up and pushed a curl of hair behind her ear. She straightened her pin-striped jacket and lifted her chin. "But if you think that baring my soul is going to make me see the error of my ways, you're wrong. All that particular memory does for me is reinforce my thinking. Sure, romance sounds like great fun. Choirs of angel song and blah, blah, blah. But underneath the hearts and flowers, it's just a sneaky way for a guy to get what he wants. Whether it's sex or money or a corner office, it doesn't matter." She slid across the seat.

Before she could get out of the cart, Dylan caught her arm. "Not all guys are jerks."

She glanced down to where he touched her. "I've heard rumors to that effect."

"Then you don't think there's any ulterior motive to me asking you to dinner?"

She smiled and plucked his fingers from her arm. "What matters is what you think."

"I think..." He hopped out of the golf cart. "I've got to stop at the office for a minute. You want to come see where I work?"

Lucky for him and all the planning he'd done, she did.

Dylan led the way inside, gave Marsha a wink when he walked past the dispatch center and headed down the hallway that led back to the cells. "Come on." He didn't wait for Sarah to follow. He took her hand. "I want to show you around."

Thank goodness Marsha was a good sport. Everything was ready.

They found the door of cell number two pushed back. Inside, exactly where Dylan left it, was a folding table covered with one of Maisie's best linen cloths. Service for two (Maisie's Sunday china) shared the table with two crystal wineglasses, gleaming silver and a flickering candle.

Dylan stepped back and with a sweeping motion, invited Sarah inside. Her face flushed with excitement, and that told him that all his preparations had been worthwhile. "I told you it was a white tablecloth kind of place."

CELL NUMBER TWO WAS neat and clean enough to do double duty as an operating room. It had a built-into-the-wall bench that also served as a bed, and it was painted a shade of gray that in the candlelight reminded Sarah of the cashmere sweater she'd worn on an *Affairs of the Heart* segment about knitting with luxury fibers. The lights in the outer corridor were off and when the air-conditioning turned on and the candle in the center of the table danced, the shadows on the wall were as feathery as an Impressionist painting.

Sarah knew it was a whole other story when the ceiling light was blazing and a couple of Saturday-night rowdies were in residence.

"I've never been in jail before," she said.

They'd just finished dinner and Dylan had stepped out into the hallway to put their dishes on the rolling cart he'd left out there earlier. He came back into the cell, a china cup of coffee in each hand. "So what do you think?"

"I think I'm lucky to be a dinner guest and not a permanent guest."

He set the coffee down and went back for a crystal creamer and a sugar bowl. "We don't have permanent guests. We're usually pretty much a quick stop. A place to sleep it off."

Her nose wrinkled when she studied the cement bunk. "I'm glad I'm not sleeping here, either." A shiver squirmed over her shoulders. "I bet it's not very comfy."

"Comfy is not the point." Smiling, he sat down in the chair opposite hers. "The point, at least for tonight, is that any place can be romantic. With the right atmosphere. The right person."

The way he said it, Sarah found herself believing it. Almost. "My guess is that the cell usually doesn't have this sort of ambiance."

He was smart enough to know a roadblock when he saw one. While he didn't slam on the brakes, he was willing to take a little detour. He sat back in the folding chair. "We don't want folks to come back."

"Then I hope you don't serve them what you served me." She poured a bit of cream into her coffee and stirred it with the silver spoon he'd left on her saucer. "Wherever you get your food, it was the best I've had in as long as I can remember. The chicken Marsala was cooked to perfection and the salad…" She smiled her approval. "Whoever put the dried cranberries and slivered almonds in there is a genius. If you treat your prisoners to that kind of food, they'll be breaking the law deliberately, just to get back in here to eat."

Dylan's eyes sparkled in the candlelight. "Thank you."

"Thank you as in aren't you a smart guy for finding somebody who cooks that well? Or thank you as in—" She sat up straight and her mouth dropped open. "You're the cook?"

"Not the jail cook!" He laughed. "But yes, I made tonight's dinner."

It wasn't like Sarah had some sort of Stone Age notion about the division of labor, men in the fields and the woman handling the mastodon meat over the open fire. It was just that she'd never pictured Dylan as the domestic type. He was too macho. Too…tough cop. She was surprised to learn that there was another side of him, but she liked the idea, too. Almost as much as she liked it that he had shared it with her.

"Dinner was remarkable. Really. You have a genuine talent. If you want to make that recipe available…" She blanched at what she'd almost said: *available to my viewers.* She washed away the thought with a swallow of coffee and gave herself a good swift mental kick for the faux pas. "That's what I get for having a couple glasses of wine." The bottle of locally made wine they'd finished with dinner was still in the center of the table. "Talking crazy. Asking for a recipe that's probably some sort of O'Connell family secret."

"I hope the compliment wasn't crazy," he said. "And I hope you left room." He got up and went into the hallway. When he came back, he was carrying two of the biggest, most luscious pieces of chocolate cream pie that Sarah had ever seen. He set one down in front of her.

She dipped her fork into the whipped topping, tasted it and sighed. "Real whipped cream! You're not going to tell me you're a pastry chef, too?"

"Oh, no!" He sat down and dug into his own piece of pie. "I do soup and salad. I'd like to try my hand at Italian entrées. And when it's not too expensive, I do a mean Lake Erie perch. Panfried to perfection. What I don't do is dessert. Meg made the pie."

"I've met Meg at the Hideaway. She's a sweetheart." Sarah took another bite.

"Had dinner with Meg and her husband, Gabe, last night. They're only in town for a couple of days this trip. Then they have to head to some big meeting in New York. Gabe's in advertising, you know. Next time they're back, we'll plan a double date."

Sarah couldn't help herself. It was too good an opportunity to pass up. She had to tease him. At least a little. She dangled her fork over her pie. "You're pretty sure of yourself. How do you know that if you ask me out again I'll say yes?"

He wasn't above a little teasing himself. He leaned forward, too, remembering at the last second to move his tie out of the way so that it didn't get coated in whipped cream. "I'd bet money on it."

"You're fairly confident."

"Absolutely. I am, after all, the chief around here. The chief is always confident."

"And not the least bit delusional."

"Nope. Like you, I know my assets and my shortcomings. As you've already pointed out, there's my cooking…"

"Definitely an asset."

"And my choice of romantic rendezvous spots."

"Another asset. At least until you arrest somebody!"

"Then there's the fact that Meg just happens to be my best friend. Pretty slick of me, yes? A best friend who's a kick-ass pie maker."

"And she claims that you're a really good kisser."

As soon as the words were out of her mouth, Sarah knew she'd made a mistake she'd never live down. Her eyes flew open. Her cheeks got hot. Her head had been pleasantly muzzy from the wine, but now she was stone-cold sober.

"I didn't mean…"

At least Dylan had the decency not to laugh. He did not, however, have the decency to ignore the comment. He cocked his head and studied her carefully and, damn, but Sarah was sure she could feel his gaze everywhere it touched. It followed the path of the blush that burned her skin, up her neck, into her cheeks. He finally settled on looking her right in the eye.

"You and Meg have been talking about me."

"Guilty." It wasn't as if she had a choice, so she might as well admit the truth.

"And you and Meg have been talking about me in the context of kissing because…"

"Because I mentioned that you were staying in the room above the garage and—"

"That's got nothing to do with kissing."

"Because I may have mentioned, just in passing of course, the fact that I asked you to help me clarify this whole notion of romance and—"

"Technically, that's got nothing to do with kissing, either."

"She told me you used to go steady and—"

"Now that had very little to do with kissing!" Dylan chuckled. "It was junior year of high school and we went out for about two weeks. The way I remember it, I kissed her once, under the bleachers at a basketball game."

"Twice." Sarah wasn't a fan of revisionist history and she trusted Meg's memory of the events more than Dylan's simply because she figured women were better at keeping track. Especially when it came to matters of the heart. "You kissed her twice. At least that's what Meg says."

"And what else does Meg say?"

"She says she's glad you guys broke up."

He planted his elbows on the table. "I'm glad we broke up, too, long before our relationship could even get close to serious. Otherwise, we wouldn't be comfortable enough with each other to be friends."

"Yeah. That's what she said."

"And she still said I was a good kisser, huh?" A smile tugged at one corner of his mouth. "Did she go into detail?"

"Detail? You mean…?"

"Oh, I don't know. Important stuff. You know, like technique. And philosophy."

Sarah had been intrigued from the moment he leaned forward and smiled at her. Now intrigue turned into flat-out attraction and attraction flirted with temptation.

She reminded herself that temptation was off-limits. But a little flirting wasn't.

Sarah took another bite of pie and licked the cream from her lips. "Meg might have mentioned technique. That is, after all, how I found out what a good kisser you are. As for philosophy…I'm not sure I've ever met anyone who had a philosophy about kissing."

"Not about the kissing as much as about the technique." He was out of his chair and standing at her side in less than a heartbeat, and in even less time than that, he had her hand in his. He tugged her out of her chair.

"You're not going to…" Sarah backed up a step. "Here?"

His smile was wide. "Hey, I'm the chief. Besides, there's nobody around. They've got strict orders. Unless there's a rash of bank robberies, a string of burglaries or an all-out riot…"

She backed up another step and scrambled for a way to save herself. It wasn't that she didn't want him to kiss her. She did. More than she wanted her next breath. But if she let herself fall prey to the temptation, she'd only end up with her heart smashed into pieces.

When he moved closer, she forced herself to hold her ground. "Romantic setting, romantic dinner, romantic bottle of wine. If you kiss me, you're admitting that I'm right. That the whole idea of romance is designed—"

"To get a woman into bed. And that's definitely not what I'm trying to do. At least not yet."

Not yet.

Those two little words and all they promised were Sarah's undoing. When Dylan stepped closer, she flattened her hands against his chest. She slid them up to his lapels and held on tight. "So, you were saying, about your philosophy."

"Ah, yes. Philosophy." He leaned toward her, his lips almost touching hers. "My philosophy, by Dylan O'Connell." He sounded exactly like Sarah had back at the marina when she listed her shortcomings and her strengths. The parallel might have been comical if he didn't whisper the words, his voice a rumble that tingled along her lips and melted all the way through her to her spine. "It's really very simple. You see, I believe in kissing with my eyes closed and my mouth open."

Just to prove his point, he did exactly that.

Chapter Nine

Of course he won't be perfect. None of them are.
Be kind when suggesting necessary improvements.
There is nothing romantic about negativity.
—*Sarah's Guide to Life, Love and Gardening*

"So that's it? That's all you want? That's all you're going to do?"

Even now, two days removed from the kiss in the jail cell, Sarah cringed at the memory of her reaction to Dylan's kiss.

She gets kissed by the hottest guy she's met in as long as she can remember, and her only response (aside from reminding herself to start breathing again) is to sound desperate? Not to mention dumb.

The laughter coming from the back lawn where the guests who were staying in Love Me Tender and the couple currently residing in Almost Paradise were playing an apparently lively game of croquet was in counterpoint to Sarah's groan.

"Incredible," she told herself.

Pretty much like Dylan's kiss.

Now, like then, a tingle ran along her spine. It prickled over her shoulders and spread warmth through her body that was every bit as hot as the touch of the June sun beginning its slide toward the western end of the lake.

Incredible. Spectacular. Terrific.

The same sensations that slammed into her in the jail cell showed up for a return engagement. And all she could think was that she'd blown it. Big time.

"What do you mean, is that all?" Dylan's words still echoed inside her head, along with the little undercurrent of satisfaction that had colored his voice. "Are you telling me you want more?"

"If I did, I'd pretty much be admitting that the whole romance schtick works. Like you were hoping it would."

"Me?" His innocent expression had been in definite opposition to the not-so-innocent suggestions that had flooded Sarah's head. "I wasn't hoping for anything. Except for a kiss."

"And you're going to leave it at that?"

"Disappointed?"

It wasn't any easier now to think about the way he smiled at her than it was then, standing there with her back against the gray cement block wall and her knees feeling like they were made of the whipped cream that frosted the chocolate pie.

Was she disappointed?

Absolutely.

At herself for being stubborn enough to stick to her guns about the sham that most folks called romance.

At him for letting her get away with it.

Now, here she was, waiting for Dylan to pick her up for what he'd promised would be another romantic evening, and all she could think about was that he might kiss her again.

All she could hope was that he would.

And all she could wonder was what she was going to do about it this time.

No closer to an answer now than she had been when Dylan kissed her, Sarah kicked at a loose pebble on the Hideaway's front walk. It skidded across the slate and disappeared into the foliage of a single lush pink petunia.

All thoughts of Dylan vanished in a rush of sheer amazement. She'd been so preoccupied, she hadn't even noticed that the beds on either side of the walk were teeming with petunias! Green-leaved, gorgeous, not-a-hint-of-brown-anywhere-in-sight petunias!

Sarah raised her eyes to the cloudless sky, thanking whatever powers were in charge of gardens and of gardeners who weren't as skilled as they pretended to be.

"Not supposed to rain. At least not until the end of the week."

No wonder Dylan was such a good cop; he had a way of sneaking up on people that made Sarah think he could get to the bottom of any mystery without the bad guys ever knowing he'd been around.

She turned to him with a smile, which widened when she saw that he was dressed in worn jeans that showed off his long, athletic legs, and a bright red shirt that molded to every inch of his muscular chest. "Told you they were only dormant," she said. "And aren't they gorgeous? They're the exact color of the little pink rosebud soaps Maisie left in my room while I was out working this morning."

He caught on instantly and his gaze traveled over the beds. "Nice." He nodded his approval. "But they're not purple anymore."

"Not…" Sarah had noticed, of course. It simply hadn't registered. At the same time she wondered how it was possible that the petunias had changed color, she scrambled for an explanation that would sound like it had even a little horticultural oomph behind it. "Well, it all has to do with hybrids," she told him. "And recessive genes."

"Uh-huh." She couldn't tell if he believed her. "Your geraniums are alive and well, too," he added. "I saw them when I came around the house from the garage. I've got to give you credit—that green thumb of yours is really remarkable!"

She basked in the compliment, poking her hands into the pockets of her denim shorts and pulling her shoulders back inside her powder-blue top. "All it takes is a little patience and a lot of skill. I'm glad you're finally coming around and admitting that there's more to this particular gardener than meets the eye."

"Oh, I've never doubted that." He smiled down at her, but before he could say another word, a movement near the street caught his eye. Two men, one wearing a hard hat and the other carrying blueprints, waved before they climbed into a red panel truck.

"Maybe I can get you to work some of your magic on those guys," Dylan said. "They promised they'd spend the day over at my place taking care of those busted water pipes. Like they've promised a dozen times before. Instead, here they are, working with Maisie on the plan for the addition she wants to put on the inn."

"It's hard to say no to Maisie."

"Tell me about it." When he started walking, Sarah fell into step beside him. "I keep telling her I can't live in the garage forever."

"Like I keep telling her I shouldn't still be staying in Close to the Heart." Sarah crinkled her nose, working through the problem. "You think she'd have guests who'd want to stay in the room. But every time I ask, she tells me that I'm fine right where I am. That it's too soon for me to leave Close to the Heart. Whatever that means."

"Maybe she's waiting for you to have some kind of romantic awakening. You know, suddenly start pouring tea from a china pot. Or dressing in linen and lace."

The idea hit a little too close to Sarah's TV persona for her comfort. She shrugged it aside. "Maybe she's waiting for you to take root back in the garage. Whoever heard of living in a garage, anyway? Is it a nice room?"

He stopped where the sidewalk led one way toward the inn's parking area and the other toward the hulking pink garage. "You want to find out?"

Did she?

Sarah reminded herself that it wasn't in her best interests, and, besides, she didn't want to look too eager to be alone with Dylan again. Even though she was.

"You told me you had a romantic evening planned for us."

"Oh, honey…" Dylan's eyes danced. "If you come up to my place, I can pretty much guarantee you a romantic evening!"

"And if I don't?"

He swept an arm toward the length of sidewalk that led to the parking area, giving in with so much good grace Sarah felt guilty. "If you don't, I can still guarantee you a romantic evening."

"Really." She wished she was able to read him better. Was he teasing? Or promising? "You want to tell me what you have planned?"

"You want to tell me what *you* have planned?"

She stopped near the back porch and the flower beds she'd been working on the first day she met Dylan and just gaped at him. She didn't have to tell him she didn't have a clue what he was talking about.

"I've decided to do the most romantic thing any guy

can ever do," he explained. "I'm going to let you decide how we spend the evening."

"That's romantic?"

He sighed. "Any woman with an ounce of poetry in her blood would recognize it as romantic. After all, I'm letting you make the decision. I'm letting you take charge. I'm asking you what you think is romantic. And whatever it is, we're going to do it. No questions asked."

She failed to see the logic of his argument, but she recognized fair when she saw it. He'd planned the dinner at the jail. Now, it was up to her to come up with some activity for them to do. One that didn't involve her ripping off his clothes and hauling him off to bed.

Thinking about that made heat shoot through Sarah's cheeks. So that he wouldn't notice, she turned to check out the resurrected geraniums.

"They're white." Just to make sure, she rubbed her eyes and studied them again. "They were..."

"Pink." So, Dylan remembered, too. "Recessive genes, do you think?" He waited for her answer.

Sarah's stomach bunched. Making a mental note to ask Becky to do some research so that they could pick up the subject of hybrids and recessive genes another time, she knew it was the right moment to steer the conversation in another direction. Eager to get him off the topic of gardening and back onto the topic of romance—or was it that she was supposed to be eager to get him off the topic of romance and onto the topic of gardening?—she got back to the matter at hand.

"So I get to choose. I mean, about where we go tonight."

"Absolutely."

"No questions asked?"

"That's what I said."

"There is one place I've been meaning to go. Most days I'm too busy and most evenings I'm too tired."

Eyebrows raised, he waited to hear her choice.

"The beach!"

"The…" Dylan's expression fell and he moved back a step. "You're sure?"

"You said no questions asked."

"I did." He swallowed hard and offered her his arm, and when she wound hers through his, Sarah wondered why his muscles were tense. It wasn't like they were talking about gardening anymore.

"IT'S BEAUTIFUL, isn't it?"

From the relative safety of the spot where the path from the parking lot ended and the beach began, Dylan watched Sarah strip off her sandals and hurry to where the water lapped against the shore. When the next wave came in and tickled her toes, she giggled.

"Come on!" She called to him and motioned him closer. "Don't stand there like a bump on a log. Come on in. The water's nice and warm."

"I doubt it." His arms crossed over his chest, Dylan kept an eye on every wave that licked the shore perilously close to where Sarah stood. "I've spent my entire life here, remember. I know it's too early in the summer for the lake to be warm."

"Well, I'm used to the Atlantic and this feels like bathwater." She took a couple of steps further into the lake and the water splashed around her.

Dylan's stomach froze.

Sarah bent down and picked up a pebble to toss into the lake.

And his frozen stomach leapt into his suddenly dry throat.

Before he even realized he'd moved, he found himself on the beach. "Careful! You don't want to…"

"What?" When Sarah turned to him, her eyes sparkled. As bright as the sun that flirted with the far horizon. "There are no great white sharks in these parts, are there?"

She was kidding.

He wasn't.

It was a calm evening and the lake seemed innocent enough. Not pancake flat the way it sometimes was before a storm kicked up. Not so lumpy that any of the sailboats he could see out on the water were hampered. The waves were modest. He supposed some folks might even say soothing. The only foam was where they broke against the shore.

The beach was part of the state park, and above them on a rise, he could see a number of tents set up for the night. Campers and day trippers frolicked in the water. Three Jet Skis zipped by, far enough out so as not to pose a hazard to any of the folks dog-paddling in the shallows.

Dylan swallowed hard and forced his gaze away from the water and back to Sarah. "You're not planning on a swim, are you?"

She looked down at her denim shorts and the light blue shirt that was loose enough to be comfortable and, as luck would have it, snug enough to show off the smooth swell of her breasts. There was a hint of mischief in Sarah's eyes. "Is there a law around here against skinny-dipping?" she asked.

The ice in Dylan's stomach melted in a rush of awareness so keen it took his breath away. He curled his hands into fists, fighting against the urge to scoop Sarah into his arms. And the panic that overwhelmed him when he realized that to do that, he'd have to get even closer to the water.

Instinctively, he backed away. The lawn to his right was dotted with picnickers and Frisbee players. "They're flying kites." He pointed up toward the cloudless sky where at the ends of strings as long as football fields, brightly colored kites danced in the evening breeze. "You want to watch?"

Sarah shielded her eyes with one hand. "I can watch from here."

She could. But if she was watching the kites and not her footing…

Dylan took another step forward, one hand automatically going out to catch her. Just in case.

"We could watch from here. But I see an empty spot of shade up there." He pointed toward a tree on the rise behind them. "And I've got a blanket back in the Tahoe. We could eat those sandwiches we stopped to pick up on the way here."

"Sure. If you're hungry." She stepped out of the water and as soon as her feet touched dry land, Dylan's heartbeat settled and his breathing evened.

She poked her feet into her sandals and joined him. "And after we eat, we can walk down the beach."

Because he didn't have much of a choice, he nodded, but he was already working on a way to get around the plan.

By the time Dylan went over to the SUV with the police emblem on the door and got the blanket and the sandwiches they'd picked up at the deli downtown, Sarah had staked out their claim under a wind-battered maple. He spread the blanket close enough to the tree so that they could sit with their backs against it and waited until she sat down.

Sarah accepted the ham-and-cheese he handed to her and caught the bag of potato chips he tossed one-handed.

"So, enlighten me." She ripped the bag open with her teeth. "Is this romantic?"

He dropped down onto the blanket next to her. "You tell me."

She took a bite of her sandwich, and while she chewed, she narrowed her eyes, thinking. "Well…" She swallowed. "We're a little lacking in the loaf of bread, jug of wine department, but I've got to admit I like the idea of al fresco dining and a warm summer evening."

"Don't forget the good company."

"Ah, yes! The good company!" She laughed and cracked open the bottle of unsweetened iced tea she'd chosen to go along with her sandwich. "So I guess we could call this romantic."

"Absolutely." It felt romantic, too, though Dylan wasn't going to tell her. At least not yet. Then again, ever since he'd kissed Sarah, the whole world had a bit more of a rosy glow. Which was exactly why, before the evening was out, he'd promised himself he was going to do it again.

"I suppose there are folks who would say that the island is too small and not nearly as classy a destination as some spots. But to me…" He spread out his arms, taking in the entire island. "This whole place is romantic."

She took another bite of sandwich and chewed slowly. "But there's no hearts and flowers. No velvet or lace." Dylan knew she wasn't being coy; she was honestly trying to work through the problem. "Some people think that romance is all about silver and china and crystal. Like a couple of nights ago. At the jail."

Dylan's hopes rose. "You ready to admit that the jail was romantic?"

"I may not be the most sentimental soul on the planet, but I recognize a good kiss when I get one!"

So, she'd been as intrigued by the kiss as he had been. Nice to know they were on the same page about something. Especially something that important.

Dylan found himself smiling as he unwrapped his roast beef sandwich. "Seems to me you should be nearly ready to admit that it can be done, then. That I can romance you. And want no more in return than a big smile and a thank-you."

"Provided that's all you want." Her smile was frisky. It warmed Dylan through and through. When she laughed and her breasts strained against her pretty blue top, he could have sworn she was inviting him to look his fill. He did, and it wasn't until he was done that he realized she was still smiling.

"What *do* you want, Chief?"

Dylan didn't have to think about it for more than a second. "I want a life here on the island," he said. "I want a wife I can love longer than forever. I want kids who will think I'm the best dad in the whole wide world and who will, some very long time from now, tell their kids and their grandkids about me. My little piece of immortality. Along with a statue of me in full uniform in the center of DeRivera park, of course."

Okay, so he was going a little too fast; the moment he'd said the stuff about a wife and the island, he could tell that Sarah got uncomfortable. But it wasn't as if he could help himself. His mind had a tendency to run a mile a minute. His imagination wasn't often far behind. He needed to remind himself to slow down. At least a little. Luckily, when he was finished and Sarah turned back to him, she didn't seem to hold his impetuosity against him.

"Gee, and all I meant was…potato chips?" She held the bag out to him, but she was smiling while she did it. "Or

corn chips?" She tossed him the bag of snacks he'd chosen back at the deli.

Dylan caught it and popped open his can of ginger ale.

"Soda from a can and iced tea straight out of the bottle." Sarah took a drink. "It would never fly with the folks
who claim that the only way to set the mood is with candles and flowers. But you know, I think you might be
right. It is romantic. The sky…" She tipped her head back.
"Those kites dancing up there like jewels." She looked
back down and right into Dylan's eyes. "The water."

Damn, but he hated it when he felt like he was under
a microscope. Especially when he knew he didn't have
anything to feel self-conscious about. At least not anything Sarah could have known about.

Dylan took a big bite of roast beef sandwich so that he
could stall for time. "Sure," he said after he swallowed and
washed the bite of sandwich down with a long drink of
soda. "The lake is romantic. The whole island is romantic. Maisie's always understood that about South Bass. It's
why she built the Hideaway here and it's a big reason the
place is so popular."

"Well, it makes perfect sense to me." Sarah nodded and
her golden hair glistened. "Blue sky. Sunshine. Long
walks down quiet roads. And oh, did I mention all that
water?"

This time, it wasn't as easy to ignore the jab. Dylan did
his best. "Laurel and Noah—that's Meg's sister and her
husband—they run the medical clinic downtown. They
love to sail and they're out on the water every day they
aren't working. Anyway, they claim this is the most romantic place to sail in the world. And with Noah lecturing at medical schools all over the country, they've been
practically everywhere."

"Yeah. I can imagine." Sarah's sigh rippled the evening air. "All that water."

"All right. That's it!" Dylan tossed what was left of his sandwich down on the waxed paper it came in. "You're fishing for information. And you're not being very subtle about it."

"Me?" Her expression was as innocent as a basket of puppies.

"You're talking about the lake." Dylan narrowed his eyes and hardened his jaw. It was a tactic that was known to make his patrol officers quake in their shoes. It didn't work on Sarah, of course. He would have been disappointed if it did. "You think you're going to trick me into making some kind of confession."

"I don't know what you're talking about." Sarah finished the last of her sandwich. She brushed her hands together, touched a paper napkin to the corners of her mouth, then rolled up the napkin in the paper the sandwich had come wrapped in. She took their dessert—two giant chocolate chunk cookies—out of the bag before she tossed the waste paper in it. "I'm altogether too practical to use trickery."

"Still, I don't think it's exactly fair to make a guy bare his soul."

"Hey, pal." She twinkled over at him. "All I was talking about baring was…" She blushed the same color as the ribbon of pink that striped the western sky. "Well, we were talking about skinny-dipping."

"No. *You* were talking about skinny-dipping. And about water."

"You're the one who brought it up."

"I simply said that the island was romantic."

"Sheesh!" Sarah wasn't a nibbler. She crunched into

her cookie. "For once, I actually agree with you. And you still get all nutso on me."

"Because you were talking about the lake."

"Well, duh! We are on an island!"

"That doesn't mean you have to rub it in. Just because you know I'm afraid of the water!"

It wasn't until Sarah's mouth dropped open that Dylan realized the words he'd never spoken out loud to anyone had slipped right past his tongue and his better judgment. He clamped his mouth shut and watched her eyes go wide and her breath catch.

Right before she burst out laughing.

Sarah laughed until tears trickled down her cheeks and she collapsed against the blanket, and when she finally got herself together again and sat up, she started chuckling again.

"You're kidding me, right?"

Dylan sat a little straighter. "Let's not talk about it."

"You're not kidding!" She swiped a hand over her cheeks. "But you live on an island!"

"I know I live on an island."

"You're surrounded by water."

"Don't remind me."

"You never leave?"

This was going too far and he decided he needed to disabuse her of the notion. "It's not like I'm some kind of hermit. I leave. But I don't do it on a ferry. Or on any of the smaller boats. When I have to go to the mainland, I fly."

She made a face. "This isn't some kind of serious psychological problem, is it? I mean, it's not why you stay, why you've got your heart set on that statue over in the park. Because you're phobic about water or—"

"Don't be ridiculous." He wadded up his sandwich wrapper and shoved it into the bag. "I live here because I

like it here. It has absolutely no bearing on how I feel
about the water. And in case you're going to ask, because
I know you're going to ask, no, it hasn't always been this
way. I used to love the water. Until I was ten and was in
a boating accident with my cousin Terry."

As fast as it had shot into her cheeks, all the pretty color
drained out of Sarah's face. She pressed one hand to her
mouth. "Oh my gosh! No one was…"

"Killed? No. But it was close."

Dylan thought about stopping the story right then and
there. He'd told her enough, hadn't he? But then he saw
the shimmer of understanding in Sarah's eyes.

"We were out on the lake on a sunny August afternoon.
Me, Terry and my uncle Mike. It was Uncle Mike's boat
and lucky for all of us, he's a first-class sailor. You'd never
know it to see the lake on a day like today, but a storm
can kick up here in the blink of an eye. Lake Erie is the
shallowest of the Great Lakes. So when a storm rolls in,
the waves are furious. A storm kicked up that day.

"We were tossed around in Uncle Mike's sailboat for
close to an hour. The radio cut out and we couldn't raise
the Coast Guard. Finally, the boat flipped over and tossed
us out. Then the thing sank. Right down from under us."

Sarah's eyes went wide. She reached across the small
space that separated them and gave his hand a squeeze. It
was that more than anything else that made Dylan say the
words he'd never dared to say to anyone in more than
twenty years. Not even to himself.

"I was scared to death." A chill snaked over his shoulders. "Terry and I had life preservers on, but the waves
were overwhelming, and I swear I swallowed half the
lake. But Uncle Mike's as strong as an ox, and he managed to haul us both to shore. I couldn't believe I was
alive."

Her hand hadn't left his, and she increased the pressure. "That must have been horrible."

Tears sprang to her eyes, and Dylan almost regretted telling her the story. "Hey, I made it. All three of us made it. But ever since then…well, the lake and I don't exactly get along."

"And nobody knows it?"

"Not a soul. Look, this gets out and I'll be the talk of the island."

"Our secret."

He twined his fingers through hers and drew her closer. "Is that a promise?"

She considered the question. But only for a second. "It'll cost you."

"I hope the price is a kiss."

He could feel her smile when he brought his mouth down on hers.

SARAH STOOD ON HER TOES to kiss Dylan good-night. After the best evening she could remember, she wasn't exactly in the mood to leave it at that, but she had no doubt it was the best course of action. And Dylan, smart guy that he was, knew better than to push. There was no doubt he was the type who would allow her ample breathing space and let her decide when the time was right for their relationship to move to the next step.

She knew it was getting mighty close.

She went inside Close to the Heart and closed the door behind her. One of the housecleaning staff or, more likely, Maisie herself had left a new set of rose-embroidered sheets on the bed while she was out. Sarah kicked off her sandals and set the sheets aside. She flopped down on the bed and waved to herself in the mirrors on the ceiling, then turned over on her stomach and gave the gold gilded cupid that hung on the wall nearby a thumbs up.

There was a whole list of reasons for her good mood: she'd had a great time tonight; Dylan was a fabulous kisser; she'd enjoyed the kite flying and the beach, and watching, Dylan's arm around her shoulders, while the sky turned to a palette of oranges and pinks as the sun went down.

Oh yeah, and did she mention that Dylan was a fabulous kisser?

As exhilarating as it was, even that wasn't the best part of the evening. That Dylan was comfortable enough to share his secret with her meant more than she could possibly say.

Sarah stared up at the ceiling and into the face of the woman who was smiling back at her.

Maybe this whole notion of romance wasn't a lot of hooey, after all.

Chapter Ten

The most romantic fantasies are the ones that come true.
—*Sarah's Guide to Life, Love and Gardening*

"It's about time!"

On the other end of the phone, Becky sounded as if she'd just run a mile. "I've been waiting by my desk all morning. Where've you been? I've got something important to tell you."

At the moment Sarah was watering the flowers in the back bed. A couple of them were droopy, but she wasn't worried. Recessive genes.

Thinking back to the evening she'd explained it all to Dylan, she smiled. Though she couldn't remember anything in any of Becky's horticultural research that said it was possible for dearly departed flowers to make a sudden, spectacular reappearance, she didn't have a shred of doubt that they would come bounding back. Like they had last time.

After all, there was a little magic in the air around Cupid's Hideaway.

"Sarah, are you listening to me?"

It was impossible to ignore Becky's question. "Listening? Nope!" Sarah grinned because she knew what

Becky's reaction was sure to be. Sarah was dependable. Sarah was reliable. Sarah always listened. To everyone. No doubt Becky was sitting at her desk with her mouth hanging open. "I'm thinking," Sarah admitted. "About a guy."

She heard Becky's sharp intake of breath. "We don't have time for this nonsense," she said. "I have to tell you—"

"Nonsense?" Sarah laughed. "You're the one who's always saying that none of it's nonsense. Not the hearts. Not the flowers. Not the romance. Becky, I'm trying to tell you, I think I finally get it. I think I finally understand what all the hoopla is about."

"Great. Fabulous. Wonderful." Becky didn't sound like she meant it. "But this is more important. Sarah—"

Sarah turned off the hose and stood in a puddle on the back walk. It wasn't even noon yet, and it was already hot and humid enough to cause her white Cupid's Hideaway polo shirt to stick to her ribs. The cold water from the hose felt good on her bare toes. "I've known you close to forever, Becky. And you've always been a big believer in romance. Now I'm trying to tell you that I might believe it, too, and all you can say is—"

"Will you stop it, already?" Becky said. "I'm trying to tell you—"

"Becky! Are you listening to me? I'm telling you I've met a guy. A wonderful guy."

Finally, her words penetrated whatever it was that preoccupied Becky's mind. Sarah heard her friend let go of a long breath of surrender. "That's great. Really, it is."

"Aren't you going to ask about him?" Sarah's gaze strayed to the garage. It had been five days since she'd had a chance to spend any real time with Dylan. Summer weekends were busy on the island, especially for its police chief. Over the past few days, they'd managed to grab lunch together once and the night before, when Dylan got home after a twelve-hour day, he'd brought a bottle of locally made wine and they'd shared it on the back porch, along with a lot of conversation and a couple of kisses that still sang through her bloodstream.

"His name is Dylan," she told Becky, "and he's a cop and I've been so anxious to tell you about him that I even tried calling you over the weekend. You didn't answer your phone and I'll bet you didn't pick up your voice mail messages, either. If you did, you would know what I'm talking about."

There was a moment's hesitation on the other end of the phone before Becky said, "I've been a little busy."

"Busy, how?" It wasn't like Becky to dodge, yet dodging was exactly what she was doing. Sarah could tell from the catch in her voice. She narrowed her eyes, exactly as she would have if she was back in Providence, staring at Becky across the studio. "And how busy?"

A flutter of excitement vibrated through Becky's words. "I've met a guy, too. We spent the weekend together, and—"

Sarah shrieked her approval. "I want all the details, Beck. Now!"

It wasn't in Becky's nature to be hard-nosed. No matter how much she tried. She softened up as Sarah knew she would, and when she giggled, Sarah could picture the way her cheeks dimpled. "I'll give you the details. I promise. But right now—"

"At least tell me his name. And where you met him."

"His name is Jason. And we talked about him before. He's the—"

"The magazine guy? The one who wants me on the

cover? I guess you changed your mind about giving him that interview."

"I didn't change my mind." Becky barely tamped down her excitement. "He still wants to interview you and he still wants you on the cover. But…well…I called him to tell him you were on sabbatical. Exactly like you told me to do. And we started talking and one thing led to another and we just sort of…connected, you know?"

"Do I ever!" Sarah laughed. "It's wild. There you are back in Providence. And here I am in the middle of Lake Erie. And we've both got the same story! Okay, my turn." Sarah talked right over Becky's attempt to interrupt her. "You've got Jason, I've got Dylan. He's gorgeous, Becky! Sandy hair, broad shoulders, eyes that are sometimes green and sometimes gray. Kind of like the lake. The lake changes color, too, depending on the weather and the clouds and—"

"I'm happy for you. Honest to gosh I am, Sarah. But if you'd let me get a word in edgewise—"

"I'll let you get a million words in!" The sun was warm on her cheeks and Sarah angled her face up to it and closed her eyes. "I want to hear all about Jason. Is he tall? Short? Muscular? Bald? Is he a good kisser? Because you know what, Beck? Dylan is a very good kisser."

Becky screeched her frustration. "Yes, Jason is a good kisser! But that's not what I need to tell you about. At least not right now. There's more. And it's important. We got—"

"I doubt it. I doubt there's anything in the world that's more important than love."

Sarah could hardly believe her own ears. Here she was, the most levelheaded woman in the Western Hemisphere, the most realistic, and she was lecturing Becky about the importance of love?

It was astounding, that's what it was. As she wound the hose back onto the reel attached to the back porch, Sarah hummed a little tune.

"You're singing." Becky was incredulous. "You can't be that head over heels about this guy, Sarah. It isn't like you."

"Wanna bet?" She finished with the hose and stepped over a geranium with brown leaves and no flowers. "It might not be like the old me, but this is the new Sarah talking, and the new Sarah is as mushy as a bowl of oatmeal. How can I help myself? I feel so terrific!"

"Bet I can make you feel even better."

"Bet not."

"Are you ready?"

The way Becky said it—with a hum of anticipation and a note of barely controlled excitement—made Sarah take notice. She stepped back onto the sidewalk and stood still, sensing that whatever it was Becky was going to say, it wasn't simply important, it was monumental.

"We got the call." Now that she had Sarah's full attention, Becky could barely contain her excitement. "We got the *call*, Sarah. From the Home & Hearth network. They're picking up *Affairs of the Heart*. Thirteen episodes!"

Sarah swore her heart stopped right then and there. The world collapsed in on itself, then expanded in a rush of exhilaration so incredible, the colors in the landscape around her seemed to intensify and the sound of the birds singing in the tree nearby was suddenly as rich and as full as a symphony.

Her heart started up again with a jolt against her ribs that made her gulp for air.

"Thirteen—" The words refused to make their way past the lump of happiness in her throat. Before Sarah even realized she was crying, a tear slipped down her cheek. "Oh, Becky!" She sniffed and laughed at the same time. "I'm...I mean, I..."

Becky was crying and laughing, too. "I *told* you it was important!"

"It is. It's...when?"

"We can keep to our regular production schedule," Becky said. "That means—" Sarah heard a shuffle of papers "—you need to be back here exactly five weeks from today. In the meantime, I'll get cracking on finalizing plans for the first couple of episodes. I could use your help, of course. And don't tell me you're too busy with that cop of yours. You can do most of this on the phone. You've got a way of schmoozing people and we need some people schmoozed. We want that antique Valentine collector from New York to appear with you the first week. And that lady who collects the vintage linens. You remember her, the one who refuses to talk to anyone except through a closed door?"

Sarah had dealt with both the Valentine collector and the linen lady before. One of them was persnickety. The other was just plain weird. But even the prospect of dealing with both of them wasn't enough to dampen her spirits. "Not a problem," she promised Becky. "I'll make the calls. After that I'll—"

After that, she honestly didn't know what she'd do. She was too excited to even try to figure it out.

"It's too much to think about right now." Sarah pressed a hand to her heart. It was pounding like a drum. "I've got so many questions to ask. I'll call you later. I'll call the Valentine guy and the linen lady later. I...I can't think straight right now."

She hung up with only a quick "Bye," and stood stock still, processing every word Becky had said, and trying to understand what it all meant.

This was the biggest event of her career. It was the most exciting moment of her life.

And all she could think was that there was only one thing she wanted to do.

She wanted to share it.

With Dylan.

The feeling was overwhelming and Sarah knew better than to try to fight it. She was headed to the back porch for her socks and sneakers before another realization hit her over the head.

If she told Dylan about *Affairs of the Heart*, she'd also have to tell him that she'd been lying. About who she was and what she was doing on the island. About how she was never going to leave because South Bass was the home she'd always been searching for.

Her excitement drained away and even the heat of the afternoon sun couldn't thaw the ice that formed in her veins. She dropped down on the bottom step, put her elbows on her knees and propped her chin in her hands.

She was still there a few minutes later when an idea struck out of the blue.

She wanted to tell Dylan about her show and about the life she had back in Providence. She had to. And now she knew exactly how to do it.

Without another moment's hesitation, Sarah got to her feet and raced up the back steps, heading for the Love Shack.

It was already after dark by the time Dylan got back to the Hideaway that night. And this time of year, dark didn't come until nine o'clock.

He parked the Tahoe and climbed out, rubbing one hand to the small of his back.

Tuesdays were supposed to be quiet.

The weekend visitors were long gone. The people who were renting cottages by the week were settled in. The beaches weren't crowded and the tourists who dutifully trudged to the top of the 1812 war memorial were few and far between. The drink-themselves-silly college kids weren't around to drink themselves silly because even college kids had to return to the mainland and get back to work.

None of which explained why this Tuesday had turned into one of the busiest days he could remember.

Dylan worked out a crick in the muscles of his neck. One stolen golf cart, two missing boaters who were later found marooned on a sandbar, a shoplifter over at (of all places) the candy store and a drunk who decided to bust up one of the local pubs and figured he could continue punching and kicking even after Dylan and his officers arrived to get the situation under control…

Dylan tentatively touched the swollen and tender skin around his left eye. As soon as he got back to the station from handling the incident at the bar, Marsha had insisted on administering an ice pack and had called Noah and Laurel over from the clinic to check him out. Their diagnosis pretty much confirmed what Dylan already knew: he had one hell of a shiner.

His muscles protesting every move and his vision blurred, he paused at the spot where the sidewalk split to head in one direction to the inn and in the other, back to the garage. All day long, he'd told himself that as soon as he got back to the Hideaway, he'd make it a point to stop in and see Sarah. It was the one and only thing that got him through the golf cart, the boaters, the shoplifter and even the guy trying to turn a nice place into a boxing ring.

The promise of a couple hours of Sarah's company. The chance to sit back and watch the way her incredible blue eyes sparkled. The not-so-remote possibility that he'd kiss her, and that just like before, she'd respond as if they were made for each other, their hearts and their minds and their desires meshing perfectly.

Unfortunately, he was so tired he felt as if he might fall over, not to mention the headache that had started up the second that guy's beefy fist connected with his face. He'd get up extra early and make sure to see her in the morning. Right now, a hot shower and another ice pack were the wisest choices.

The door that led to the stairs was on one side of the garage, and as he turned the corner, he stopped, sure that his eyes were playing tricks on him. South Bass wasn't the kind of place where doors needed to be locked but still, cops were cops and Dylan was a cop through and through. In spite of Maisie's protest that he shouldn't bother, he made sure to lock the door every day when he left for the station. But tonight, it was standing open a crack.

A groan probably wasn't exactly a professional response, but Dylan couldn't help himself. He wasn't up for another confrontation. Not to mention any more paperwork. If someone had broken in...

If someone had broken in, he owed it to Maisie to get to the bottom of it as quickly as he could.

Dylan shook away his exhaustion, pulled back his shoulders and inched the door farther open.

When he did, he stopped dead in his tracks.

In front of him was a wall where Maisie (always conscious of first impressions even when the first impression was of the garage) had hung a picture of a knight in shining armor and a red-haired maiden. To his right were the stairs.

On every second step, a candle glowed from a small colored glass holder. Royal blue. Purple. Red. There were no other lights on, and in the dark, the colors shone like jewels. There was music playing from somewhere upstairs.

And flower petals…

Not sure if he was so tired that he was hallucinating, Dylan bent down for a better look.

They were flower petals, all right, and they were strewn on the steps. He ran them through his fingers and was rewarded with the spicy scent of carnation, the soft smell of lilac and another perfume that was musky and exotic, like patchouli.

Cops were men of action. Yet suddenly, Dylan found himself unable to move. He decided instantly that burglars, no matter how well bred, didn't usually care much about atmosphere.

Which must mean…

Suddenly his muscles didn't ache nearly as much. Dylan took the steps two at a time.

The stairway opened into what Maisie called a room but was really more of a suite. There was a bathroom straight ahead with a whirlpool tub and a shower big enough for two. There was a table against the wall of windows that faced the lake. It was set with two crystal champagne flutes. And two flickering candles.

There were other candles burning around the room, too. A good thing since there weren't any lights on. A whole row of candles flickered on the fireplace mantel. Another pair glimmered on the low table in front of the couch. A few more were placed on either side of the flower-petal path that led from where he was standing to the canopy bed that dominated the far side of the room.

Dylan was keenly aware of every inch of his body. He felt his heartbeat where it slammed against his chest. And his throat became suddenly as dry as a desert. He felt a fierce aching in his gut, and damn if it didn't feel good!

"So what do you think?"

The voice, soft and sweet and feminine, came from somewhere across the room.

"I think…" He took a couple of steps and when his shoes crushed the flower potpourri, the scent of it filled the air. Before tonight, he would have described the suite as comfortable. More than comfortable. It was spacious. It was nicely decorated. Now, with the lights off and the candles flickering, it was positively—

"Romantic." Dylan's voice echoed in his own ears along with the Puccini playing from the stereo near the couch. He took another step toward the bed and as he did, Sarah came out from the alcove where a bay window offered the perfect spot for Maisie to pamper a number of tropical plants and African violets. His eyes were still adjusting, and all he could see was the glimmer of her golden hair.

"I'm completely blown away. This is the most incredibly romantic thing I've ever seen in my life," he told her.

"Thank you." For the first time, he realized that Sarah was wearing a long satin robe. It was ivory with an edging of fat satin roses that brushed the floor. Dylan recognized it instantly. He'd seen the robe in the Love Shack.

He remembered it because the demure robe came with a surprising addition—a nightgown in the same material. Cut up to here. And down to there. With skinny spaghetti straps made to be slipped off a woman's shoulders.

Dylan smiled.

Suddenly he wasn't feeling very tired anymore.

Chapter Eleven

> Not sure what to do? Follow your heart. In any situation.
> With anyone. Your heart will never steer you wrong.
> > —*Sarah's Guide to Life, Love and Gardening*

Sarah took a deep breath and swallowed hard.

Not exactly the right way to begin a romantic encounter. Even a left-brained woman knew that. Still, it was hard not to be nervous. Dylan stood fifteen feet away, all smiles and surprise, so delicious in his blue uniform that it was hard for her not to throw herself into his arms.

Not yet, she had to remind herself. Just as she'd been reminding herself since she'd come up with this crazy idea.

First, they would talk. Then…

Her heart did a rat-a-tat against her ribs and she braced herself against it, folding her thumbs into her palms and wrapping her fingers over them. She held on—to her self-control and to what had sounded like a really good plan until Dylan had walked into the room and she realized she didn't have the strength to resist him any more than she had the nerve to face him with the truth.

"We have to talk."

She knew the words came out of her mouth, but they

sounded disembodied, no more lasting than the candle-light that flickered against the walls and puddled on the high ceiling. They would talk all right, then if he was still interested in a woman who would be leaving in a little less than five weeks to begin a whole new phase of her career on a national stage and in the national spotlight...

Then they'd see what might happen next.

But for now...

Sarah held out her hand.

He leaned forward and squinted through the dark. "Is that—"

"An ice pack."

Dylan's smile faded in disbelief. "What, you're psychic?"

She shrugged. "Word travels fast around here. Marsha called Laurel. Laurel called Maisie."

"And Maisie told you. Great." He touched a hand briefly to his left eye. "Not exactly the right way to make a good impression. A black eye and word going around the island that the police chief isn't fast enough on his feet to dodge a slobbery drunk."

Because he didn't make a move to retrieve the ice pack, Sarah went to him. In this light, it was hard to see how badly he was hurt, but even candlelight couldn't hide the dark blotch that stained his cheek or the fact that the skin around his eye was swollen. Just thinking about all he'd been through made her wince. She raised the ice pack and held it against his face, careful not to press too hard. "That's not exactly the story I heard."

"Really?" He sighed. Maybe because the ice felt so good on his bruised face. Maybe because when she stepped nearer, he tensed as if he'd been waiting for this moment and now that it was here, he didn't want to waste it or wish it away too quickly. He settled his hand over hers where she held the ice pack to his skin. The pulse in his wrist beat out a message against her hand. "What exactly did you hear?"

"That your slobbery drunk was actually trying to clock one of the bar patrons, a friend of Mr. Slobbery's who was doing his best to get the situation under control before it...well, before it got out of control."

"It was way past out of control by the time I got there," Dylan tried to roll his eyes. Not the best plan in light of the broken blood vessels and swollen tissue. He flinched. "Yeah, the guy's friend tried to stop him. And I don't think he was doing it out of the goodness of his heart, either. I got the impression he was a practical sort of guy. He could see the dollar signs flashing above the drunk guy's head. Court costs, attorney fees, payment for the couple of bar stools he'd already busted into a million little pieces and the pinball machine he'd smashed beyond repair. Not to mention the tickets I'm going to write first thing in the morning: disturbing the peace, inciting a riot, inducing a panic. By the time I'm done with him, this is going to be his most expensive vacation ever."

"So here was this guy, trying to keep his friend from getting into any more trouble. And Mr. Slobbery went after him."

"You got that right."

"And that police chief you mentioned..." Briefly, Sarah lifted the ice pack and brushed a finger against his swollen cheek. The skin around Dylan's eye was cool. As opposed to his hand where it rested against hers. His fingers were warm. His palm was hot. She settled the ice pack back in place. "I hear that police chief walked right in and took charge. He stepped between those two friends. It was the only way he could keep Mr. Slobbery from really hurting Mr. Practical. I also hear that the police chief got in a few licks of his own. He had Mr. Slobbery down on the ground and in handcuffs practically before the guy knew what hit him."

"But not before he hit me." There was a sparkle of laughter in Dylan's eyes. At least in the eye she could see. "Guess I should have been faster."

"Oh, I don't know. I have a feeling that you're fast enough."

"You have no idea!" His pulse quickened. Just like Sarah's heartbeat. "So is that what this is all about?"

She didn't have to ask what he was talking about. She could tell he was impressed by the candles and the music. Not to mention her satin outfit. "You don't think you deserve a hero's welcome?"

His expression brightened and he looped his fingers around her wrist and lowered her hand and the ice pack. He didn't let go. His hold on her tightened. "Just doing my job, ma'am. But that doesn't mean I'll turn down a reward." He grinned and his gaze traveled around the room. "My guess is that you and I are pretty much on the same wavelength."

"That's a distinct possibility. But first…" It was the hardest thing she'd ever done. Ruining a moment as good as this. Taking the chance that once the spell was broken, it couldn't be cast again. Evidently, Sarah was as practical as Mr. Slobbery's friend.

Before she could remind herself that for the first time in her life she didn't want to be, she tugged Dylan toward the table. "Let's sit down. First we need to talk."

"First I need to kiss you."

No, that was wrong. It was all mixed up. It wasn't the way this was supposed to work!

Sarah never had a chance to tell him. Before she could, Dylan brought his mouth down on hers and her words were lost beneath the sensations that coiled through her like liquid fire. There was nothing tentative about the kiss. It was firm and insistent. It was temptation, and so convincing that when she felt his tongue touch her lips, she never considered doing anything but opening to him.

The moan she heard might have come from her. Or him. It didn't matter. Her muscles relaxed. Her nerves unwound. The ice pack splatted against the floor and Dylan's hands skimmed the length of her satin robe.

"Mmm." He made an attempt to nuzzle a kiss against the right side of her neck, but when it put his bruised cheek in contact that was too close for comfort, he slanted his head the other way and pressed the kiss to the left side, instead. "You taste good," he said. "And you feel…" His hands slipped over the satin, across her butt, up her back and down again. With each caress Sarah found her mind wandering.

She was supposed to stay on track, she reminded herself.

And she would.

As soon as she remembered what that track was. Where it was heading. And why she was on it in the first place.

"Dylan!" He slipped the knot on the sash that tied her robe closed, and she did her best to protest. It might have sounded more genuine if it hadn't escaped her on the end of a trembling sigh. "What about talking?"

"You talk. I don't want to talk." He slid a hand inside the robe. "So tell me…" He glided a hand along her thigh and up to the short, short hem of her nightgown, his fingers skimming the satin before they moved on to brush the edging of lace where it caressed Sarah's breasts. "Is this what was inside that mystery bag?"

"I can't believe you're still thinking about that auction." Sarah laughed. Not easy, considering that her insides were liquid and her outsides were standing at attention, especially when his fingers played across the bare skin exposed by the low-cut nightgown.

"So…" He trailed a series of kisses as light as butterfly wings against her shoulder and the hollow at the base of her throat before he dipped another kiss, longer and hotter, into the shadowy place between her breasts. "You don't want to talk about the auction. Then maybe you want to talk about Tony DiMarco."

Sarah had practiced what she was going to say to Dylan. All afternoon in front of the mirror. She had the words down pat. The part about how much her career meant to her. The bit about how she could tape *Affairs of the Heart* in Providence and still visit Put-in-Bay often. She wasn't even above pulling out the old, hokey proverb about absence and how it made the heart grow fonder. She'd anticipated all his objections and prepared a reasoned answer to every one.

Every one but this one.

As if it actually might help her figure out what he was talking about, Sarah scrunched up her nose and narrowed her eyes. "Tony DiMarco? What does he have to do with this?"

"Maybe a lot. That is why you're hedging, isn't it?"

"I don't hedge. I never hedge." It wasn't until after she stepped back and crossed her arms over her chest that she realized she was hedging.

Sarah forced her hands to her sides. "You think some guy I knew years ago who was enough of a Philistine to play on my emotions and then laugh about what a sucker I was…" She hauled in a breath. "Do you really think I'm thinking about Tony?"

"Are you?"

"Don't play that game with me." Sarah caught herself

as her hands were about to curl into fists. She forced them to relax. "The only thing Tony DiMarco has to do with this is—"

"That the last time you tried this whole romance routine with a guy, you got your heart diced and sliced and handed back to you on a platter. Don't worry, I understand. That explains the hedging."

"But I'm not—" Sarah barely controlled a screech of frustration and reminded herself that it was better to show and tell than yell. She took another step back and yanked open her robe. "Does this look like hedging to you?"

She didn't even have to watch Dylan to know what he was doing. She felt the heat of his gaze where it grazed her thighs and flirted with the short hemline of the nightgown. She gasped at the fire that erupted within her when he studied the wisp of satin where it hugged the mounds of her breasts.

"It looks like heaven." Dylan sounded the way he had the day he watched her step into the lake. As if he couldn't catch his breath.

Sarah wrapped her robe around her. "Heaven. Not hedging?"

"No, ma'am." His smile sparkled like the candlelight. He stepped closer, his voice as soft as the light that flickered around them. "So this whole bit about how we have to talk…"

Dylan unlaced her fingers where they were clasped over the front of her robe.

And Sarah's insides caught fire.

"It's not because you think I'll do a Tony DiMarco on you?"

Starting at her waist, he slipped his hands up, one on either side of the robe.

And Sarah's knees turned to rubber.

"You're not worried that I'll spend tomorrow around the water cooler at the station, laughing about how you succumbed to my romantic gestures?"

He twitched the robe over her shoulders and down her arms, and once it was free, he tossed it across the room where it landed on the couch.

And Sarah held her breath.

"So tell me…" Her nipples were outlined against the satin by the firelight and he fingered first one, then the other, a deceptively simple action that caused a not-so-deceptive reaction. Heat pooled. Flesh sizzled. Sarah wasn't the only one feeling it. Dylan's pupils were wide with desire. "If it's not Tony DiMarco, what is it you want to talk about?"

"Talk?" The response might have been more convincing if Sarah's voice hadn't come out an octave too high. "Are we supposed to be talking?"

His laugh rumbled in his chest and his chest was close enough for Sarah to feel the vibration all the way down to where her toes were poked into ivory satin slippers. She braced herself against the sensations and tried to pretend her good intentions weren't completely destroyed by the undisguised longing on his face.

"We need to talk about us," she said.

Even swollen, Dylan's face was handsome. He touched his nose to hers. "I've got an idea. I'll admit it right now and I'll tell the world if you want me to—you wanted to learn about romance, and you did! With flying colors. This is the single most incredible thing I've ever seen. And the most romantic." He kissed her again. And even though she told herself it was too soon to surrender, she had no choice but to coil her arms around his neck. Just in case her knees gave way.

He liked her response. Almost as much as he liked the way her tongue met his, the way her fingers brushed the shoulders of his crisp blue shirt. She fingered the edges of his badge where it was pinned over his heart. "There's a lot I haven't told you," she said. "You've already guessed that. Every time you ask about my past, I manage to change the subject."

"And I manage to let you." He flattened his hand and brushed his palm against her nipple.

Sarah sucked in a breath against the incredible sensation. "But you're the police chief around here and—"

He stepped back, unpinned his badge and tossed it onto a nearby table. "There," he said. "I'm not the police chief anymore."

"But you're still a cop."

The firelight danced in his eyes. "Can't prove it once I'm out of this uniform. You want to help?" He stepped nearer, fitted his hands against her waist and tugged her close enough for her to feel the evidence of his arousal. When she caught her lower lip in her teeth, he undid his belt. He slid it out of its loops and dropped it on the floor.

Sarah knew an invitation when she saw one. And this one was as good as they got.

Fortunately, she still had enough sense to know that none of it would matter if she didn't tell him the truth. "Maybe if we could talk a little first. If we could—"

"Is that what you want?" He didn't seem hurt. Not exactly. But he was so eager to get her in bed that he was about to burst. And so anxious to make sure that it felt right—for him and, more importantly, for her—that he was willing to slow down and take it easy. If that was what she needed him to do.

It was that moment of compromise from a guy who never vacillated and couldn't afford to waffle that tugged at her heartstrings.

Dylan, on the other hand, was tugging at the lace at the low-cut neckline of the nightgown. "You were saying?"

"Saying?" Sarah's eyes drifted shut. "I was saying. Yeah. I was talking. About us. I was saying—"

He inched down one of the spaghetti straps of the nightgown, and when it slipped far enough, he dipped his head and took her breast in his mouth.

"I was saying that—"

He cupped her breast in his hand, learning its shape while his thumb stroked her nipple.

"I was saying that—"

The desire in his eyes pushed her over the edge.

"I was saying that there are all these candles around us on the floor and it could be dangerous. We'd better get over to the bed!"

He wasn't about to argue. Laughing, Dylan followed when Sarah tugged him to the other side of the room. She sat on the edge of the bed and when he made a move to pop the button on the waistband of his uniform trousers, she pushed his hands away. Before she could remind herself that she was getting carried away from both her common sense and her good intentions, she undid the button, slid the little zipper down and slipped her hand inside.

After that, talking was running dead last on the list of what was on her mind.

It was Dylan's turn to suck in a sharp breath. His chance to relax and simply enjoy the sensations she stirred with every movement of her fingers. She measured the length of him against her palm, gave him enough of a playful squeeze to let him know that even though she wasn't romantic, she wasn't the shy, retiring type. When her own urgent need reminded her that though they had all night she didn't want to wait nearly that long, she knelt on the bed, slipped off his pants and unbuttoned his shirt.

Dylan's chest was granite-hard and so muscled that regardless of the blow to Dylan's eye, Mr. Slobbery must have come out on the losing end of the confrontation. She couldn't help but smile.

"What's that all about?" Dylan shrugged out of his shirt, got rid of the T-shirt he wore underneath and chucked a finger under her chin.

She cocked her head and let her fingers drift over his bare chest. There was a sprinkling of fine golden curls that arrowed down to his waist, and her fingers played through them, then toyed with the elastic band at the top of his boxers. "A girl can't smile?"

"Oh, she can smile, all right." He was smiling, too. "It's gotta make a guy wonder, though, you know? What she's smiling about."

"About us. About this." She inched the boxers over his hips and watched him step out of them and when he was done, she slipped out of her nightgown. The satin shimmied down over her hips. She scooted back on the bed and dragged him along with her. "About what I'm planning to do to you."

He grinned down at himself. Naked as the day was long, every masculine, wonderful inch of him gilded by the firelight. And when she opened herself to him and he slipped inside and filled her, Sarah took a breath of pure pleasure.

They rocked each other to mind-numbing ecstasy, and when they were done, their bodies slick with sweat, he gathered her into his arms and kissed her.

"Still want to talk?" he asked.

She didn't.

Not now.

Maybe not ever.

WHEN HE WOKE UP the next morning, the first thing Dylan saw was Sarah.

Fingers of early light poked their way through the branches of the oak tree outside the back window, painting her eyelashes with gold, washing her features with color as soft as the kiss he couldn't help but press to her forehead.

"Amazing." He breathed the word, along with a sigh of appreciation. "You're simply—"

"Thank you!" She popped one eye open and brushed a finger against the nasty black-and-blue splotch on his cheek. "You're pretty amazing yourself."

"Yes, I am!" Laughing, both at being caught and because of the exhilaration that bubbled through him, Dylan flopped back against his pillow, his arms bent and propped behind his head.

It wasn't often a guy had the feeling that he could fly. That he could take on the world. Today was one of those days he felt like the owner of the universe, and the reason was pure and simple: Sarah. All through the night, she had proved that she was more than amazing. She was spectacular. Giving and loving. Tender as a flower and as sizzling as summer lightning.

Dylan stretched beneath the sheets, his thigh grazing hers, setting off a new barrage of fireworks in him. Content and aroused by memories of all they'd done together and the certainty that they'd do it all again—and soon— he grinned. "I haven't felt this good since—"

His words froze beneath the sudden onslaught of memories that filled his head and drowned the heat in his groin with a rush of ice water.

Sarah didn't miss the sudden change. "What?" She flipped to her side and propped up her head on one elbow. "You keeping secrets?"

Dylan twitched the pillow from behind his head and put it on his lap. "It's no secret. Just a woman I used to—"

Sarah's laughter cut him short. She poked his arm. "Oh, come on! We're not kids. We're adults. And adults have pasts. It's certainly not worth getting all bent out of shape about. Everyone has baggage. Heck, I have Tony DiMarco. And you have—"

"I have an ex-wife."

It wasn't fair to hit her with the facts square between the eyes without even making an attempt to soften the blow. But it wasn't fair to hold back, either. He'd been doing that. Practically since the day Lisa had left. It had led him here, to a morning that should have been nothing short of wonderful with a woman who was nothing short of perfection. And now he had no choice but to ruin the moment and cool the warm afterglow of what they'd done and shared the night before.

All because he hadn't been man enough to come clean about Lisa in the first place.

Dylan scrubbed a hand over his chin. "It's been eighteen months," he said, justifying the situation to Sarah and to himself. "I shouldn't have even mentioned it."

"Except that it's kind of important."

"It was. Eighteen months ago."

"And now?"

"Ancient history." It was true. Of course, that didn't explain why thinking about it left him chilled to the bone.

He leaned over the side of the bed and plucked his boxers off the floor. He slipped into them under the sheets, then sat up and swung his legs over the side of the bed. His back was to Sarah when he said, "She left."

Behind him, he heard Sarah shift uncomfortably beneath the sheets. A few minutes ago, the sensual sound of bare flesh against the crisp cotton would have reminded him of the things they'd done together beneath the sheets all through the night. It would have reignited a passion that had been so close to the surface that it took only a look from Sarah, a touch, and even though they might have finished making love only a couple of minutes earlier, he'd been ready, willing and able to start again.

He forced himself to face her when he shrugged. "Like I said, ancient history."

"Yeah, I can see that." Her gaze level, her expression as calm as the lake he could see outside the window, she sat up and tucked the sheet securely under her arms and over her breasts. Maybe it was her own attempt to distance herself from him. Maybe it was pure instinct. Either way, the body language was unmistakable.

So was her detached tone of voice. "Ancient history," she said. "That would explain why you're not looking me in the eye?"

"It's not like she matters to me anymore." Dylan was damned if he was going to allow Sarah to think for one minute that it might not be true. "I'm over Lisa. I have been for a long time. It's just that..." The coffeepot was on a timer and Dylan crossed the room to where it sat atop an antique desk. Beside it were a microwave and a couple of white ceramic mugs with big gold cupids on them.

He poured, and remembering their dinner at the jail and how Sarah liked her coffee, he added cream from the small refrigerator. Though he hadn't noticed her get up and hadn't heard her move, by the time he walked back across the room to hand the mug to her, she was standing near the window. She was wearing the ivory satin robe.

There was a certain finality about the moment, as if the robe was a roadblock, a sign that the magical night was officially over. The realization didn't improve Dylan's mood.

He handed her the coffee and took a swallow of his own.

"Lisa wasn't a native," he said, turning and leaning against the desk. He cradled his mug in both hands. "She was here for the summer, working over at the hotel."

"And you fell in love."

It wasn't a question. But then, it never had been for Dylan, either.

"Head over heels," he said, and though the ending wasn't the happily-ever-after he'd always dreamed about, he couldn't help but remember those first heady months. He smiled, but the movement hurt his cheek, so he wiped away the expression. He supposed that was appropriate, too. Like his relationship with Lisa, he started with a smile and ended up hurting like hell. "Lisa was exactly what I'd always hoped for in a woman. She was smart and she was funny. Pretty, too." He took another swallow, watching Sarah over the rim of his cup. "But not as pretty as you."

If she appreciated the compliment, she didn't show it. She studied him. "So what went wrong?"

"Not a thing. At least not at first. Lisa grew up in foster care, so when she came to the island, she found the whole small-town-America atmosphere a little overwhelming. You know, everyone knowing everyone else. Everyone knowing everyone else's business. But you also know how warm the people around here are. They welcomed her with open arms. Pretty soon, it was like we'd all known her all our lives."

There was a table near where Sarah was standing and she set her coffee down. "Sounds like the way I've been treated."

"Exactly." Dylan contemplated his coffee, then returned his gaze to Sarah. He wasn't sure what he'd been expecting from Sarah when he sprung the news about Lisa—a little emotion maybe, a little spark of jealousy so that he could jump right in and tell her she didn't have to worry, that Lisa was officially out of his system. When he didn't get any response except a sort of detached interest, it gave him the hope that this would be a lot easier than he'd anticipated. "Put-in-Bay was nuts about Lisa and Lisa was nuts about Put-in-Bay."

"And about you."

"Yeah." For a second, Dylan remembered that there was a time when he actually believed it was true. His satisfaction faded in light of the cold, hard truth.

"We were married at the end of that summer," he told Sarah. "And I thought every one of my dreams had come true. Lisa wanted a home. So did I. Lisa wanted a family. So do I. Lisa told me I was the most important person in her world."

"But I already know the ending to this story." Sarah turned to him, her coffee apparently forgotten. "What went wrong?"

"August turned into September. And September faded into October. By the time November rolled around, Lisa woke up to the fact that she got more than she bargained for."

"More?"

"More island." Suddenly his coffee tasted bitter and Dylan set down his mug. "One afternoon, she showed up at the station and told me she was headed out on the last ferry of the season. Said she couldn't stand island life anymore. Too quiet, she said. Too boring. I reminded her that not so long before that she'd said that I was all she ever needed to be happy. And she…" Now that he considered it, Dylan realized he'd never told all this to anyone. Not even to Meg. She'd been living in Baltimore at the time and the minute she heard that Lisa walked out on him, she'd called Dylan twice a day for three months or more.

"Lisa laid it on the line. She told me that I wasn't enough," he said. The words were as bitter as the coffee. "She told me that she needed more out of life and that she could never find it here in Put-in-Bay."

"She had to leave." Sarah's cheeks looked ashen. Or maybe it was a trick of the early-morning light.

Before Dylan had a chance to figure out why, she disappeared into the alcove where Maisie nurtured her African violets. When she came out again, she was clutching a pair of black shorts, a T-shirt emblazoned with the inn's grinning cupid mascot and her sneakers. She made a grab for the ivory nightgown and added it to the pile.

"I've got to go."

When she turned toward the stairway, Dylan knew that all the magic they'd made together was about to leave, too. He hurried after her.

"I shouldn't have hit you with this out of nowhere," he said. "All the stuff about Lisa. I know it's a shock. Nobody around here talks about it, because after it happened, I made sure no one ever did. Not Meg. Not Maisie. Lisa was one topic that was strictly off-limits. I would have mentioned the whole thing to you sooner. I should have. I hope you're not—"

"I'm not." At the stairs, she turned to face him. It might have been a more tender moment if that pile of clothes hadn't been in her arms. Like a shield. "Honest, Dylan, I meant what I said. We're adults. We all have pasts. People in our pasts. I'd be crazy to think that you've been living like some kind of monk, waiting for me to come along."

"But I have been waiting for you to come along." He reached over and cupped her face in his hand.

"I've been waiting for you, too. It's just…" She stared down at the floor. "I really better get going," she said. "If Maisie sees me coming out of your room, we're never going to hear the end of it. I'll see you later."

And before Dylan could tell her that *later* was way too long to wait, she scrambled down the steps and out of the garage.

SARAH NEVER STOPPED until she was inside the Hideaway and up the winding stairway that led to the guest rooms on the second floor. Never stopped walking. Never stopped reminding herself that she was the biggest fool on two feet.

"Now you can't tell him," she grumbled to herself. "Not about Providence or *Affairs of the Heart*. Not about how you're going to be the hottest hostess on cable. Or about how in order to do that, you're going to need to kiss this little island goodbye. Because if you do, if you leave, you'll be a carbon copy of Lisa. And then…" She stopped at the top of the stairs, and even though there were no windows in this part of the inn, she didn't have to see it to know exactly where the garage was located.

She looked that way, and a single tear trickled down her cheek. She swiped at it with the back of her hand. She'd blown her opportunity to tell Dylan the truth. She'd let herself get sucked in by all the romantic claptrap, and because of that, her emotions—not to mention her hormones—got in the way of talking to him about her real life. As a result, the most incredible night ever had morphed into the most miserable morning of her existence. Because now she knew she could never tell him. Not without breaking his heart. And hers.

"Damn!" The ivory nightgown fell from the pile of clothing in her arms, and just for good measure, she kicked it down the hallway. It landed right outside the door of Close to the Heart.

On top of the bunch of long-stemmed red roses sitting on the floor right outside her door.

It seemed that even before she'd bushwhacked him with the satin and the candles, the music and the champagne, Dylan had planned another romantic gesture. Sarah's heart sank even lower.

She picked up the flowers and carried them into the room. She started sneezing even before she closed the door behind her.

Chapter Twelve

There is nothing as important as romance. And nothing
says romance like consideration. Don't ever take your
lover for granted. Even for the little things, always say
thank you. There's no way it's ever the wrong thing to do.
          —*Sarah's Guide to Life, Love and Gardening*

As much as Dylan loved his job, he was never so glad to
see a shift end. Even before he was out of the station and
into the Tahoe, his heart was doing a version of "River-
dance" inside his chest. He had to see Sarah—the need
was fierce. The past twelve hours without her, he felt like
an electrical line with a short in it.

He'd soon fix that. Sarah had had all day to process the
news about Lisa, and she must've come to grips with the
facts by now. Fact number one: Lisa was gone, from the
island and from Dylan's heart. Fact number two: he was
in love with Sarah. As soon as got back to the Hideaway,
he would gather her into his arms and kiss her doubts
away.

The promise of what was to come made Dylan smile,
and smiling, he turned off on the road that led to the northern part of the island. Like he did every night when he left
the station, he drove past his house. It didn't hurt to make

sure that the house was still standing, and besides, Phil, the head of the construction crew, had called that morning and assured him that—finally—Maisie had given him something of a reprieve while she made final decisions about paving tiles and outdoor lighting. They'd get some work done today on Dylan's house. Phil had promised.

It wasn't that Dylan didn't trust Phil, but he'd heard the promises before. Like cops everywhere, he only believed what he saw.

He pulled into his driveway, hopped out of the truck and waved to Mrs. Grassi, his neighbor.

"The workmen aren't here anymore!" she called to him, and Dylan nodded. Maybe *aren't here anymore* meant that they'd been here for a change. He headed into the house for a quick look around. Satisfied that—finally—the upstairs bathroom (scene of the broken pipe) was almost back to normal and that the collapsed kitchen ceiling (result of the broken pipe) was ready for plaster, he dropped the dirty clothes he'd brought home to be washed in the laundry room and packed some clean jeans and shirts. As anxious as he was to get back to the Hideaway, it was impossible for him not to step out back and check his garden. At this time of the year, he was especially fond of walking around and seeing which of his plants were poking out of the soil, which needed staking and which were doing better even than he hoped.

This year, like most years, every plant was doing better than he hoped.

He watered his vegetables and checked to see how the herbs he'd planted along the south side of the house were doing. He was growing oregano for the first time, and because it was drooping, he filled a watering can and sprinkled the oregano, as well as the sage, the dill and the thyme. Once the renovations to his house were finally finished, he told himself, the oregano would be big enough to cut. When it was, he'd make a pot of his island-famous spaghetti sauce and invite Sarah over for a private celebration.

Sarah in his house.

He liked the sound of that, and it didn't take much imagination for him to picture her sitting beside him on the front porch swing or puttering in the kitchen, which he'd refinished himself a couple years before and would need to refinish again as soon as Phil and his crew were out of there.

Sarah in his garden.

He liked that thought, too, because his garden was his pride and joy, and he couldn't think of anyone else he'd rather spend time in it with. He might yet teach her a thing or two about growing flowers.

Sarah in his bed.

He liked that idea most of all, just as he liked picturing lazy mornings when they'd lie under the sheets and read the paper together and not-so-lazy nights when like last night, they would lose themselves in passionate lovemaking.

The now-familiar ache tightened his body. He couldn't wait to get Sarah alone again. He finished with the herbs and tucked the watering can next to the back steps. He kept a satchel of garden tools on the patio and he searched through it for a trowel. Though he'd been too drunk with satisfaction to notice much at the Hideaway that morning, he had noticed that a couple more of Sarah's geraniums had kicked the bucket.

"Too much water," he told himself, and for the first time since he'd picked up on her less-than-adept gardening skills, he found that it didn't irritate him. So Sarah didn't know how to take care of a garden. So what?

Every time Sarah overwatered, underwatered, overfertilized or just plain messed up, it gave him another opportunity to play hero and surprise her. And every opportunity he had to play hero in Sarah's eyes...

Dylan plunked the geraniums into plastic pots and loaded them into the back seat of the Tahoe. Once everyone at the Hideaway was asleep, he'd replace the dead geraniums, exactly the way he'd replaced all the other dead-and-gone flowers in Sarah's garden.

Because doing things for Sarah...

A grin on his face and the hum of anticipation in his bloodstream, Dylan climbed back in the Tahoe and started for the Hideaway.

He was beginning to think that he wouldn't mind doing things for Sarah for the rest of his life.

"THE ROSES ARE BEAUTIFUL, but you really shouldn't have gone to all that trouble. There's no florist on the island, and that means you had to have them shipped over from the mainland. That's a huge effort and it was probably expensive and it's not that I don't appreciate it, it's just that I'm not sure I deserve it. After all, I am going to end up ripping out your heart and handing it to you on a platter."

Right sentiments. Wrong words.

Sarah made a face. She paced the Hideaway's backyard, keeping one eye on the site that would soon be home to the private patio and hot tub, and the other eye on the parking lot. So she'd have plenty of warning when Dylan arrived.

Of course, she'd already had all day to try to figure out how she was going to break the news to him about *Affairs of the Heart* and how she'd always known she was going to be heading back to Providence at the end of the summer. That didn't mean she was any closer to finding the right words. Or nearer to figuring out the right way to say them.

"The roses you left by the door of Close to the Heart are romantic. I know, I know." She held up one hand, the way she would if Dylan were standing in front of her and she was anxious to hold back the tide of his disbelief. "I know you never expected me to admit that I finally understand that romance can be alive and well in the modern world. But thanks to you, I've learned a lot this summer and…"

Simply thinking about all they'd done and shared together reminded Sarah of how Dylan was going to feel when she dropped the bomb. And how she was going to feel dropping it. Tears wouldn't help. Neither would choking on her words, so she cleared her throat and tried again.

"Okay, so the roses are gorgeous. Even if they do make me sneeze. But before you get the wrong idea and we get too involved…"

She didn't need to remind herself that they'd already gotten too involved. Way too involved.

Not that she was complaining. Last night with Dylan…

At the spot where the lawn was roped off to establish the dimensions of the new patio, Sarah stopped and pulled in a breath of pure wonder. She let it out slowly, savoring the memories that zinged through her like high-octane fuel. Last night had been incredible, but, she reminded herself, she'd been less than honest. And that wasn't fair. Especially since Dylan had been so honest with her.

All the more reason to set the record straight. Instead of his heart on a platter, she needed to serve up a big helping of the truth.

She'd do it, too. As soon as he got back to the Hideaway.

As soon as she figured out what to say and how to say it.

Dead set on doing what she had to do, she spun around and marched back the other way. "When you left those roses for me, you probably didn't realize that the whole story I gave you about me staying here on the island was nothing but bull." Not pretty, but at least it was closer to the truth. "You see, I'm a lot like Lisa."

Too close to the truth!

Sarah shivered. Rather than remind herself, she started into her dry run once more. "I finally find a guy I really like," she said, and this time the truth sang through her. "I mean one I really, really like, and you gave me the most incredible night of my life and twelve of the most gorgeous roses I've ever seen, and now I'm going to—"

"Going to what?"

The sound of Dylan's voice close behind her caused the blood to drain from Sarah's face. Before she had a chance to recover, he stepped up behind her and slipped his arms around her waist.

He kissed her ear. "I don't have a clue what you're talking about, but I'd like to go on the record as saying it doesn't much matter. Whatever you have in mind, I can't wait to get started."

If only it was that simple!

While she tried to figure out how to tell him it wasn't, she turned and smiled up at him. His cheek was an ugly shade of purple. His left eye was bloodshot. His face was swollen.

He was the handsomest man she'd ever seen.

"Okay," Sarah said. "What exactly do *you* have in mind?"

He slipped his hands down to cup her butt and hitched her a little closer. Sarah instinctively angled her hips up to meet his. "Oh, I don't know," he said. "I was hoping that maybe we could go up to my home away from home.

Make some dinner that we won't bother to eat. Put on some music that we'll be too busy to listen to."

Sounded like a great plan.

One Sarah knew she shouldn't let herself get sucked into...

Which didn't explain why the next words that popped out of her mouth were, "The roses are beautiful."

"Yes, they are." Dylan glided his hand up to her ribs and back down again. He kissed her on the nose. "You're beautiful, too," he told her. "And I've been waiting all day to kiss you. You're all I've been able to think about." He moved in close enough for her to know he wasn't kidding.

Desire flashed through her and her determination wavered. When he inched up her white polo shirt and slipped his hand inside, it went up in smoke. She fought against the tightening between her legs at the same time she enjoyed it.

They'd talk, she promised herself.

They had to.

Later.

Right after she was done melting into a puddle of mush.

As usual, Dylan was on the same wavelength. He grabbed her hand and by then, Sarah couldn't have resisted if she tried. Which she'd pretty much stopped doing the second he kissed her. They hurried to the garage, but never made it all the way upstairs. Halfway there, Dylan sat down and unzipped his uniform pants. Sarah struggled out of her shorts, ready to combust. She straddled him and he pushed into her and if Sarah felt as if she was ready to go up in flames before, it was nothing compared to the way she felt now. He nuzzled her breasts and she raked her fingers through his hair. He cupped her butt and held her so close and so tight, she couldn't move. And that only aroused her more.

Orgasm? The word seemed pale to describe the sensations that racketed through Sarah. She could tell Dylan felt the same way. Because when they were done, he was as dazed and as winded as she was.

His voice rumbled in her ear. "So...still want to talk about how pretty the roses are in the garden?"

Still too shaky with the sensations that vibrated through her, Sarah inched back enough to see his eyes. "Not the roses in the garden. The red roses that were delivered to the door of Close to the Heart. The ones you sent me. Thank you."

"You're welcome." He kissed her chin and her cheek. He nibbled her earlobe. "Only, I didn't send you any roses."

It took one heartbeat for the words to sink in.

It took another for Sarah to consider what they meant.

She didn't believe him. He was teasing.

"Yeah, right," she said. The night before, she'd learned that he had a sensitive spot on the back of his neck, and she wasn't above taking advantage of it. She tickled her fingers along his skin and ruffled his hair. "No need to be modest. So they cost an ungodly fortune? I'm worth it! And you're a lousy liar."

"Yes, I am. Which is why I don't even try. You might have gotten roses, but they didn't come from me."

"You're serious," she said. "You really are."

Sarah's heart banged to a painful stop. She swallowed down the sudden sour taste in her mouth and slid off Dylan's lap. There wasn't much room on the stairway and no graceful way to get her clothes on, so she grabbed them and hurried up the steps.

"What?" She heard him start up behind her, but by then, Sarah was too close to panic to care. While she stepped into her clothes, he stood near the kitchen sink, watching her carefully. "You're as white as a sheet."

"I…" She turned away from him, but just as quickly forced herself to turn back. "It isn't a game," she said.

"I'm not playing a game."

"But then why…" It wasn't until she swiped a hand over her cheeks that she realized she was crying.

"Sarah?" Dylan knew better than to push, but he also knew that he had no choice but to try. "You want to start at the beginning?"

"The beginning. Yeah. I think maybe the beginning goes back to those rosebud soaps in my room and the towels embroidered with roses. And that set of sheets in rose print. I assumed that Maisie left them there. I mean, I figured there was no other way—" Her voice was choked with tears, but she refused to give in. Instead, she squared her shoulders. "I think maybe somebody followed me."

"Followed? To the Hideaway? To the island?" He cocked his head, considering the implications. "You mean like a stalker?"

"Yeah, that's exactly what I mean."

"A stalker who sends roses."

"Fresh roses. Pictures of roses. Clothing decorated with roses. Maybe I'm jumping the gun, and I'll ask Maisie to make sure. But if you didn't send the flowers and she didn't leave that other stuff in my room…" She found herself considering what she'd spent the summer trying to forget. "Tell me you sent the roses and I'll feel a whole lot better."

"I wish I could. I'd do anything for you. But I didn't send the flowers." He stepped closer and she could practically see the war of emotions inside him. The cop part of Dylan wanted to take names and kick butt. The lover wanted to comfort her. She sensed it was the first time he'd ever had to choose, and the fact that he folded her into his arms and held her close to his heart, instead of reaching for a notebook so he could start filing his report, helped Sarah make up her mind.

Good time or bad time. It didn't matter. It was time.

"It started in Providence," she said.

A spark of anger flared in his eyes. "That's why you came to the island? To hide from this creep?"

"Yes. And no. It's only part of why I came to the island." She couldn't stand that close to him. Not when she was about to break his heart. She backed out of Dylan's arms. "I'm the hostess of a TV show," she said.

He gave her a blank stare.

"TV. You know? That box that lights up and shows pictures?" She'd hoped this was going to be easier. She'd hoped wrong. "You've been right all along about me and my nonexistent gardening skills. I'm not a gardener. Back in Providence, I host a TV show called *Affairs of the Heart.*"

At least he had the good grace not to laugh. "And that's how this scumbag targeted you? He saw you on TV?"

Sarah shrugged. "I guess. I don't know. I never really thought about why he focussed on me."

"What did the local police say?"

Back in Providence, keeping her secret had made so much sense. Now it didn't just sound lame, it sounded downright stupid. "I haven't told anyone," she said, and before he could point out the part about the lame and the part about the stupid, she hurried right on. "When I'm on TV, I'm different."

"Different good? Or different bad? You show porn movies? Or do you dress in a purple dinosaur suit?"

"No. I'm the queen of romance."

One moment of stunned disbelief. Then a smile quirked one corner of his mouth. He controlled it. Barely. "So this TV show. It's all about…"

"Romance. Yeah." Her cheeks flamed. "But you know me. You know that romance and I…well, we aren't exactly on speaking terms. And back in Providence, I'm sort of well-known. If I went to the cops, they'd be sure to find out that I'm not the Sarah Allcroft their wives and girl-friends watch on TV. The one who hosts Valentine's Day tea parties to promote her show. The one who never trips over her own feet and always knows which perfume to wear. The perfect Sarah who doesn't exist."

"That's why you didn't report a stalker?"

"That and the fact that if I did, there was bound to be a media circus. Come on!" When it looked as if he was about to contradict her, she pinned him with a look. "Tell me you think the media would have stayed out of it once the police report was filed."

"Which is why you didn't report the stalker."

"Exactly." Sarah exhaled some of her tension. "I didn't think you'd understand."

"No, I don't! That's just plain dumb." Dylan's reserve cracked along with his voice. "Don't you know how dangerous stalkers can be? And you thought you could hide out from him here? That's why you came to the island?"

"The stalker. The reporters." Sarah shrugged. Like that would explain it. Like it even could. "They were always hounding me for interviews. And calling for quotes. I had this plan. Or maybe it was just a wild hope. If I could lie low for a while, they might lose interest. Or maybe I'd fig-ure out how they wanted me to act. That way, when I went back…"

Dylan had been deep in thought, no doubt plotting strategy. Now, his head snapped up and in spite of how much it must have hurt, he narrowed both eyes. "*When*. Not *if.*"

Sarah tried for a brave face. "Yesterday Becky called

with really good news. Becky's my producer. She's been keeping an eye on things while I've been gone and well...*Affairs of the Heart* has been picked up by one of the cable networks. We're going national."

"And you're going home."

Funny, it had always felt like home before. Now hearing Dylan say it, the word didn't click. "I've got a book to write," she said. "And a publisher champing at the bit, waiting to see if we'd be on cable before planning a huge promotional campaign. The book is all about color-coordinating bed linens and how to be the perfect hostess and what it takes to keep your garden in tip-top shape. And I've got this line of stationery products...." Her words dissolved against the misery that welled inside her. There was no use telling him about the sealing wax or the scented ink. Her shoulders slumped under the weight of her guilt. "I never had any intention of staying."

"You should have told me."

"If I had..."

"Maisie never would have given you the job. Yeah, I get it."

It wasn't what she was going to say. She was going to say that if she *had* told him, if he knew from the start that she was as come-and-go as any tourist who visited the island, she knew they would have never gotten close. And her heart would still be in one piece.

"I sort of got carried away with the lie," she told him. She wasn't sure why she bothered. It was pretty clear from the thundercloud expression on his face that he really didn't give a damn. "I talked about staying and everyone glommed on to it."

"Yeah, we bumpkins out here in the middle of nowhere are like that. We actually give people the benefit of the doubt and believe that what they say is true."

"Then this morning...when you told me about Lisa..."

Dylan's shoulders stiffened, but she had to give him credit. His gaze never wavered and a single muscle kept right on working in his jaw.

Which is more than she could say for herself. The way her stomach was jumping, she felt like she was back on Pete the Perch. Or worse yet, in front of the cameras.

"I lied from the get-go. About being a gardener. About sticking around to watch the winter storms and the crocuses poking their heads out in the spring. But I never lied about us, Dylan." Sarah scrambled to find the right words, but the harder she tried, the more impossible it seemed. "I never lied about the way I feel about you."

"But you are leaving."

It wasn't a question.

She didn't answer it.

What was the use, anyway?

As if he was getting rid of every last memory of her, he shook his shoulders. "I guess I should offer my congratulations," he said.

"About the show?" Sarah couldn't believe he could be so gracious. "It's sweet but—"

"Not about the show." He stepped back and stepped aside, so she could leave. "I've got to hand it to you. When it comes to the whole part about being a liar and a phony who can step on a guy's heart and crush it into a million pieces, you outdid Lisa."

Chapter Thirteen

Don't believe the country songs that say there's nothing as
terrible as love gone wrong. No lesson in love is ever
without a purpose. All you need to do is find it.
Look for the silver lining—and plant some
geraniums to brighten your outlook.
—*Sarah's Guide to Life, Love and Gardening*

Sarah didn't need to see it in writing. The moment she
walked out of the garage, she knew it was over between
her and Dylan. Kaput. Finished. Done for.

Just like that.

At the time, she was feeling pretty done for, too, but
there was no done for like the done for she felt when the
next morning, Dylan sent Jake over to take her report
about the stalker. In a little less than twenty-four hours,
she had gone from Dylan's bed to his to-do list. And she
couldn't even be angry at him for it.

"There you go, ma'am." Jake's voice cut through the
ache that had taken up residence where Sarah's heart used
to be. He tore off one of the self-carbon copies of the report he'd finished and handed it to her. "You keep that for
your records. In case there are any questions. In the meantime, we'll do our jobs. We're watching the Hideaway to

make sure no one comes around who doesn't belong here.
And we're talking to everybody, checking to see if there
are any strangers on the island."

"At this time of year, isn't everyone here a stranger?"

Jake scratched a finger behind one ear. "Why, yes,
ma'am. I guess there are a lot of strangers on the island.
But those strangers, they're visitors. I mean, they're here
taking advantage of our hospitality and they'll be headed
back to their own lives pretty soon. You know what I
mean?"

She did. The way Jake described it, she was a stranger
here, too.

"What I mean, ma'am..." Apparently Jake figured she
was still confused. He removed his uniform cap and wiped
a hand over his forehead—it was a warm morning, and it
promised to be a hot and sticky afternoon. "I mean *suspicious* strangers. You know, like somebody asking too
many questions about you and your routine. Or somebody
who's out of place. Somebody who isn't acting normal."

"Is Dylan acting normal?" It was wrong to put Jake on
the spot, but now that the words were out of her mouth,
Sarah felt a wave of relief. It was the one subject she'd
wanted to bring up since Jake walked through the door of
the Hideaway.

"The chief?" Jake hesitated. "He's acting—"

"Sullen. Preoccupied. Fidgety." Maisie walked out of
the swinging door that led from the kitchen into the dining room where Sarah and Jake were talking. It was clear
from the start she'd been listening at the door and equally
as clear that she didn't care if either of them knew it. "Of
course Dylan isn't acting normal." Maisie tsk-tsked away
the very idea. "Everybody knows that."

Everybody but Sarah.

She knew better than to question Maisie's sources or

her information. That didn't mean she couldn't try to wrangle at least some of the details out of the old lady. "And you know this because…?"

Maisie had a vase of fresh flowers in her hands. She carried them over to the table and set them down. "Ask Jake. He's the one who helped Dylan move his belongings out of the garage this morning."

The young policeman blanched. "He told me not to—"

"Don't be silly, dear." Maisie dismissed his concern with the kind of forbearance she gave to children who didn't mind their manners. "I know everything that happens here at the Hideaway. You know that and so does Dylan. It's not like he had to tell me he was leaving. But the least he could have done is given Sarah some sort of explanation."

Sarah shook her head. "He didn't need to. I know why he left. He wanted to get away. From me."

Maisie didn't seem surprised. She nodded to Jake, effectively putting an end to the conversation, and once he was gone, she dropped into the chair beside Sarah. "I was wondering how long it would take you to tell me."

"You knew?" Sarah was awestruck. "How could you? It only happened yesterday."

It wasn't worth the effort of finding out how Maisie knew what she knew. Besides, the *how* didn't matter. Not as much as the *why*. And the *what was she going to do about it*.

"I blew it," Sarah said. "Big time."

Maisie didn't argue the point. "You should have listened to some of your own advice."

"Except I'm not very good at giving advice."

"Of course you are." She patted Sarah's arm. "Tea etiquette and antiques shopping. Lace handkerchiefs and luxurious bath products. Romance in all its glory. You're always right on the button when it comes to advice."

It took a second for what Maisie said to sink in, and when it did, Sarah shot out of her chair. "Wait a minute!" She pointed an accusatory finger at the old woman. "You know. You know about the tea and the antiques and the—"

"Know? Of course I know. I've known all along." Smiling, Maisie rose and wound her arm through Sarah's. There were French doors on the east wall of the dining room and on the other side of them, a stone patio where this time of day, the sun filtered through a veil of blue morning glories. She led her outside to a wrought-iron bench. "I know everything that happens here at the Hideaway, remember."

"Yes, but—"

"Come, come, dear." There was a pitcher of ice water on a nearby table and chilled crystal glasses, each containing a single, paper-thin slice of lemon. Maisie poured and handed Sarah a glass before she dropped into the rocking chair across from the bench. "You don't think I would have hired you if I didn't know all about you, do you?"

"But—"

"How? Well, yes, I suppose that's a legitimate question." Maisie sipped her ice water. "I saw *Affairs of the Heart*, of course. About six months ago when Gabe and Meg were in Boston visiting his grandfather and I met them there for a long weekend. I was so taken by you and the show that I've had Grandpa Morrison tape every single episode for me. Watched your *Salute to Chocolate* again last night. I have to give you credit, dear, you know your way around a ganache."

"I know exactly zip. About ganache. And certainly about romance."

"Don't be so hard on yourself." Maisie waved away the criticism. "You're a terrific hostess."

"But not such a good liar."

"Oh, you're a wonderful liar!" Maisie laughed. "I knew the truth all along, but everyone else supposed you were a gardener."

"Everyone but Dylan."

"Ah, Dylan." Maisie took another sip of ice water and rocked back and forth. "You know why he's taking this so hard, don't you?"

"I know about Lisa."

"And you think that's what this is all about?"

"Of course it is." Sarah was too restless to keep still. She hopped off the bench and walked to the far side of the patio where broad stone steps led into the garden. The sun shone brightly on row after row of droopy geraniums.

"I'm sorry," she said, glancing over her shoulder to where Maisie sat perfectly calm and composed. "I've made a mess of all of it. I've ruined your garden and probably your reputation. Your guests come here expecting the best and they always get it. They must be disappointed."

"Oh, pooh!" Maisie grinned. "They don't come here for the flowers. They're too busy up in their rooms taking care of business, if you know what I mean."

"That doesn't excuse the fact that I've left you high and dry. Or is it wet? You knew I didn't have a clue about gardening. Why did you give me the job?"

Maisie set her glass on the table. "Let's just say that when you called, I recognized your name and voice immediately. I have to admit, the fact that I hired you was a bit self-serving. I wouldn't mind a plug on your show. Especially if you're going to be on cable. But aside from that, I knew if you wanted to come here and work as a gardener, there must have been a very good reason for it."

"But you never asked me what that reason was."

"It didn't matter. It still doesn't, except for this nasty stalker business. I'm worried about you, Sarah."

Sarah supposed she might be worried, too, if she wasn't so busy being miserable. "It's nothing," she said.

"It was enough to make you leave Providence."

She shrugged. "I thought if I could put some distance between myself and the stalker, between myself and the Sarah Allcroft on TV…I thought it might make a difference."

"And what you discovered was that you can't run away from your problems. They follow right along after you."

"My stalker sure did." Sarah frowned.

"And those unreasonable expectations you have for yourself?"

"I guess those followed me, too. I imagined that I could change things, that I could learn about what romance is really all about and that with a little more time, I could be the Sarah everyone wants me to be."

"You're already who Dylan wants you to be."

The statement caught Sarah off guard. She didn't think she could feel any worse. Until she did. "I've let him down most of all," she told Maisie.

"You think he knows it?"

Sarah gave a humorless laugh. "If the fact that he pulled up stakes and went back home to a house that is only half repaired doesn't mean squat, then every word he said to me yesterday sure does. I should have told him the truth from the start. I should have told you the truth, too. At least then your garden wouldn't be the mess it is. And why is that, anyway?" Sarah bent down to examine the flowers more closely. "Every other time they've been droopy, they've bounced right back."

"Maybe that was because of the magic."

"The magic in the air around the Hideaway?" Sarah stood and looked around. That proved that she was a fool because somewhere in the back of her mind, she believed that if she looked hard enough, she could still see the magic.

All she saw was dead flowers and a strip of lake that was rough with whitecaps, promising wind and rain.

"The magic is gone," she told Maisie. "At least for me. And it's nobody's fault but my own. I never should have lied to Dylan."

"He wouldn't have listened if you told him the truth. It wasn't what he wanted to hear."

"It wasn't fair."

"Dylan isn't the type who worries about fair. He's a cop, remember, and no one is better at sizing up the black-and-white of a situation than a cop. You see shades of gray. All Dylan sees is you walking out on him."

"Like Lisa did."

"Yes, exactly like Lisa did. But you know, you really aren't giving him enough credit." Maisie got up out of the rocking chair and headed back into the house. "It's not déjà vu all over again and I'd bet every cupid in the place that Dylan's already figured that out. After all, that time it was Lisa and this time it's you."

"And you're saying…?"

Over her shoulder, Maisie gave Sarah a smile. "I'm saying that he's in love with you."

"He was in love with Lisa, too. He married her."

"Yes." Maisie's silvery brows dipped low over her eyes before she walked into the dining room. "But that was different," Sarah heard her say right before she disappeared into the kitchen. "Dylan just doesn't know it yet."

PAINTING WASN'T AT THE TOP of Dylan's want-to-accomplish list. His eye hurt and he had a headache. Breathing in paint fumes, keeping his hand steady and paying attention to woodwork detail was not exactly what he felt like doing. But it beat going to talk to Sarah, and if he didn't keep himself busy and his mind off everything that had happened between them, going to talk to Sarah was exactly what he'd end up doing.

Not a good idea.

He wasn't sure what he would say when he got there, and besides, if he went to the Hideaway, everybody on the island was sure to catch wind of it.

And humiliation, he decided, was not an experience he wanted to share with his friends and neighbors.

Not again.

Reminding himself not to forget it, he put the finishing strokes on the last of the woodwork in the kitchen and used a hammer to tap the cover back onto the paint can. When he was done, he swore he still heard a knocking sound.

Since it was exactly the same sound his heart had been making since the day before when he heard from Marsha who heard from Jake who heard from Laurel who had it on good authority from Maisie that Sarah was leaving, it took him a second to realize the noise was coming from his front door.

He grabbed a rag and wiped his hands, heading through the maze of ladders and drop cloths in the kitchen into the tiny dining room and from there into his living room and the front door. When he yanked open the door and saw Sarah standing on his front porch, his heart stopped its steady, painful beat. It thudded instead, so hard that he swore every last man, woman and child over on the mainland could hear it loud and clear.

It was already after dark and in her light shorts, her white polo shirt and her sneakers, she reminded him of a ghost. Or a figment of his imagination. The fantasy was blown away by the stiff breeze that came in off the lake and slapped him in the face.

"Hi," she said. Her voice, too, was strangely like a slap. One that woke him up to the reality of everything that had happened. She chewed on her lower lip and pretended to be interested in the pots of cherry tomatoes he kept here on the west side of the house where they got the right amount of sun. "We need to talk."

Maybe. Maybe not.

Before he could decide, he realized the street was empty.

"Where the hell is Bill?" he asked.

Whatever kind of reception she expected, this wasn't it. It took her a second to process the question and another to remember that Bill was the officer assigned to the patrol car that was supposed to be watching the Hideaway. "It's not his fault," she said.

Dylan didn't want to hear it. He had already turned around to reach for the phone so that he could call and remind Bill that he had a duty to the people here on the island. Even people who had no intention of staying here.

Sarah stopped him, one hand on his arm. "I said, it's not Bill's fault. He didn't see me. I snuck out the back door."

He twitched away her hand. "And you think that was smart?"

"I didn't say it was smart. I said I did it." Another gust of wind blew her hair over her face, and she scooped it out of her eyes with one hand. She shivered and looked over his shoulder toward the house. "Do you suppose we could talk inside?"

"Sure." As soon as she stepped over the threshold and the door was closed behind them, he tossed the rag he had clutched in one hand onto the plastic runner the workers had put down to protect the hardwood floors. It wasn't as easy to get rid of the anger that churned his stomach. He didn't invite Sarah to sit down. All the stuff from the kitchen had been moved into the living room and the place was a mess. Besides, he wasn't sure he wanted her to sit. He didn't want her to stay.

He moved back and crossed his arms over his chest.

"That's the dumbest thing I've ever heard."

"That I want to talk?"

"That you went out of your way to avoid the officer who is supposed to be protecting you. Do you think this is a game?"

"Are you talking about the stalker? Or about us?"

"You know exactly what I'm talking about. If you're worried about a stalker, you shouldn't be walking around the island by yourself."

"I know. It was dumb. I admit it."

"Nice to know you can be that smart. Did you also think how much of an inconvenience you are to the department? We're not exactly big-city cops with a big-city staff or a big-city budget. I've got a car assigned to the Hideaway. That means overtime pay for Bill. Not to mention the fact that it takes one car off the street where it belongs."

"I hadn't thought of that. I'm sorry." She perched on the arm of the couch. Maybe it wasn't comfortable. Maybe she didn't feel like sitting. She was up again in an instant. She stuffed her hands into her pockets. "All I could think was that I had to talk to you."

"There's always the telephone."

All right, so that was a little harsh. He knew it. He

didn't need to see Sarah's cheeks pale. Instead, he picked up the rag from where he'd dropped it and carried it into the kitchen. He was half hoping that when he got back, she'd be gone. No such luck. When he got back to the living room, she was studying the photographs arranged on the fireplace mantel.

"You and Meg." She pointed toward the picture. "She looks so happy."

"That was her wedding day."

"And you and Maisie." She picked up the next picture and turned it toward the light. "You're all puckered, like you've got a sour taste in your mouth."

"It was the Girl Scouts' annual lemonade contest. I was a judge and I did have a sour taste in my mouth." He plucked the photo out of her hands and put it back where it belonged. "Did you come here to talk about lemonade?"

"I came to explain."

"I don't think you can."

"You could at least give me a chance."

"I could." He moved toward the door, because he knew if he stood there for one more second, he was going to take Sarah into his arms and kiss her. He didn't need to show that kind of weakness. Not with a woman who'd ripped out his guts and served them to him along with a great big helping of *This happened once before and you were a fool for not seeing it coming*. "You can tell me on the way back to the Hideaway."

IT WASN'T FAR from Dylan's house to the Hideaway, no more than a couple of minutes.

They were the longest couple of minutes of Sarah's life.

"So…" Now that they were stopped in front of the inn, she looked over to where he was drumming his fingers against the steering wheel. "Since you haven't said a word, I guess it's safe to say that you don't want to talk."

He stared straight ahead to where Bill's patrol car was parked. "I don't think we have a whole lot to say to each other."

"That's what Maisie said you'd say."

"Maisie? What does Maisie have to do with this?"

"You know Maisie. She's got her nose into everybody's business here on the island. Besides, she's smart. About people. And life. She said that maybe you didn't real-ize—"

"Oh, no, you don't." Dylan spun to face her. "Don't put this on me. You're the one who's leaving."

"It's not like I planned it from the start." Brave words. They were also completely untrue. Sarah sighed. "Okay, so I did plan to leave from the start. But it's not like I came here and knew I'd meet you."

"And where does telling me the truth fit into the pic-ture?"

"I just didn't want anyone to know. And after all I did to try and hide my past, it turns out to be no secret, any-way. Maisie knew all along. Where I was from, who I was."

He stayed silent. She knew Maisie was going to receive a lecture sometime soon.

Sarah put a hand on the door, ready to get out of the truck. At the last second, she hesitated. "There was a whole lot I wanted to say to you. If I don't say it—"

"If you don't say it, then neither of us will have any-thing to regret."

His words were as chilly as the wind that made the big pine tree on the lawn of the Hideaway dance. Sarah braced herself against them and against the anger that suddenly filled her, head to toe. She'd tried. She'd set aside her pride and held her emotions in check. She'd taken the chance of appearing foolish—simply so they could clear the air.

This was what she got in return?

She slapped the door open.

"You're right," she said before she climbed out of the truck. "We don't need to say a word. I've already got quite enough to regret."

She slammed the door closed behind her. She pounded up the steps of the Hideaway, opened the front door and entered the lobby. It took a lot of self-control not to slam *that* door closed behind her, too.

Her hands shaking as much as her knees, her knees as wobbly as her insides, Sarah crossed the lobby. She was already on her way up the steps when she thought she heard a noise from the kitchen.

"Maisie?" She called, but there was no answer. Then she realized there wouldn't be, at least not from Maisie. Doc Ross had taken Maisie to the mainland early that afternoon. They had a day planned in Cleveland: the Art Museum, the Rock and Roll Hall of Fame, dinner. They weren't due back until the last ferry, and that wasn't for a couple of hours.

Sarah knew she could go get Bill and have him check out the noise, but since it was probably nothing, what was the point? Besides, she didn't want to risk coming face-to-face with Dylan again.

She drew in a breath and marched down the hallway toward the kitchen. Why shouldn't she? The Hideaway was being watched by the police. The back door was locked. There wasn't one chance in a million that her stalker could have slipped by the surveillance.

Sarah pushed the door open. The light was off and she stepped into the room and felt along the wall for the switch.

She was so busy trying to find it that she didn't hear the noise behind her....

Not until it was too late.

Chapter Fourteen

Nothin' says lovin' like a surprise.
    —*Sarah's Guide to Life, Love and Gardening*

Sarah didn't recognize the man she found standing behind her. It was that, more than anything, that frightened her. If he'd been an acquaintance—somebody she worked with, maybe, or one of the guys at the gas station where she got the oil changed on her three-year-old Saturn—she'd know what she was dealing with. Or at least she'd have the ghost of a chance of figuring it out.

But this was a stranger. And that meant she had no point of reference. She was completely at sea.

From what she could tell in the bit of moonlight leaking through the window, the man was medium height and bulky.

She backed up a step. "Who are you? What are you doing here?"

The man didn't say a word. He had one hand behind his back, and though she tried to keep her cool and appear tough, Sarah couldn't help herself—she kept glancing that way. She weighed the idea of running against the concept of screaming.

But if he had a gun in that hand. Or a knife...

Sarah swallowed hard. "I think you've got the wrong place," she said, her voice shaking. "Or the wrong person. I think…"

He whipped his hand out from behind his back, and her words dissolved in a little shriek.

"For you." He held out a single red rose.

There was something about the flower—its color like blood in the moonlight—that worried Sarah even more than a gun or a knife.

"It's not that I don't appreciate the sentiments." She tried to act like the TV Sarah, but her smile kept wilting. "It's just that I think maybe you have me mixed up with someone else."

He narrowed his eyes. "You're that Sarah, right? From the TV show back in Rhode Island?"

So much for that argument. She cursed her luck as well as Maisie's penchant for cleanliness. An empty champagne bottle would come in handy right about now. Or a nice, hefty wooden cutting board. Where was a good frying pan when a girl needed one?

"Here." The man shoved the rose at her. "This is for you. You have to take it."

Sarah accepted the offering. At least the darkness prevented him from seeing her hands tremble.

"Thank you," she said. Stupid to worry about being polite with a stalker. Stupid to be talking at all. She took another step back. If she could put Meg's marble-topped bread table between her and the man…

He took a step closer. "You're not going anywhere, are you?"

Sarah sneezed. "I'll just get a vase," she said, holding up the rose. "And some water. I wouldn't want my flower to die or—"

Bad choice of words. She cringed. "What I mean, of

course, is that it's so beautiful." She held the rose to her nose, sniffed and sneezed again. "I'd like to keep it fresh as long as possible. It needs to be trimmed and the petals should be peeled back. I'll get a knife and—"

That was no better.

She regrouped and tried another approach. "It's not like I don't appreciate your gift. It's beautiful. Everything you've sent has been beautiful. The nightgown and the soap. And those really great sneakers with the little roses painted all over them. I really appreciate it all. But, hey, it goes back to my childhood. My mother always told me not to accept gifts from strangers, and I really don't have a whole lot of time for any new friends. So you see, a relationship with me is really a sort of dead end."

Another poor choice.

"Oh, forget it!" Sarah turned and ran.

She didn't get far. The man clamped a hand on her arm and dragged her closer. "You can't leave. Not yet," he said.

Sarah was suddenly tired of being polite.

She squirmed and she kicked. She screeched and she punched.

But the man had a grip like a bench vise. The more she struggled, the tighter he held.

"Let me go!" she screamed. "The cops are outside and—"

No sooner were the words out of her mouth than the kitchen door burst open. A man raced into the room and grabbed her attacker by the throat. They scuffled, shoving back and forth, and Sarah heard the sound of flesh pounding flesh. Her attacker got in the final punch. He pushed aside her rescuer and headed for the door. By the time Sarah's breathing slowed enough for her to hear any sound other than her own drumming heartbeat, all she heard was the back door slam.

The room spun. Sarah's knees went limp. She braced a hand against the bread table and bent at the waist, feeling a whole lot like she had when she was sitting atop Pete the Perch.

"Pete the Perch!" The memory sparked an awareness that flashed through her like wildfire. She shoved off from the table and over to her rescuer. "Oh, Dylan! Thank goodness—"

At that moment, the man flicked on the lights.

And Sarah froze in the middle of the kitchen with her mouth hanging open.

She scrubbed a hand over her eyes, sure they were playing tricks on her. But when she was done, nothing had changed.

"Matthew?"

Her brother held up one hand. "Don't even say it. I know. It was heroic. But, hey, I *am* your big brother." The knuckles of his right hand were scraped, and he shook out his hand and flinched. "It's the least I could do for my little sister. No thanks necessary."

"I wasn't exactly thinking *thank you*. I was thinking more like what the hell are you doing here? You're supposed to be in California!"

"I was in California." Matthew flexed his fingers. A wave of pain crossed his face. Rather than watch him suffer while she tried to make sense out of what had just happened, what it all meant and how Matthew figured into the picture, Sarah went over to the drawer where Maisie kept the dishcloths. She took one out, ran it under cold water, wrung it out and tossed it to Matthew.

"You're going to have to excuse me," she told him. "I'm a little confused. I was sure—"

"You were sure that I was some guy named Dylan." Matthew's eyes lit up the way they used to when they were teenagers and he was teasing her about her latest boyfriend. "Is there a story here somewhere?"

"No. No story. Not until you explain what's going on." She pointed toward the hallway. "That was the guy who's been stalking me for months."

"I know. I'm sorry I didn't get here sooner. I tried." Matthew adjusted the cloth against his hand and winced. "It's my fault. If I was a little bit faster—"

"Hold on! Wait a minute!" Like a cop directing traffic, she held up both hands. "Let's start at the beginning. Are you telling me you knew about the stalker?"

"Of course."

"And you knew he followed me here?"

"I didn't know. Not for sure." Of all three of her brothers, Matthew had always been the brother no woman could resist, and even now, over thirty and with a few added pounds, Sarah could see what still attracted them. He had the same golden hair as she did and eyes the color of a California sky. There was also the added temptation of his six-figure salary, his Corvette and the bachelor pad on the beach. Matthew could put on the charm as easily as other guys pulled on their blue jeans. But Matt had the tendency to forget that charm didn't work on younger sisters.

Sarah added up the two and two of what he'd told her. It came out to five and a half. She narrowed her eyes. "How?"

"How?" He adjusted the cold cloth and winced again. "You mean how did I know? About the stalker? That's easy. A few weeks ago, I flew back home to see the family. You weren't there, of course. But, hey, they're worried. They told me all about the stalker. And I got worried, too. Naturally."

Sarah crossed her arms over her chest and cocked her head. "Naturally."

"Right. So…" Matthew tossed the cloth onto the countertop. "I did what any big brother would do. Any kind, considerate, concerned big brother. I decided to keep an eye on you. Lucky I did, huh? You really might have gotten hurt."

"Yeah. Lucky. Only, Matt…" Sarah bent and picked up the rose that she'd dropped when she fought with her attacker. She slapped it against her hand. "Mother and Dad don't know about the stalker."

"What?" Matthew tried to hide his surprise with one of his trademark charming smiles. Too bad it didn't work. "Of course Mother and Dad know about the stalker. You never keep secrets from them. And this—"

"—is way too creepy. So I didn't tell them. I didn't want them to worry."

"Of course not! What I meant to say was that I didn't hear it *from* Mother and Dad. I heard it from—"

"Stop lying, Matthew. You didn't hear it from anybody. Nobody knows about the stalker. Nobody. And nobody knows I'm here on the island, either. Nobody but…"

Sarah's eyes widened. "Becky! She's the only one who knows where I am. I had to tell her so she could send me some contracts. That means she's the only one who could have told you and that means…" Like a thunderbolt, another idea struck, and Sarah felt as if she'd taken a punch to the solar plexus.

Her surprise melted into amazement. Her amazement solidified and suddenly, it was as if a bright light had been turned on the cold, hard facts. Matthew had always had too much chutzpah for his own good. Looked like he was out to prove it again. "Let me guess. Jason from *El-*

egant Living magazine. It was you! You lied to Becky. About the magazine. To find out where I was."

Matthew shrugged. A curl of golden hair hung over his forehead and into his eyes. "It's not like I wanted to lie. Not to anybody. But I couldn't think of any other way. I had to find out where you were so I could protect you. You know, there's bound to be more of this. Once you're a star. Yeah, Becky told me about the cable network. You're going to need someone to watch out for you, kid. I feel lucky that I was able to do it today."

"Uh-huh. And as Becky is so fond of saying, I just fell off a turnip truck." Another realization struck and fire flashed through her belly. Before she could remind herself that she was regressing into the annoying kid sister who had spent the better part of her growing-up years going out of her way to drive her brothers crazy, she whacked Matthew over the head with the rose. Petals scattered. She sneezed.

"Hey!" He brushed rose petals off the shoulders of his designer shirt. "What was that for?"

"That's for Becky, that's what it's for. You spent the weekend with her. You made her think you cared about her so you could sweet-talk her into telling you where I was."

"I did it for you!"

"Bull." Sarah tossed what was left of the rose down on the kitchen counter. "What are you up to, Matthew?"

"You know me better than that."

"Yeah, I do. That's why I'm asking. How did you know about the stalker? Like I said, nobody knew but me and the stalker, and that means…" Sarah's stomach bunched, and this time, she knew if she walloped Matthew, she'd do some serious damage. She forced herself to keep her distance. "You set me up! Either you told that big guy all about me or you did it all yourself. That would explain how stuff got delivered to my home address, as well as to my office. And how the stalker knew what size shoes I wear. *You* sent all the stuff to me! *You're* the one who's been making me crazy all these months. And then you send this big guy in to scare the living daylights out of me!" She slapped a hand against the marble-topped bread table, and the sound reverberated like a gunshot. "What the hell are you up to, Matt?"

She had to give him credit; Matthew did pathetic really well. He hung his head. "I need a job."

"You what?"

"I need a job. All that stuff about my being a successful real estate developer? It was a lot of bull." His eyes flashed with desperation. "I've got an image to protect. I can't let people know that my business went south."

"So you decided to scare me to death?" Sarah pressed a hand to her heart. "What does stalking me have to do with you finding a job?"

"I knew that if I could prove how resourceful I was…" Matthew raised his chin and had the nerve to look her in the eye. It was that whole chutzpah thing again. Cute when he was sixteen. Not so cute coming from a grown man who'd made the last few months of her life a living hell. "I figured once you went national, you'd need someone to be responsible for security."

Sarah hadn't realized how tense she'd been ever since the day the first package had arrived. Now all the tension drained out of her. She sank into one of the chairs next to the kitchen table, and feeling both relief and a weird appreciation for the absurdity of the whole situation, she started to laugh.

She laughed until tears streamed down her cheeks and she could barely find the breath to talk. "Matthew…" Her brother stared at her as if she'd lost her mind. Maybe she had. She started laughing again. "You're such a doofus! Don't you realize..." Her face muscles hurt and she wiped her smile away and fought for control. "All you ever had to do was ask. I would have been happy to give you a job."

"I don't need your charity."

"Good. Because I'm not offering any. But honestly, Matt..." A giggle bubbled out of her. "This has got to be the dumbest, most boneheaded plan I've ever heard. You planned on jumping in and being my hero. Is that it? And then when you did, you figured that I'd be eternally grateful and offer you some big fat paycheck in return?"

"Even scraped my knuckles on the back sidewalk so you'd think we were actually fighting." He held up his hand to show her and tried again for that hangdog look.

Sarah was way past that. "You've been watching too many really bad TV shows."

"You don't know what it's like." Matthew dropped into the chair next to hers. "You haven't spent the last twelve years listening to your parents brag about how you got a four-year scholarship to Harvard."

"No. I've spent the last twelve years listening to my parents brag about how *you* got a four-year scholarship to Harvard."

The subtleties of her argument were lost on Matthew. Once self-absorbed, always self-absorbed. "Everyone expects me to be this brainchild," he said. "The golden boy. What would they say if they knew that I've been mooching off my friends for the last six months? I made some stupid investments. I lived way beyond my means. And now I've lost it all, the house and the cars and the women, who only stayed because of the house and the cars." He sighed. "I even had to borrow the money to send you all those gifts. How pathetic is that? So you see, I couldn't let anyone know. I had to keep up the image. It's hard trying to be someone you're not."

He didn't have to tell her. Not about that.

The truth hit and Sarah's smile evaporated. She reached over and gave Matthew's uninjured hand a squeeze. "I guess it's kind of a family failing."

"You? Not a chance! You're the one who's got it all together. You've got the TV show and you're going to have a decorating empire. You're going to be famous, Sarah. And you're going to be rich."

"Big deal." It wasn't. Now that she thought about it, it never had been. The familiar ache started up inside Sarah again. "Famous doesn't mean a thing," she said. "And rich doesn't keep you warm at night."

"But—"

"No buts. I won't tell a soul that you've lost whatever you had, Matthew. It's none of my business, and besides, you need to take care of that yourself. But I do have to tell Dylan—he's the local police chief—that there's no stalker." She pushed back from the table and stood. "He's got officers working overtime and he's going to be—" She'd been about to say *worried*. She changed her mind. Mostly because it hurt too much to think that if Dylan was worried, he was worried in a strictly professional sort of way. "Bill's out front in his patrol car. He might as well know that he can go home and go to bed. Speaking of which…do you have a place to stay for the night?"

Matthew stood, too. "I'm renting a place," he said. "Over on the other side of the island. Greg is supposed to meet me back there later." He saw his partner in crime outside the kitchen window and waved the man back inside.

"Greg Posner—" Matthew pointed toward the man who'd surprised Sarah in the dark kitchen "—Sarah Allcroft. My sister."

Greg apparently wasn't sure what to say. And who could blame him? The last time they were face-to-face, he'd been some big bad stalker with a fondness for roses and an obsession with Sarah.

"It's okay." Sarah stuck out her hand. "Matthew told me what's going on. I know you were only playing a role."

Greg didn't shake her hand. Instead, he scraped a hand over the stubbly beard on his chin. "Good. Then I don't have to go back to your place, Matthew. We can wrap this up right now."

Matthew didn't answer.

He didn't have to for Sarah to understand what was really going on. Her blood turned to ice, and whatever warm family sentiments she might have been feeling froze solid. "You said this guy was a friend of yours," she told Matthew, and when he didn't say a word, her temper snapped. "You actually recruited a stranger to play my stalker? And let me guess, now you owe him money."

"Damned straight," Greg snarled. Sarah's initial impressions of Greg were pretty accurate. Medium height. Medium weight. Darned big shoulders. He turned to Matthew and somehow, when he was standing next to her slim brother with his shaggy hair and Left Coast good looks, Greg was more menacing than ever. "Three hundred bucks. That's what you promised me. So pay up, pal, and I'm outta here. Can't wait to get off this freakin' island."

"Well, that's just it, you see." Matthew poked his hands into the pockets of his khakis. "I'm a little short of funds right now and—"

"Oh, good grief!" Sarah couldn't believe it. "Are you telling me you expect me to pay for my own stalking? Well, you can forget that, buster. I don't have three hundred dollars. Not on me. And even if I did, I wouldn't pay this big oaf for the privilege of scaring me out of my wits." She tapped the toe of one sneaker against the floor. "Pay up, Matthew."

Matthew shrugged. "I can't."

"What?" Greg wasn't happy with the news. He took a couple of steps toward Matthew, and Matthew blanched and backed out of reach. Unfortunately, Sarah wasn't as fast.

"All right then." Greg latched on to her arm. "She's coming with me." He dragged Sarah toward the door. "You'll get her back. When I get my money."

"Matthew?" Sarah waited for her brother to jump in and explain. She waited for him to be the bodyguard he wanted to be and take a swing at Greg. She waited for him to take action. And when he didn't do anything but stand there and look scared, Greg dragged her out of the back door.

DYLAN FINISHED checking in with Bill, discussing the evening's events and complaining that he should never have let Sarah slip by him. He got back into the Tahoe to start for home. By that time, he'd already decided he'd been too hard on Sarah.

Not that it made a whole lot of difference.

"Regret." He slammed the truck door closed and jammed the key into the ignition.

"Funny, I thought what we had was way better than that."

He might have had a chance to think about it—and feel worse than he already did—if a man who resembled Sarah didn't race out of the front door of the Hideaway. He caught sight of the police cars and pounded down the steps.

Dylan was already out of the truck by the time the man got to him.

"He took her." The guy gripped Dylan's arm and pointed toward the inn. "He wanted the money and I didn't have it. I mean, I figured a coupla beers and he'd be perfectly happy, and that's the only reason I agreed to the three hundred dollars in the first place. Of course, I didn't have it and—"

Dylan was not in the mood for long stories or longer explanations. Bill had hopped out of his patrol car and Dylan handed the stranger over to him. "You're talking about Sarah?" he asked the man. "Sarah Allcroft?"

The young man nodded. "I'm Matthew Allcroft and she's my sister. And I never meant for her to really be in danger. I just wanted to scare her a little. You understand, right?"

Dylan didn't. He didn't want to. From what Matthew had already told him, he had a feeling that once he knew the whole story, Matthew would be minus a few teeth.

As appealing as it was, he set the fantasy aside. There was no room for panic. Or for anger. Not right now.

Not if he intended to find out what happened.

"Who took her?" Dylan asked. "And where?"

Matthew ran a hand through his hair. The gesture was so like the one Sarah sometimes used, it tore at Dylan's heart.

He couldn't take the time to think about that, either. Emotion would get in the way of doing his job. And now, more than ever, he needed to do his job and do it right.

"His name is Greg Posner," Matthew explained. "I met him in a bar this afternoon. He seemed like a nice enough guy and I figured he could take a joke, but…well…"

While Bill ran back to his patrol car to get on the radio, Dylan got the details. "This Posner guy, he's the one who's been stalking Sarah?"

Matthew's face paled. He eyed Dylan's gun in its holster and the black eye that made him appear tougher and meaner than ever. "Actually, officer, that was me." As soon as the words were out of his mouth, he jumped back, out of Dylan's reach.

"It was supposed to be a joke," Matthew said. "I never wanted her to get hurt. But then when I couldn't pay Posner, he said he was taking her."

Dylan already had the door to the Tahoe open. "Where?"

Matthew shrugged. He choked over his words. "I don't know. I can't say. I hardly know the guy." He squeezed his eyes shut, thinking really hard. "He said he's from somewhere outside Toledo. But he didn't say where he was staying. He said... That's it!" Matthew's eyes flew open. "He said he had a boat."

Didn't it figure?

Dylan stopped dead in his tracks.

But only for a second.

The next instant, he was behind the wheel of the truck. He put on the flashers, hit the siren and headed for the marina.

Chapter Fifteen

> You are a different person than you were when
> you began to read *Sarah's Guide to Life, Love and
> Gardening*. You are more romantic, more aware of
> the subtleties of romance—color, scent, texture,
> style. Take these suggestions and give them your
> own special touch. Don't be afraid to improvise.
> —*Sarah's Guide to Life, Love and Gardening*

Too bad stupidity wasn't illegal.

Dylan would have loved to slap the cuffs on Matthew
Allcroft and haul him off to jail. As it was, he didn't have
the luxury. Or the time. He promised himself he'd talk to
the prosecutor about Matthew and the cockamamie scheme
he'd admitted to, but for now he had to forget about Matthew.

He couldn't afford to let anger get in the way of what
he needed to do. He couldn't afford to be preoccupied.

He had more important things to worry about.

There were seven different places on the island where
boats could be docked and Dylan sent officers to every one
of them

Trouble was, it was already late. By the time he got his
staff roused from their homes, their beds and (in one case),

their every-Thursday-night pizza after the softball game, time had gone by.

Too much time.

He took the municipal marina himself and because it was large enough to accommodate hundreds of boats, he had Jake stick around to help.

Jake headed off in one direction, and it wasn't until he was headed in the other that it registered with Dylan that he was standing in the middle of one of the three large docks that stuck out into the lake. A fierce wind blew in from the north and the waves kicked up and slapped the underside of the dock. Water licked the soles of his shoes. It splashed up and polka-dotted his face. It churned under him. And ahead of him. And around him.

And no one could have been more surprised than Dylan when he realized he didn't give a damn. ·

There wasn't any room inside him for his fear of water or the lake. He was too busy being scared to death about what might happen to Sarah.

By the time he'd talked to a dozen of the boat captains who were docked for the night and hadn't seen anyone around, Jake was headed his way from the far side of the marina. Dylan flagged him down. "Anything?" he called over the sound of the wind and waves.

Jake gave a noncommittal shrug. "Boat left a little while ago," he said. "But no one knows for sure who was on it."

"I think it's safe to say that whoever *is* on it has got to be a little nuts." Dylan hadn't bothered to grab a jacket before he left his house and the wind was chilly. He shivered. "Any idea where they're headed?"

Jake pointed over his shoulder. "Dave McGuire is docked up the way. You remember him, he's the captain who won the regatta last year. Says he thinks the boat that left was headed east."

Dylan didn't wait to hear any more. He headed for the slip reserved for the police department boat and Jake trotted along beside him. When they got there and Dylan hopped in, Jake held back.

"You're not going, are you, Chief?"

If Dylan wasn't so anxious to get a move on, he might have spared the time to care what Jake was talking about. Instead, he checked the fuel gauge and cast off the ropes. "Of course I'm going. Sarah's out there somewhere. And who knows what this Posner guy is up to." He started up the engine and waved Jake aboard. "We can call the Coast Guard once we're under way. And we'll call Bill, too. We'll let him know where we're headed and see what he's found out. Come on!"

"But, Chief…" Jake toed the edges of the dock It was long past dark and even this close to shore, the whitecaps made the water look like it was boiling. "You're afraid of the water!"

His hand on the throttle, Dylan spun around. "How did you—"

Jake hopped onto the boat. "Heck, Chief, everybody knows that."

SARAH WASN'T ALL THAT AFRAID when Greg Posner grabbed her. How far could they go with him hauling and her dragging her feet?

She wasn't all that afraid when he forced her into the pickup truck he had parked around the back of the Hideaway where nobody could see it, either. South Bass was a small island and someone was bound to see them sooner or later. How far could they get without being noticed?

In fact, it wasn't until they got to the marina and he

shoved her on a boat, started the motor and pushed off from the dock that the real panic set in.

And by that time, of course, it was too late.

She watched the island get smaller and the waves get bigger, clinging to the plastic bench to the right of where Posner stood to steer the boat. "You know what you're doing with this boat?"

Posner didn't answer.

"You do realize you're going to be in big trouble for this."

He didn't say a word about that, either.

"Can you even see where you're go—" A wave splashed over the side and drenched Sarah, washing away her words. She shivered and groped around for a towel to wipe her face. She didn't find a towel, but she did find an orange life vest, and since she knew they weren't going to have smooth sailing any time soon, she slipped it over her head and cinched the buckles on the front to tighten it.

The boat bucked and Sarah slid along the bench.

"This is insane!"

At least this time, she got some sort of reaction out of Posner. Even if it was only a grunt.

"Matthew can't pay you if he doesn't know where to find you."

Greg had both hands on the wheel, fighting to keep the boat steady. "He never had any intention of paying."

He was probably right, but Sarah didn't think this was the right time to mention it. "Well, he's my brother and I'll make good on his debts. I'll pay you. But it would help if I could get to an ATM machine."

"It will help more when we get over to the mainland and we give that brother of yours a call." Posner's smile was sleek. "By that time, he should be willing to pay a whole lot more than three hundred dollars."

Maybe.

If they lived that long.

The boat rolled up and splashed down. The engine sputtered. Sarah hoped Posner was a better boater than he was a kidnapper.

They rounded Buckeye Point and turned south. From this direction the waves seemed a little less intense and the rocking wasn't quite as bad. Sarah dared to stand up. Hand over hand, she clung to the side of the boat and made her way over to where Posner struggled to keep both hands on the wheel.

"You could pull over and let me off." She knew it wasn't that easy, not when it came to five-foot waves and a coastline that, in places, had jutting rocks, but it was worth a try. "If you're willing to cooperate, I'm more than willing to forget all this ever happened."

Posner spat. "I ain't the kind of guy who forgets. Not when it comes to money. Besides, if that brother of yours—"

Whatever he was going to say, he didn't have the chance to finish it.

An airhorn blast split the night. Loud enough to make Sarah jump. The next second, a searchlight flashed across the lake. It stopped on Posner's boat.

"This is the Put-in-Bay police!" It was Dylan's voice over a bullhorn. Staggering step after staggering step, Sarah lurched to the back of the boat. A hundred feet or so behind them was the police department boat. Dylan was standing on the prow, bullhorn in hand and a very pissed-off expression on his face.

Sarah's throat closed over a lump of emotion. She waved. Partly to let him know she was there. Mostly to remind him not to get too close to the edge.

She'd been so worried about Dylan, she didn't hear

Posner come up behind her. One arm around her, he yanked her closer. "They get too near…" He flashed a knife in front of her nose.

This time, the emotion that closed Sarah's throat was fear. She watched the light glint off the knife blade. She felt the boat's forward motion—obviously Posner had left the throttle on and somehow locked the steering wheel—then felt another wave lift the boat and plop it back down. For a second, Posner lost his footing and loosened his hold.

It was just the second Sarah needed.

While he was still off balance, she pushed away from him. She struggled to the side of the boat and from there, she knew she had exactly two choices: she could stay right where she was and take her chances with Posner and that knife of his. Or she could move ahead. Into the water. Toward Dylan.

Sarah liked to think that she did the brave thing and jumped. But she knew that in all honesty, she never had much of a chance to make the decision for herself. Another wave kicked up and rocked the boat, and the next thing she knew, she was in the water.

The waves were rough and even in the life preserver, she went right under. She gulped in a mouthful of water, and it wasn't until the next wave spit her to the surface that she was able to spew it out. She dragged in a deep breath.

"Sarah!" Dylan called her name. The light played over the surface of the lake. She tried to lift a hand to signal him, but before she ever could, the waves battered her. She went under again.

Below the surface, the noise of both boat engines was muffled. The light was very far away. Nothing in her *Sarah's Guide* had ever prepared her for anything like this.

Her hair was in her eyes and she tried to scrape it away, but the life preserver made it hard for her to maneuver her arms. She kicked her feet and moved her arms as best she could to help herself stay afloat. The light got closer.

Until another wave crashed over her and pushed her down again.

Sarah's lungs burned. Her body ached. The life preserver was buoyant, but the strength of the waves was too much. They forced her back down. She bobbed to the surface a dozen feet away from the light and hauled in a breath, but even before she closed her mouth, she went under again.

Water filled her mouth and she swallowed and gagged. Her body responded automatically, demanding a breath. No matter how much Sarah tried not to, she couldn't help herself. She opened her mouth. Instead of air, she got another mouthful of water.

She choked and kicked, fighting to make her way to the surface and the light she saw only a few feet away. The next second, the light flashed off the water above her head and moved on. She was left in the dark.

Sarah closed her eyes. She stopped fighting. She allowed her body to drift. Away from the boats. Away from the light. Away from Dylan.

Farther out into the lake.

When a hand grabbed her wrist, she figured she was imagining it. When she felt a tug, she knew it was wishful thinking.

When she opened her eyes and found herself face-to-face with Dylan, she knew it must be a dream.

He wrapped an arm around her waist and clipped a safety line to the metal clasp on the front of her life preserver. He was wearing the same sort of bright orange vest, and he tugged on the line attached to his. As if by magic, Sarah felt herself skimming the water, getting closer by the second to the police boat. A minute later, Jake carefully hoisted her aboard.

Her legs wouldn't hold her. Lucky for her, she didn't even have to try to make them. No sooner did Dylan step onto the deck and strip off his life preserver than he wrapped a blanket around her. He lifted her and carried her to a seat inside the enclosed pilothouse.

Away from the wind and the pounding of the waves, she struggled to breathe again. She hauled in breath after breath, but even though the air was chilly, her lungs were on fire.

"Don't worry. You're going to be fine." Dylan pushed the wet hair off her face. He rubbed her cheeks to warm them. He dropped onto a bench and scooped her into his arms, holding her close enough to warm her with what little heat was left in his own body and his drenched clothing.

"What were you thinking?" He kissed her nose and her cheeks and her forehead. "Why did you jump?"

Sarah snuggled against Dylan's wet clothing and the blanket that was already soaked through, and she found herself smiling through the tears that sprang to her eyes. Her throat was raw, and the words croaked out of her. "Let's just call it a leap of faith."

"BUT YOU'RE AFRAID of the water."

Sarah figured she'd already mentioned this a dozen times, but she just couldn't get over it.

"You hate the water. And you got on a boat and went out onto the lake when it was that choppy and—"

"And lived to tell the story. More importantly…" Dylan handed her a mug of the steaming hot chocolate Maisie had sent up to Close to the Heart. He dropped down on the floor next to her in front of the fire that roared in the fireplace and slipped an arm around her shoulders. "*You* lived to tell the story." He drew her close and Sarah put her head on his shoulder. They were dressed in identical Hideaway robes, white terry-cloth with a red cupid embroidered over the heart. The fabric was soft and Sarah rubbed her cheek against it.

"I can't believe you did that. For me," she said. "After what I did to you."

"You mean all that stuff about you leaving?" He nudged her far enough away so that he could gaze into her eyes. "What does that have to do with me conquering a mind-numbing fear, going after a dangerous kidnapper and risking my life?"

She knew a joke when she heard one. Which was why she gave him a playful elbow in the ribs. But there was a lot of truth in what he said, too, and realizing it, Sarah felt her throat tighten.

"You could have been hurt." She skimmed a finger along Dylan's jaw. "You could have been killed. What if—"

"It didn't happen." He cupped her chin with one hand. "I'm okay, you're okay, and that scumbag Posner…" He pictured Greg Posner's face when the Coast Guard arrived and assisted in his arrest. Dylan always felt a certain satisfaction at putting a bad guy where he belonged. But this time, he felt better than ever. "He'll be enjoying the hospitality of one of our jail cells for a bit. Minus the gourmet dinner, of course. Then we'll transfer him to the county jail over on the mainland. You going to be okay with testifying against him?"

Sarah grinned. "Anything to help out our men in blue."

"Anything?" Dylan's smile was soft, but his eyes glinted with mischief.

She knew exactly what he had in mind. It was a good idea, but she knew she couldn't give in to the temptation.

Her moment of hesitation spoke louder than words. The glimmer in Dylan's eyes faded.

"Yeah." He sat back. "I'm okay, you're okay, and nothing's changed between us."

"Good thing." She laughed when his mouth dropped open, but she wasn't about to be discouraged. It seemed a lifetime ago that she'd gone to his house to talk to him. Then, he hadn't given her a chance to say what she wanted to say. Now, she wasn't about to be put off again. Call it a little bit of family chutzpah. Or plain old narcissism. Maybe a near-death experience had a way of making a person see that what's really important in life is worth fighting for.

She wound her fingers through his. "Dylan, I love you."

"Yeah, but—"

"And I know you love me. You might be the bravest police chief in a hundred-mile radius, but even a brave police chief doesn't put himself on the line like you did tonight."

"Yeah, but—"

"And even if you didn't, I'd know how you feel about me. You show it in everything you do. You say it, even when you're not talking."

"Yeah, but—"

"And if there's one thing I learned tonight other than the fact that I never want to jump into a choppy lake in the middle of the night again, it's that I don't want to live without you."

"Yeah, but you're leaving."

"Dylan…" She leaned in close and tried for a smile, but she was worried about how he might react and far more terrified of what he might say than she'd ever been out there in the middle of the lake surrounded by water and blackness. Her smile wobbled around the edges. "You never asked me to stay."

"And if I did?"

Sarah kissed him. "Give it a try. I bet you'll be surprised by the answer."

Epilogue

Romance isn't simply a word, it's a lifestyle. A hint of elegance, a touch of refinement and a big dose of panache
combine to create your ideal world. Whether it's life or
gardening, you design and nurture your own reality and
that reality can be everything you've ever dreamed.
And when it comes to love…
Dreams can come true there, as well. All it takes is the
right place. The right person. And a little bit of magic.

—*Sarah's Guide to Life, Love and Gardening*

Nothing was as blatantly romantic as a Valentine's Day
wedding.

Which was exactly why Sarah chose that day for the
big event. The ceremony (taped for airing at a later date)
was held in the Hideaway's parlor, and in spite of the fact
that it was off-season and there was eight inches of snow
on the ground, the place was filled to the rafters.

Laurel and Noah were there, along with Teddy, their
little boy. Meg and Gabe made the trip from L.A. and
brought Diana the dog, even though she was starring in a
new weekly sitcom and her absence held up production.
Maisie was there front and center, of course, along with
Doc Ross. Sarah's parents had adored Dylan from the

moment they met him and they, along with her brothers, were the first to offer hugs and congratulations. Matthew was just about finished with the community service time he'd been sentenced to and he was none the worse for the wear in spite of spending twenty hours a week at a juvenile detention facility over on the mainland. No one was more surprised than he was to discover that he had a real way with kids. He talked about heading back to school to get his master's in social work.

Becky and the rest of the *Affairs of the Heart* crew were there, too, mostly because they were friends but partly because this was a business trip for them. They were checking out the island, pricing real estate and setting up the new *Affairs of the Heart* production center. After all, a TV show could be taped on an island almost as easily as it could be in a big city. Books could be written in the quiet of an island winter. And as for personal appearances…Sarah had already decided that when she needed to leave, she'd fly, instead of taking the ferry. So Dylan could come with her.

A time or two, Sarah saw Becky and Matthew exchange uncomfortable glances. No way was Becky prepared to forgive Matthew on sight, but she was still smitten. And Matthew was charming. They'd work it out.

As for Sarah and Dylan…

By the time the reception was over and they'd said thank-you and goodbye to every last one of their guests, they were more than ready to be alone.

Maisie had wanted them to stay in Close to the Heart, but common sense prevailed. Maisie had a lot of guests, and they needed rooms. Sarah and Dylan went home.

Her white gown bunched in one hand and held up above her black galoshes, Sarah trudged over to the front steps while Dylan parked the Tahoe. She'd left a surprise tucked between the porch swing and front door, and before she retrieved it, she waited for him and watched him unlock the front door.

"Home." His smile was filled with the promise of forever. "You ready, Mrs. O'Connell?"

She reached behind the swing and brought out the brown grocery bag she'd bought at the auction. She dangled it between two fingers. "The question is, are you ready?"

She didn't think it was possible for Dylan to be any happier. She was wrong. He gave the bag a tap and it swung back and forth. "You mean you're finally going to show me what's in that bag?"

"Not only am I going to show you, I'm going to let you help me use it for the very first time."

His smile inched up a notch. He stepped aside so she could walk into the house. "Then let's get going."

"Not so fast, officer." Sarah stopped him with a quick kiss. "Aren't you going to carry me over the threshold?"

"Over the threshold and right up to bed. That sound all right with you?"

"It sounds—" he scooped her up into his arms and Sarah laughed "—very romantic."

* * * * *

Welcome to the world of American Romance!
Turn the page for excerpts from
our July 2005 titles.

A SOLDIER'S RETURN
by Judy Christenberry

TEMPORARY DAD
by Laura Marie Altom

THE BABY SCHEME
by Jacqueline Diamond

A TEXAS STATE OF MIND
by Ann DeFee

We hope you enjoy every one of these books!

Bestselling author and reader favorite Judy Christenberry delivers another emotion-filled family drama from her Children of Texas miniseries, with *A Soldier's Return*. Witness a touching reunion when the Barlow sisters meet their long-lost older brother, and find out how the heart of this brooding warrior is healed by an impressible beauty—an extended member of his rediscovered family.

Carrie Abrams was working on her computer when she heard the door of the detective agency open.

She turned her body to greet the entrant, but her head was still glued to the computer screen. When she reluctantly brought her gaze to focus on the tall man with straight posture standing by the door wearing a dress uniform, she gasped.

"Jim! I mean, uh, sorry, I mistook you for someone I—um, may I help you?" She abandoned her clumsy beginning and became as stiff as he was.

"I need to speak with Will Greenfield."

"And your name?" She almost held her breath.

"Captain James Barlow."

"Thank you, Captain Barlow. Just one moment, please." She got up from her desk, wishing she'd worn a business suit instead of jeans. *You're being silly.* Jim Barlow wouldn't care what she was wearing. He didn't even know her.

She rapped on Will's door, opened it and stepped inside.

"He's here!" She whispered so the man in the outer office wouldn't hear her.

"Who—" Will started to ask, but Carrie didn't wait.

"Jim! He's here. He's wearing his uniform. He wants to speak to you."

Will's face broke into a smile. "Well, show him in!"

Carrie opened the door. "Captain Barlow, please come in."

She wanted to stay in Will's office, but she knew he wouldn't extend the invitation. And she wouldn't ask. It wouldn't be professional.

As she leaned against the door, reluctant to break contact with the two men inside, her gaze roamed her desk.

"Oh, no!" she gasped, and rushed forward. Jim's picture. Had he seen it? She hoped not. How could she explain her fascination with Vanessa's oldest brother? She'd been enthralled by his square-jawed image, just as Vanessa had been. He was the picture of protective, strong…safe. The big brother every little girl dreamed of.

Her best friend, Vanessa Shaw, had probably dreamed those dreams while being raised as an only child. Then, after her father's death, her mother had told her she had five siblings. That revelation had set in motion a lot of changes in their lives.

Carrie drew a deep breath. It was so tempting to call Vanessa and break the news. But she couldn't do that. That was Will's privilege.

All she could do was sit here and pretend indifference that Jim Barlow had returned to the bosom of his family after twenty-three years.

Temporary Dad is the kind of story American Romance readers love—with moments that will make you laugh (and a moment now and then that'll bring you to tears). Jed Hale is an all-American hero: a fireman, a rescuer, a family man. And Annie Harris is just the woman for him. Join these two on their road trip from Oklahoma to Colorado, with three babies in tow (his triplet niece and nephews, temporarily in his care). Enjoy their various roadside stops—like the Beer Can Cow and the Giant Corncob. And smile as they fall in love….

Waaaaaaaaaaaaaaa! Waa huh waaaaaaaaaAAAHH!

From a cozy rattan chair on the patio of her new condo, Annie Harris looked up from the August issue of *Budget Decorating* and frowned.

Waaaaaaaaaaa!

Granted, she wasn't yet a mother herself, but she had been a preschool teacher for the past seven years, so that did lend her a certain credibility where children were concerned.

WAAAAA HA waaaaaaa!

Annie sighed.

She thought whoever was in charge of that poor, piti-

ful wailer in the condo across the breezeway from hers
ought to try something to calm the infant. Never had she
heard so much commotion. Was the poor thing sick?

WAAAAAAAAA WAAAAAAA WAAAAAAA!

WAAAAAAA Huh WAAAAA!

WAAAAAAAAAAAA!

Annie slapped the magazine back to her knees.

Something about the sound of that baby wasn't right.

Was there more than one?

Definitely two.

Maybe even three.

But she'd moved in a couple weeks earlier and hadn't
heard a peep or seen signs of any infant in the complex—
let alone three—which was partially why she'd chosen
this unit over the one beside the river that had had much
better views of the town of Pecan, Oklahoma.

WAAAAAA Huh WAAAAAAAAA!

Again Annie frowned.

No good parent would just leave an infant to cry like
this. Could something else be going on? Could the baby's
mom or dad be hurt?

Annie popped the latch on her patio gate, creeping
across grass not quite green or brown, but a weary shade
somewhere in between.

WAAAAAAAAAA!

She crept farther across the shared lawn, stepping onto
the weathered brick breezeway she shared with the as-yet-
unseen owner of the unit across from hers.

The clubhouse manager—Veronica, a bubbly redhead
with a penchant for eighties rock and yogurt—said a bachelor fireman lived there.

Judging by the dead azalea bushes on either side of his
front door, Annie hoped the guy was better at watering
burning buildings than poor, thirsty plants!

Waaaaaa Huhhhh WAAAA!

She looked at the fireman's door, then her own.

Whatever was going on inside his home probably wasn't any of her business.

WaaaaaAAAAA!

Call her a busybody, but enough was enough.

She just couldn't bear standing around listening to a helpless baby—maybe even more than one helpless baby—cry.

Her first knock on the bachelor fireman's door was gentle. Ladylike. That of a concerned neighbor.

When that didn't work, she gave the door a few good, hard thuds.

She was just about to investigate the French doors on the patio that matched her own when the forest-green front door flew open—"Patti? Where the—? Oh, sorry. Thought you were my sister."

Annie gaped.

What else could she do faced with the handsomest man she'd ever seen hugging not one baby, not two babies, but three?

Like Alli Gardner, the heroine of *The Baby Scheme,* Jacqueline Diamond knows about newspapers. She worked as an Associated Press reporter for many years. You'll love this story of a woman who puts her investigative talents to the test—together with a very attractive private investigator—as the two try to unravel a blackmail scheme targeting parents who've adopted babies from a Central American orphanage.

"I'm here about the story in this morning's paper," Alli said to her managing editor. "The one concerning Mayor LeMott."

"Ned tells me you were working on something similar." J.J. eased into his seat. "He says Payne warned him you might have a complaint."

"It wasn't similar. This *is* my story," Alli told him. "Word for word."

"But you hadn't filed it yet."

"I'd written it but I was holding off so I could double-check a couple of points," she explained. "And there's a sidebar I didn't have time to complete. Mr. Morosco, Payne's planted spyware in my laptop. He stole every bit of that from me."

The editor's forehead wrinkled. He'd been working such long hours he'd begun to lose his tan and had put on a few pounds, she noted. "The two of you have never gotten along, have you? He'd only been here a month when you accused him of stealing your notebook."

"It disappeared from my desk right after he passed by, and the next day he turned in a story based on my research!"

"A guard found your notebook outside that afternoon, right next to where you usually park," the M.E. said.

"I didn't drop it. I'm not that careless." Alli hated being put on the defensive. "Look, you can talk to any of the people I quoted in today's story and they'll confirm who did the reporting."

"Except that most of your sources spoke anonymously," he pointed out.

"I was going to identify them to Ned when I handed it in!" That was standard procedure. "Besides, since when does this paper assign two people to the same story?"

She'd heard of a few big papers that ran their operations in such a cutthroat manner, but the Outlook couldn't afford such a waste of staff time. Besides, that kind of competition did horrible things to morale.

"He says Payne asked if he could pursue the same subject. He decided to let the kid show what he could do, and he beat you to the punch."

How could she win when the assistant managing editor was stabbing her in the back? If she were in J.J.'s seat, she probably wouldn't believe her, either.

"Give Payne his own assignment, something he can't steal from anyone else," she said. "He'll blow it."

"As it happens, he's going to have plenty of chances." J.J. fiddled with some papers. "I'm sure you're aware that I've streamlined two other sections. In the meantime, the publisher and Ned and I have been tossing around ideas for the news operation. I'm about to put those proposals into effect."

Why was he telling her this? Allie wondered uneasily. And why was he avoiding her gaze?

"The publisher believes we've got too much duplication and dead wood," he went on. "Some of the older staff members will be asked to take early retirement, but I'm going to have to cut deeper. After careful consideration, I'm afraid we have to let you go."

American Romance is delighted to introduce a brand-new author. You'll love Ann DeFee's sassy humor, her high-energy writing and her *really* entertaining characters. She'll make you laugh—and occasionally gasp. And she'll take you to a Texas town you'll never want to leave. (Fortunately you can visit Port Serenity again next June!)

Oooh, boy! Lolly raised her Pepsi in a tribute to Meg Ryan. Could that girl fake the big O! Lord knows Lolly had perfected the very same skill before Wendell, her ex, hightailed it out to Las Vegas to find fame and fortune as a drummer. Good old Wendell—more frog than prince. But to give credit where credit was due, he *had* managed to sire two of the most fantastic kids in the world.

Nowadays she didn't have to worry about Wendell's flagging ego or, for that matter, any of his other wilting body parts. Celibacy had some rewards—not many, but a few.

Meg had just segued from the throes of parodied passion to a big smile when Lolly's cell phone rang.

"Great, just great," Lolly muttered. She thumped her Pepsi on the coffee table.

"Chief, I hate to call you right at supper time, but I figured you'd want to handle this one. I just got a call from Bud out at the Peaceful Cove Inn, and he's got hisself something of a problem." An after-hours call from the Port Serenity Police Department's gravel-voiced night dispatcher signaled the end to her evening of popcorn and chick flicks.

Chief of police Lavinia "Lolly" Lee Hamilton La-Tullipe sighed. Her hectic life as a single mom and head of a small police force left her with very little free time, and when she had a few moments, she wanted to spend them at home with Amanda and Bren, not out corralling scumbags.

"Cletus is on duty tonight, and that man can handle anything short of a full-scale riot," Lolly argued, even though she knew her objections were futile.

Lordy. She'd rather eat Aunt Sissy's fruitcake than abandon the comfort of her living room, especially when Meg was about to find Mr. Right. Lolly hadn't even been able to find Mr. Sorta-Right, though she'd given it the good old college try. Wendell looked pretty good on the outside, but inside he was like an overripe watermelon— mushy and tasteless. Too bad she hadn't noticed that shortcoming when they started dating in high school. Back then his antics were cute; at thirty-seven they weren't quite so appealing.

"I'd really rather not go out tonight."

"Yes, ma'am. I understand. But this one involves Precious." The dispatcher chuckled when Lolly groaned.

Precious was anything but precious. She was the seventeen-year-old demon daughter of Mayor Lance Barton, Lolly's boss and a total klutz in the single-dad department. She and Lance had been buddies since kindergarten, so without a doubt she'd be making an unwanted trip to the Peaceful Cove Inn.

"Oh, man. What did I do to deserve that brat in my life?" Lolly rubbed her forehead in a vain attempt to ward off the headache she knew was coming. "Okay, what's she done now?"

"Seems she's out there with some guys Bud don't know, and she's got a snoot full. He figured we'd want to get her home before someone saw her."

Lolly sighed. "All right, I'll run out and see what I can do. Call her daddy and tell him what's happening."

She muttered an expletive as she marched to the roll-top desk in the kitchen to retrieve her bag, almost tripping over Harvey, the family's gigantic mutt. She strapped on an ankle holster and then checked her taser and handcuffs. In this business, a girl had to be prepared.

Amanda, her ten-year-old daughter, was immersed in homework, and as usual, her fourteen-year-old son had his head poked inside the refrigerator.

"Bren, get Amanda to help you with the kitchen." Lolly stopped him as he tried to sneak out of the room and nodded at the open dishwasher and pile of dishes in the sink. "I've got to go out for a few minutes. If you need anything call Mee Maw."

Her firstborn rolled his eyes. "Aw, Mom."

Lolly suppressed the urge to laugh, and instead employed the dreaded raised eyebrow. The kid was in dire need of a positive male role model. Someone stable, upright, respectable and…safe. Yeah, safe. It was time to find a nice, reliable prince—an orthodontist might be good, considering Amanda's overbite.

"I'm leaving. You guys be good," Lolly called out as she opened the screen door.

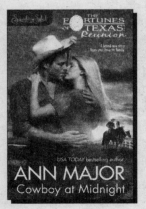

HARLEQUIN *Super*ROMANCE®

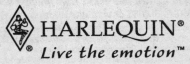

HARLEQUIN®

AMERICAN *Romance*®

is thrilled to bring you
a heartwarming miniseries
by bestselling author

Judy Christenberry

Children of TEXAS

Separated during childhood, three beautiful
sisters from the Lone Star state are destined
to rediscover one another, find true love and
build a Texas-sized family legacy they can
call their own....

You won't want to miss the third installment
of this beloved family saga!

A SOLDIER'S RETURN
(HAR #1073)

On sale July 2005.

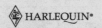
COMING NEXT MONTH

#1073 A SOLDIER'S RETURN by Judy Christenberry
Children of Texas
Ever since he was a kid and his orphaned family split, sending him into
foster care, Captain James Barlow knew he was a jinx to anyone he loved.
He'd hidden out safely in the marines…until a detective found him and most of
his siblings. The captain had seen battle, but no enemy made him uneasy like his
newfound family—and the beautiful Carrie Rand.

#1074 TEMPORARY DAD by Laura Marie Altom
Fatherhood
After her last "romantic" experience, Annie Harnesberry has sworn off men—
especially single fathers. Now she just wants to start her new job and redecorate
her condo. But when her neighbor—of the gorgeous male variety—needs help
with his five-month-old triplet niece and nephews, it's Annie who can't seem to
help *herself*.…

#1075 THE BABY SCHEME by Jacqueline Diamond
Alli Gardner may be out of her reporter's job thanks to an underhanded
competitor on her newspaper, but she's not out of story ideas—or an
investigative partner. She and hard-nosed private detective Kevin Vickers
are about to have their hands full looking into a blackmail scheme involving
babies from a Central American orphanage. Soon Alli and Kevin will also
have their hands full with each other.…

#1076 A TEXAS STATE OF MIND by Ann DeFee
Lavinia "Lolly" LaTullipe, a single mother of two, is busy enough as police
chief of the little Texas town of Port Serenity, but her job becomes even
more complicated when the bodies of drug dealers start floating into the
town's cove. Enter Christian Delacroix, undercover DEA cop sent to help
solve the murders. When he and Lolly meet the sparks fly—literally!

CNMHAR0605